A Study In Crimson

The Further Adventures of
Mrs. Watson and Mrs. St Clair
Co-Founders of the
Watson – Fanshaw Detective Agency

Molly Carr

Paperback ISBN 978-1-907685-40-8
ePub ISBN 978-1-907685-41-5
Mobipocket/Kindle ISBN 978-1-907685-42-2
Published in the UK by MX Publishing
335 Princess Park Manor, Royal Drive, London, N11 3GX
www.mxpublishing.co.uk

Cover design by www.staunch.com

Chapter One

'"Ever since Raffles rolled Moriarty into the River Thames," said I, "London has been..."

"Very quiet," responded Lestrade from the other side of the fireplace.

"I was about to say, 'very dull'. But have it your own way. Sherlock's vanished again. My former consulting room has been changed into a nursery for at least two obvious reasons. Mary has broken with Mrs. St. Clair..."

"The woman who calls herself Emily Fanshaw? The one who is so fond of dressing as a man?"

"Yes. Although I dare say they'll be back together again as like as not. Maybe you remember going with us to that opium den in Upper Swandam Lane to arrest the street beggar, Hugh Boone, on a charge of murdering her husband. Only to find he *was* her husband. But in disguise, and done up to look more like an old tramp than anything else."

"'The Man with the Twisted Lip'? It wasn't me who went with you and Mr. Holmes to Upper Swandam Lane. It was Inspector Bradstreet, who told me all about it. It sounded a right caper, I can tell you. I was amazed to hear how Mr. Holmes went to work with that sponge."

"No more than I. He took it out of the bathroom and put it in a Gladstone bag before we left Baker Street. But he wouldn't say what it was for. The thing that most intrigues me at the moment, however, is why you should have called round this evening."

Lestrade shifted uneasily in his chair and, after a lot of throat clearing and whatnot, said in a conciliatory tone, "It's like this, Doctor Watson, I feel real sorry for arresting you and causing you to go into court... " [1]

"Not 'Doctor' if you please. The Judge and Jury made quite sure of that." I rose heavily to my feet and went towards a small side table. "It's not too early for a whisky-and-soda," I muttered. "I could certainly do with one. How about you?"

He gave an appreciative nod and held out his hand. Meanwhile I grabbed two glasses, put a generous slug of whisky in each and then added a little soda water from the gasogene. "Your calling me, a ward orderly from the Military Hospital at Netley, 'Doctor' is now out of the question," I said. "Why I ought to be calling you, 'Sir'!"

Lestrade sniggered complacently. "Especially as I've just been promoted. But you were saying your wife and this Fanshaw woman may soon be back in harness again. Sometime in the near future, I take it?"

I leaned back in my chair and stared at the ceiling. Then I said, "As you know, I am extremely fond of Mary. She has managed to find a really good nursemaid to look after the Little Nipper.

1. *The Sign of Fear* by Molly Carr

The girl takes him for an airing every day in the park and sees to his collywobbles. But my wife *will* go sleuthing. First thing in the morning it's 'Watson, see you answer the door promptly while I'm out. It could be a client. John, try not to get your feet wet at the race course. Taking time off to look after you if you are ill means that we will lose money. Did you write this down correctly? I can't make out if there's been a robbery in Richmond or a burglary at Barnet.'

Lastrade laughed so hard his hand shook and the whisky went all down his crumpled shirt front."What a life," he gasped. "If I recall, you were always being nagged by Mr. Holmes. Now it's..."

"Not quite as bad as that," I said huffily, holding out the whisky bottle since I was well aware this very irritating Scotland Yard man was off-duty. "She doesn't make me feel small; and always gives me a kiss before she leaves the house."

For some reason this set the visitor off again. Emptying his glass at a gulp, and wiping his eyes with a none-too-clean handkerchief, he got up and made for the door. I followed him, my slippers (about which Holmes had so much to say during the investigation into the Stockbroker's Clerk business) flip-flopping as I went. But before he left the house Lestrade turned to me and asked, "Why exactly did your wife fall out with that woman?"

"I have an idea it was the other way round. You see, we were staying with the Duke and Duchess of Loamshire..."

"Don't I know it," said the new Chief Inspector sourly. "Letting somebody pinch her diamond necklace, calling in The Yard, and then expecting me to sleep in that draughty attic and eat below stairs with the servants. As it was, we never did recover the damned thing. Although I'm sure she had others. Though probably not quite so valuable."

"You didn't recover the necklace because the gardener went down to 'The Hammer and Pincers' and gave it to Emily."

"I don't see what that's got to do with your wife."

"I asked her to help persuade Miss Fanshaw to let me lodge the diamonds at my bank in Charing Cross. It was much safer that way. Raffles was threatening to kill her and..."

"What, Cox & Company?" Lestrade suddenly changed his mind about going away and stepped hurriedly back into the hall. "Surely that means we can recover them, even after all this time. It'll be quite a feather in my cap, I can tell you."

"No, you can't recover them," I said, suddenly realising what I'd done and wishing I had kept quiet. I was also wondering how to get out of the mess I found myself in before Mary came home. I looked at Lestrade in horror and started to stammer helplessly. Finally I blurted out, my face red and a choking feeling in my throat, "They're lost!"

The policeman's face took on an even more sallow shade than usual. "Lost?" he said scornfully. "They can't be lost if they're in a bank."

"Burned down, went bust," I shouted desperately.

"What rot! We're not talking about Overend and Gurney's. That Bank went bust some years ago. I'm going home now, and tomorrow we'll take a cab to Cox's. You can ask them to open your box. I assume it was your box the necklace was put into since you seem to know so much about it?"'

Well my name is Mary Watson, née Morstan, co-founder with Emily Fanshaw of The Watson-Fanshaw Detective Agency. I have just come in after being out at work all day, in one of London's thickest fogs, trying to get to the bottom of a mysterious death. My head aches and I badly need a night's rest. Coming into the house, so exhausted that I feel almost done for, taking off my damp cloak, hanging it on the hall stand and going into the room Emily had agreed we should use as an office, in spite of feeling so dog-tired I am suddenly jolted wide awake by the dreadful thing I find lying on the desk.

Watson had been here before me. Well, there was no harm in that. He often helped with the business side of things. But the paper dancing before my weary eyes showed he'd once again been trying his hand at writing a story. After the fiasco of 'The Riddle of the Rotterdam Packet', when he borrowed sentences he (or Sherlock Holmes) had already used for several so-called 'adventures' written for 'The Strand Magazine', I didn't hold out much hope for this latest effort. But I nearly had the vapours when I read it. Watson is almost incapable of making up a coherent story by himself, and out of his own head. What I saw could only be the unvarnished truth: the way he had spent the evening while I was out hunting all by myself round London. Set down here word for word as a record of the conversation he had with that fellow Lestrade.

As soon as I finished reading this ridiculous effusion I rushed into the drawing-room. Where I could see Watson sitting staring into space with his hands between his knees and looking very glum indeed. One glance at my face showed him I'd read what he'd written, and he looked almost frightened for someone who had once posed as an experienced army officer with war service in Afghanistan.

"I suppose you realise what you've done?" I screamed.

He looked up at me and nodded ruefully. "Let Lestrade think we still had the necklace. I'm afraid I got rather carried away. It was so much like old times when I used to sit comfortably by the fire with Sherlock, while the wind whistled in the chimney and the rain came down in torrents."

"I'm beginning to agree with what that high and mighty man thought of you. How could you be so stupid when you know you finally gave the Duchess's diamonds to A. J. Raffles outside that pawnshop? I said at the time they were the rightful property of the new Duke of Loamshire. Now that rat-faced copper's coming round here in the morning and will probably accuse us of the devil knows what."

"Do you think he would give the diamonds back? Raffles, that is."

"Not a chance. They were probably fenced as soon as he and that Bunny of his left Cox's, with them in his dratted pocket. Wait while I put on a dry cloak. I'm going down to Lambeth and I want you to come with me."

"Lambeth?"

"Yes, Lambeth. Pinchin Lane to be precise. I'm going to call on old Sherman."

"What good will that do? He's a bird stuffer, with a side line in renting out dogs!"

"I'm almost sure I heard somewhere that he's diversified a little. Now please hurry, John. We've very little time left."

I knew the shop in Pinchin Lane would be closed by this time. But the owner lived above his premises; and we arrived there in double-quick time, thanks to Watson offering a very generous fare to a sleepy cab driver. I stood impatiently tapping my foot on the pavement while John threw stones at an upper window. It was still showing a light and, after what seemed an age, opened just enough to reveal a pair of rheumy eyes glaring balefully at us through the fog.

"Go on, you drunken vagabond," said an angry voice, "and stop disturbing respectable traders at this time of night!"

"It's me, Watson," said John.

"Watson? What Watson? I don't know any..."

"I called on you one evening to borrow a dog during 'The Sign of Four' investigation."

"And no doubt disturbed me then, I shouldn't wonder."

"It was for Mr. Sherlock Holmes. And this lady..."

"Lady, what lady?"

"She's here with me now."

"Oh she is, is she? Worse and worse."

"Don't be such a fool," said John. "She's my wife, and needs to speak with you urgently."

The window slammed shut. Ten seconds later the outer door of the shop opened and a lanky old man stood panting on the step and staring into the street. He gestured to us to come in and I saw the place was crammed with cages, each containing its own little animal. Sherman had threatened to set one of the poisonous snakes on John if we didn't go away, and I was thankful when he directed us out of the shop and into a little back-parlour. Where he asked in a rasping voice what it was Mr. Holmes wanted this time.

Seating myself in the nearest armchair and ignoring the question, I said I'd heard he'd branched out and become a pawnbroker in a small way. Did he by any chance have an unclaimed diamond necklace on the premises?

"A diamond necklace?" he demanded sarcastically. "What do you think this place is? I'd be lucky if it was paste, always supposing I were ever to have one hocked at all. Claimed or unclaimed."

"It would be worth your while to look," said John.

Sherman got up, grumbling, and went into a room situated even further back from the front door of the shop. After a long time, and a lot of banging about and bad language, he came back carrying a flat jewel case – a case which was decidedly oblong in shape. It was similar to the one I'd shown Sherlock Holmes on my first visit to Baker Street at the beginning of the investigation into 'The Sign of Four'. So this seemed promising. I could see Watson felt the same. Hadn't he given a whistle of surprise when I opened that case to reveal the six pearls from the Agra Treasure? Holmes, of course, had simply looked at them with half-closed eyes and made no sound at all.

Now Sherman opened *his* case, and I saw at once that the rope of diamonds was paste. But the situation had become desperate. John took the necklace, handed over enough money to satisfy the bird stuffer and we hurried home through the fog, the cabby narrowly missing several obstacles looming into sight an inch or two from his horse's hooves. "We know that Lestrade ate with the servants while we were at the Loamshires," I said, "so he never saw the diamonds close up. We might get away with it."

"I doubt if he saw the diamonds at all," said John. "Even the Duchess didn't wear them in the day-time. But what about the old Duke's Secretary?"

"I can't be certain, but I believe he left for foreign parts as soon as the young Lord St. Vincent succeeded to the title. Said that after all the years spent serving the late Duke he wanted to do something for himself."

"Has he ever seen the diamonds, Lord St. Vincent I mean?"

"Quite possibly. But, even if he had, he'd ask for them to be locked away without bothering to look at them again. No nephew wants to be reminded that his uncle was murdered, and his aunt hanged."

When Lestrade called the following morning we told him Watson and I had already been to the bank. Slightly peeved because he hadn't been in time to accompany us, he took away the heavily wrapped and taped-up parcel in a huff saying he would deliver the diamonds to the Loamshire Town House himself. Even if the young Duke wasn't there he, Lestrade, would still get the credit for recovering the necklace. John, very relieved at not having to answer any awkward questions, asked me later over the luncheon table how I'd got on the day before with my investigation into the mysterious murder. If it was murder, and not just a dead body in a district unremarkable for corpses.

I told him that, although I had been following other leads, I'd also spent part of the morning in a tavern in Whitechapel trying to find out why a business man had died so suddenly. My better half, fork poised, looked at me as if he couldn't believe his ears.

"You went into that notorious area again, and by yourself, after you were nearly murdered by Leather Apron? I noticed you had started wearing a worn-out cloak whenever you left the house, and a tatty bonnet. But think what that constable said to you both when you went there for the first time with Mrs. St. Clair."

I leaned towards him to pour out a second glass of wine. "The tavern is on the outskirts of the stews," I said, "but near a very populous and quite good commercial district. The man who died was one of the customers."

"All the same you should have asked me to go with you," said Watson. "No respectable woman would enter a public house by herself. In fact, no respectable woman would be seen in a public house at all."

"Well, *I* went straight in and ordered a pint of porter. I wanted to see what the landlord did with it."

"Did with it? What do you mean, 'did with it'? Handed it over the counter, I should think. Once he saw the colour of your money, that is."

"I've been going in at different times for a week. Not once has the rascal cleared the pipes."

John pondered this for a moment. "You're saying he just draws the beer? Well, that wouldn't matter normally. It's only the first pull of the day that's crucial."

I stared at John, put down the decanter and went round to his side of the table to give him a hug. "Sherlock," I said, trying not to laugh at his look of surprise, "it seems you have hit the nail on the head. Something's been puzzling me for days."

I could see he was pleased but also perplexed (even though he made an unsuccessful attempt to appear blasé), so I went on hurriedly. "The man who died so mysteriously was quite well-to-do and had a very good job in the City. But he also had a taste for low life. Every morning he went into this particular hostelry for a drink before work, and was nearly always the first customer. If what you say is correct, that the first drink of the day is the important one..."

"Of course it is," said John, busy finishing off the roast lamb. "Any landlord worth his salt draws off two or three pints and flushes them down the sink before the place opens. Otherwise some poor devil has a very good chance of being poisoned.

14

Don't forget, the beer has had time to settle and been in the pipe since the place closed the night before."

"And it's the same for any pub?"

"Any pub with lead pipes leading from the barrel to the bar. The old inns with their wooden pipes would be all right. This chap's habit of going in every morning and being the first to be served means the lead built up in his system and eventually killed him. It wouldn't take long. It's a wonder there hasn't been wholesale slaughter if all the innkeepers around that area are the same. I sincerely hope, Mary, that you were never the first customer?"

"Only once, when the man I'm talking about was delayed for some reason. But I imagine it would have to be a pretty regular practice before it did away with somebody. And the pubs can't all be the same. Otherwise..."

"Several landlords in that part of the world would certainly be in the soup and no mistake," finished John. "Of course you are quite right in saying that the effect of any lead poisoning could be cumulative. But it was because the man went in every day at more or less the same time, and usually before any other customer, that he died. It would only take a small amount of lead to kill him in those circumstances. If he'd taken the same amount in one go instead of over several days he'd probably still be here, funnily enough."

I began to clear the table and said, "The body was found one morning in an alley near this chap's offices. The police suspected foul play, of course. But there wasn't a mark on him, and he hadn't been robbed. His family said he had always been in the best of health, even if rather irritable recently, so it was unlikely he'd died from disease. Thanks to you, I think we have found out exactly why he did pop off so suddenly."

"There were some advantages to working with Holmes," said John with a satisfied smirk. "That is, when we did actually work and not sit over the fire swapping yarns, studying form or reading sea stories. But how did you get involved in this particular incident?"

"A letter came from the family asking the Watson-Fanshaw Detective Agency to investigate. They weren't satisfied with the official police, or the doctors."

"But how did you get on to the Whitechapel pub?"

"I heard through the grapevine about the man's rather eccentric habit and thought it was the best place to start."

With a happy smile at dear John, I carried the empty plates into the kitchen on a handy tray. "While I'm washing up," I said over my shoulder, "I want you to get in touch with the relatives and tell them what we think. If we're right, there should be a cheque in the post for us pretty soon. It won't be as big as the one the Gold King gave you for saving his life in Ballarat. In fact, it won't come anywhere near it. But at least it will keep the wolf from the door."

Going down to Whitechapel and sampling beer every day for a week had left me feeling queasy. I decided to take a rest from detective work and was actually darning a pair of Watson's socks when a loud ring at the front door bell made me jump out of my skin. I knew it couldn't be Moriarty, who had once danced madly in our hall but was now very dead, and I sincerely hoped it wasn't Raffles or his dear friend Bunny. It could be Wiggins of the Baker Street Irregulars who had helped us to discover the thief when most of our worldly goods were stolen while we were in Australia but it didn't seem likely. The best thing to do was to go and see.

The woman on the doorstep looked a perfect stranger. Tall and slim, with dark hair done up in a neat bun on the back of her head, she wore a pale blue dress with a fashionable peplum at the back and a tight-fitting jacket with long sleeves. She was also very well shod. In the act of telling her politely that she had come to the wrong house, I suddenly noticed a sardonic gleam in her eye. "You're never Emily Fanshaw?" I shrieked.

"Why not, Muriel?" she said, stepping over the threshold and calling me by the name Moriarty dreamed up when he suggested I should become one of his agents. A suggestion which in the end fortunately came to nothing.

"But the hat," I said weakly. It was a very fancy affair. Straw, with a fetching ribbon and a great bunch of artificial flowers on the crown.

"Neville's at home," she replied briefly, as if that explained everything.

Maybe it did. Her husband hadn't any profession to speak of, but he'd usually been away whenever Emily and I were out catching criminals. Nevertheless, he appeared to become a bit straight-laced after Sherlock warned him off begging – and would certainly not approve of his wife going about in male attire, as she had done when we went searching for Leather Apron in the environs of Whitechapel. I sometimes wondered where the money for the St. Clair family to live on came from these days.

Mr. St. Clair had once earned a colossal sum, more than seven hundred pounds a year, simply by coming up from the country to London every day and sitting on the pavement selling matches. He wore a grotesque make-up and had developed a nice line in repartee. This set him apart from the less talented cadgers, and was the reason people were only too happy to put so many small coins into his cap. The matches, of course, were a blind to stop the police from moving him on. Street begging was illegal, and very much frowned on by the authorities who always wanted it cleared up.

But as Emily Fanshaw was forever reminding me, after Holmes unmasked him Neville St. Clair had to sell the house in Kent (described by the estate agent as 'a large villa with very nicely laid out grounds') and move with his family to a smaller place in Bayswater. It could be that they were still living on the proceeds of that sale. If so, how long would it last? Maybe this was why Mrs. St. Clair now sat opposite me in the kitchen probably hoping for more work. Well I wasn't averse to having her back. After all, she'd been the one who'd gone off in a miff. I decided, however, not to tell her about my investigation in the East End of London. The cheque would be small – and we needed the money. Instead I made some tea, got out the chocolate biscuits and asked her if she had any idea where our Agency should go next.

Emily traced a pattern on the floor tiles with the inevitable parasol, the one she had bought in Paris on our way to Nantes at the time of the de Luc episode. "I think," she said, "that I would like to go to New York to investigate the Long Island cave mystery." So she hadn't forgotten that?

I put away my darning with a feeling of relief and asked calmly, "Why? And what's in it for us? Besides, where's the cash to come from to get to America?" I was in no mood to poke my nose into something I knew nothing about, and travel so many miles to solve a mystery which might not even exist.

"Neville gave me quite a lot of money for my birthday," she said, opening her purse and showing it to me. "I don't mind standing treat. As to what we'll gain from going over to the other side of the Atlantic, who can tell?"

"Is Watson to come as well?"

"If he wishes," said Emily indifferently.

"What about the Little Nipper? I'll have to bring him with me."

"Not a good idea," she said decisively. "He's much too young."

"Then what do you propose I do with him?"

"Leave him with that nursemaid of yours."

"John wouldn't be too happy about that," l said, wondering how she knew so much about my domestic arrangements since we hadn't met for some time.

"Then bring him to Bayswater."

Where there was a governess, a cook and a couple of live-in housemaids of rather more advanced age than our girl Millie. "My two would love to have a baby in the house. Especially Griselda," continued Emily. "She's developing into quite a little mother."

"So much for heredity," I thought to myself. But I was still occupied with the question of money. As I stated earlier, nothing had been said about what the American mystery might be, whether it needed investigating at all or if we were the most suitable people for the job. It could so easily become a pleasure trip. I felt that, although she was offering to pay, I couldn't spare the time from consolidating my position as a Female Sherlock Holmes here in Britain. I was also mighty suspicious at seeing my dear friend so flush with cash.

"Emily," I said, "has Mr. St. Clair been..."

She looked at me defiantly. "Neville doesn't tell me everything."

I reflected that he didn't tell her *anything* if, with all her brains, she hadn't cottoned on to what he'd been doing in Threadneedle Street. How did she reconcile the large sums her husband brought home with his being (at different times) a not altogether successful reporter and an amateur actor, the only two jobs he was ever known to have done but which had helped him considerably in his role as a beggar? Where did she think the money for their lavish lifestyle at Lee had come from?

Saying he went up to London every day because he was interested in 'several companies' shouldn't have deceived anybody, least of all her. And how did he account for the sale of 'The Cedars' and the enforced move to 'The Laurels' in Bayswater if he told Holmes he didn't want his family to know what he'd been up to in that little alcove near the Bank? Then I recollected how, in the early days of our acquaintance, she told me Neville St. Clair suddenly appeared in Kent from nowhere and seemed very well supplied with what it takes to impress the neighbours. The two were instantly attracted to one another and lost no time in getting married. I recalled what Moriarty had once said to me when we met in The Haymarket: 'One villain can always recognise another villain.' Knowing some of the things she got up to, it struck me that Emily might be well aware of what her husband was like and where all those pennies and half-pennies were coming from. If she wasn't, then why did she resent it so much when the begging had to stop?

If that former expert mendicant, Hugh Boone, told Sherlock Holmes the truth: that he was going off the game, not only because Bradstreet told him he would have too if he wanted to avoid prison and have everything hushed up, but also because he didn't want his family to be ashamed of him (as he thought they would be if things did leak out), how come his wife knew anything at all about his begging? Had there been some confessing going on in the sacred privacy of the nuptial bedroom after all?

Deciding it was too much bother to think about, but determined not to let her go on nagging me on the subject, I made up my mind to forget the whole thing for the time being – and stood waving to her on the doorstep with a sly smile (which I hastily hid with my other hand) as she went off. Looking, I couldn't help noticing, like any other respectable matron and mother of a family.

When she left, and I told Watson we might be going to New York at Emily Fanshaw's expense, he looked extremely dubious. Even more so when he found we were leaving the Little Nipper behind. But I managed to reassure him by saying there would be several competent female persons of advanced age residing at 'The Laurels', as well as Mr. St. Clair himself. Emily had managed to convince her husband she needed a complete break from family responsibilities, and what could be better than a prolonged visit to The United States of America?

I reflected cynically that Mr. St. Clair might possibly have some devious plans of his own and be very willing to let his wife go where she liked. But after she had spoken to him, and I had had another word or two with Watson, everything was arranged quite quickly. Emily went round to the steamship company and, two days later, we entrained for Liverpool. The journey by ship was smooth and uneventful and the weather journey by ship was smooth and uneventful and the weather fine. I got the impression John rather enjoyed squiring two women around, and turned a blind eye to his occasional attempts at a mild flirtation with Emily while we were at sea. That would soon stop if he got as seasick as he had done on the way to Norway when searching for the mythical Sigerson.

Chapter Two

So the quiet days passed in what seemed no time at all. We arrived safely at one of the Hudson River piers and disembarked without any untoward incident. Watson reminded me of the last time we were in New York, and how the Gold King's luggage had been put through Customs so much more quickly than ours and that of the rest of the passengers. Then, as we docked, I was surprised to see my husband waving enthusiastically to someone on the Quay. Was it Neil Gibson? The man looked much too weedy. As soon as we came off the ship he ran up and greeted John like an old friend. "I saw your name in the Passenger List," he said with a grin. "You remember 'The Red Circle'?"

"Yes, by Jove!" said Watson. "Some crook bleeding to death all over the white woodwork. How are you, Leverton?"

"I get along."

"And Pinkerton's American Agency?"

"It gets by."

"If you don't mind my saying so, you sound a bit down in the mouth," said John sympathetically.

"It's all this fuss over the Long Island cave business. People will keep treating me as a kind of hero. It's been going on for some time. Soon I'll be so well-known I won't be any use to my bosses. Detection involves such a lot of undercover work."

"I take it you're free at the moment?"

"Yep. But hopefully not for long. The work will soon start to come in again."

I could see Emily pricking up her ears at the mention of Long Island. Now she went over to Watson and asked sweetly if she could be introduced to his friend. She told Mr. Leverton that, after a few days enjoying the sights of New York, we were going over the Brooklyn Bridge to the Railway Terminus on the Island. From there we hoped to travel to Peconic Bay.

Mr. Leverton looked startled. "'The Line to Nowhere'. That sure is some distance," he said, as if he desired to put us off. "I'd say at least a hundred and twenty miles. But for the moment you'll be wanting to get to your hotel and rest a while till you get back your sea legs."

Thanks to the American, we soon found a cab, and were pleased when he offered to accompany us. But after shepherding us safely into the foyer he gave Emily and me a low bow, shook hands with John, hoped we would have a pleasant evening and then went off with a bright smile and a cheery wave. But not before he expressed a hope of seeing us all again very shortly.

"A comely young man, forsooth," said Emily as we went towards Reception. "I'm sure I don't know why he would think a journey of one hundred and twenty miles by train is at all arduous, or that it is any great distance. Especially as he must have done it at least once himself. But I really ought to find out

25

as much as I can about Pinkerton's. From a professional point of view, of course."

Was that just vulgar curiosity, her thirst for knowledge or a reason to meet up again with the gallant Mr. Leverton? Watson winked at me and raised his hand to give the bell on the desk a push. Before he could do so, a tall man wearing steel-rimmed spectacles and a green eye-shade materialised as if by magic through a door behind the counter. He gave the three of us a thin-lipped smile and reached for the Hotel Register.

"Mr. and Mrs Watson," he muttered, "and Miss Fanshaw." So she had even provided herself with a different passport than the one she used when going abroad with her family. Now, that could only be done by going into some very shady places indeed, meeting some very shady people and parting up with a lot of money. However, I was still occupied with the desk clerk. Turning his back on us, he took down two sets of keys from some hooks hanging near a number of cubby holes meant for letters and banged them on the counter. At the same time 'a boy in buttons' and wearing a page's hat appeared from nowhere. With a cheery word he began gathering up our luggage which had already arrived from the steamship.

"A bell-hop," whispered John, taking the keys off the counter and preparing to follow the youth into the elevator. "Two adjacent rooms on the fifth floor."

"I only hope Emily doesn't start grumbling," I said as soon as we were alone. "After all, she booked the rooms in this hotel..."

"I don't care if she does," said Watson, busy taking off his boots. "Go next door and ask her if she's also booked dinner."

"Of course I have," said Emily indignantly. She'd removed her outdoor things and was sitting on the bed gazing at an open wardrobe, trying to decide what to wear for the evening. "Don't tell me your husband's doing the unpacking..."

"No," I said, "he isn't. In fact I've left him lying on the bed having forty winks. He found the whole journey rather exhausting in spite of the calm crossing. But I can see you have been busy. I had no idea you had so many dresses."

"Well you couldn't expect a shirt and trousers. Not with Mr. Watson in tow. Now, if we had come here by ourselves..."

She'd be marching about Manhattan with her hands in her pockets pretending to be my brother. Just as she had when we visited that Music Hall in Nantes. And was it my imagination or did she dwell on the 'Mr.'? She seemed to me to hold the word a little too long. "Damn it," I thought to myself. "If that's the case poor old John can go back to being 'Doctor'. At least for as long as we're abroad."

As luck would have it, this was what was fated to happen. Soon after we took our seats in the dining-room that evening a young man rushed at us. He was waving a little book made up of pages of coloured paper. Pulling his hat off his head, in much the same way as Wiggins of the Baker Street Irregulars had done when he'd met me one day in the street for the first time, the stranger said breathlessly, "It is Doctor Watson, isn't it? The man who helped Sherlock Holmes in his investigations? It would be such an honour for me to have your autograph."

The boy, he really was only a boy, looked eager. John looked embarrassed; and Emily sat gloating, obviously waiting for what might happen next. "Certainly you can," I said loudly, taking the autograph book and passing it to John. "*Doctor* Watson would be only too delighted to give it to you."

"Would you like ours too?"asked Miss Fanshaw sarcastically. "I run a famous Detective Agency and..."

But the youth had already vanished, so I felt it unnecessary to give her a vicious kick on the shins under cover of the tablecloth. Instead I contented myself with sampling the Idaho potatoes in their foil jackets and the meat swimming in the most delicious gravy I have ever tasted.

"So much for the 'Roast Beef of Old England'," said Watson. "At the risk of sounding unpatriotic, I'd say this was even better."

"It's not roast beef," said Emily sourly, cutting viciously into her meat and spearing a large portion of it on her fork. "It's Porterhouse steak."

28

"Beef, steak, spare rib," said John cheerfully. "What does it matter? Just let's make sure we enjoy it. Don't forget, there may be tough work ahead."

It was while we were sampling a strawberry sorbet with whipped cream and pistachio nuts that Emily asked, "How did that young man know who you were?"

Watson shrugged mildly. He had heard how good American coffee was and looked forward to lingering over a cup of it in the lounge. I saw him swallow hurriedly before saying, "The Hotel Register?"

"There are lots of Watsons all over the place," said dear Mrs. St. Clair, as if she resented the very name.

"Never mind that now," I said, getting up and carelessly throwing my table napkin down on the cloth in the way I had seen the best people do. "I'm for a shot of Bourbon in the bar."

But John wouldn't hear of it. We were to sit drinking coffee in the lounge or we could have a bottle of the best Bourbon sent up to our room. Emily looked at me coldly. I knew she was wishing Watson miles away. What I didn't know then was that he very soon would be.

Things continued to go well for the moment, however. The next day the ubiquitous Mr. Leverton called (as we had suspected he might) to take us on an outing. He suggested Fort Wood for a closer look at the Statue of Liberty which was fast becoming a tourist attraction. After a short discussion, John and I decided to accompany him and Emily as far as something called The Battery. From there they would catch a ferry to Liberty Island and we would do a little sightseeing by ourselves. Referring briefly to The Battery as we sped in a trolley car back the way we had come the day before, our guide told us it was in Castle Clinton Park and that Castle Garden used to be a place of entertainment. Jenny Lind, said Mr. Leverton, came over from Europe to sing there and was known as 'The Swedish Nightingale'.

"How clever of you," said Emily with an uncharacteristic simper. "That's just the sort of information my friend Mrs. Watson loves to collect." I could tell she would have liked to say 'useless information'. But the desire to impress the Pinkerton man held her back.

"Now it's used to process immigrants," he said, referring to the Battery and making it sound like a canning factory. I craned my neck out of the window and thought what a sad sight it was to see the place where hoards of hopefuls, each with his or her pathetic little bundle of possessions, were waiting to be checked out or, rather, checked in. Ellis Island, that 'Isle of Tears' where some arrivals would be welcome and others sent back to their homeland, wasn't in use yet. Although, according to Mr. Leverton, it would be very shortly.

I recalled my first sight of the Statue of Liberty on my way to Australia. Her height doubled by the pedestal on which she stood, this gift to the United States from the French Nation a year before John and I were married was an inspiring sight, with her torch held so proudly aloft, and with such a calm and thoughtful face. "No wonder so many oppressed people want to come to a new land of the free, I thought; and suddenly felt so sentimental, I hoped the cynical Miss Fanshaw was steadily looking the other way.

After seeing Emily and her escort off, John and I decided to watch the small ships dodging in and out of the harbour, welcoming the bigger liners as they steamed into port. But our plan was spoilt by some kind of trouble near the water. An immigrant had apparently drowned the day before and his body was only just now being recovered. A sound that we heard was a horse ambulance come to take the body to the mortuary. "Do you think he committed suicide because he was going to be sent back to Europe?" I asked.

"Could be," said John. "There might be something about it in the papers tomorrow."

But there wasn't. With so many people trying to get into America the death of one poor, lonely stranger didn't prove worth reporting. John laid 'The New York Times' on the table at breakfast and opened his tobacco pouch. Emily, however, begged him to delay smoking until we left the dining-room. She looked tired after her day out with Mr. Leverton, and complained that she had a splitting headache.

Watson said huffily that he wouldn't dream of smoking while people were still eating. He was just checking he had enough 'Ships'. Or, failing that, 'Arcadia Mixture'. It turned out he hadn't either of his favourite brands of smokers' weed. With a hasty apology, he said he'd better go out and find some. If he couldn't then perhaps he'd be able to 'make do' with Havana cigars.

After sitting over our coffee (the tea was undrinkable) for some time, I began to wonder why my husband wasn't back. There were plenty of tobacco kiosks, with their distinctive 'Cigar-Store Indians', within walking distance if one went the right way. We had migrated to the lounge, where Emily sat reading a fashion paper while I grew increasingly fidgety. At last she looked up and said, "If you're that worried about the man hadn't we better pay a visit to Leverton's office? How long has Mr. Watson been gone?"

"At least three hours."

"What's his bump of direction like? Would he be able to find his way back to this hotel by himself?"

"Just because John isn't allowed to practice medicine anymore," I said crossly, "doesn't mean he's a complete idiot."

"Nevertheless, he's a difficult person of which to paint a portrait. Connected to the army but not in it..."

"What do you mean? Ward orderlies at Netley are trained soldiers, part of the Army Medical Service. Besides, the army is in Watson's blood. His great-grandfather, John T. Watson, was a quartermaster in The Northumberland Fusiliers and fought in the Peninsula War. When he earned the Peninsula Medal."

"Which your husband no doubt wears on his watch-chain," said Miss Fanshaw with heavy sarcasm, implying that it must be a very small medal indeed. "He has acquired a middle-class veneer of a sort because of his long association with Sherlock Holmes," she continued nastily. "Although this is inclined to slip now and again. But it came out at the trial that he was by no means an educated man. Not Public School, University and trained in Medicine, as everyone had been led to believe. So how could he understand all that French and German Mr. Holmes was so fond of throwing at him, to say nothing of when Sherlock said something in Persian?"

"Holmes quoted Hafiz in English," I said, very rattled. "At least, he said it was Hafiz. Although no-one has ever been able to discover it anywhere in the Persian poet's works."

"Shortly before, in another of the stories, your husband brought out some Latin all by himself. Something about a miser, wasn't it?"

"I can't say anything about that as it was before my time. It's a very well-known saying anyway. On a par with 'Beware the Greeks when they come bearing gifts.' Or if you prefer it in the original..." I was becoming increasingly angry at what I saw as a useless discussion. One which would do nothing to help John if he had really lost his way.

"I've never heard of that, whatever it means, in any language!" Emily interrupted. "But Neville said some of the French and German wasn't transposed correctly. But that's not surprising, I suppose." Shifting her seat a little she went on, "They don't, as far as I myself am aware, teach foreign languages in the Board Schools."

"Watson did very well in the circumstances," I said.

"It's quite on the cards that you helped him, of course."

"Well I did no such thing." Meanwhile, I thought to myself, didn't Holmes say he wrote up the investigations, Watson signed them and Arthur sold them? It would be Sherlock who was at fault when it came to translating foreign languages and not my John.

"What's the weather like I wonder," said Emily, suddenly changing the subject and looking out of the window. "Do you think it's hot enough for me to need my parasol?"

Drat her parasol. It was hardly ever unfurled anyway. She simply carried it around because she thought it made her look elegant. Jumping up in a fury, I said I was going to find Leverton immediately – even if I did make a fool of myself and Watson had simply been delayed for some silly reason. Leaving a note for him in case he came back while we were away, I asked the desk clerk with the green eye-shade the way to the nearest Pinkerton office. We would have to take a cab, he said, but we couldn't miss it.

"Do you think it has the name blazoned all over its front?" said Emily to me with a snigger. "So much for undercover work."

Well it wasn't as bad as that. But everyone seemed to know where the office lay. It was a different matter with Emily's *beau* of the day before. Mr. Leverton hadn't been seen in Pinkerton's for a week, and he wasn't there now. "He told us he was on leave," said Emily.

"That's not till next month," said the girl at the counter. "You had better see Mr. Castalotte."

I stood there for a moment, rather puzzled, sure that I'd heard the name before. But where? Suddenly the door of an inner sanctum opened and a swarthy man came out with a bundle of papers.

"This is Mr. Castalotte," said the young woman, deftly relieving her boss of his burden and preparing to do some filing. He, meanwhile, ushered Emily and me into a large comfortable room and asked how could he help us? I could see Miss Fanshaw enviously eyeing the fixtures. But this was America, where everything was done on a grand scale. Before she could pass any remarks, or make any odious comparisons between our office and this one, I told the handsome and well set up man before me that my husband had gone out that morning to buy tobacco and hadn't come back.

"Which is the habit of many husbands in your experience I suspect," said Emily with an arch smile.

"But not my husband," I said angrily.

However, she wasn't to be put off speaking to the man in her usual flirtatious manner. "Are you the same Castalotte whose family owns a Fruit Importers?" she asked, making it sound the most glamorous job in the world.

"That was my uncle. Unfortunately he is now dead. But he wanted me to go into the business because, as a bachelor without any children of his own, he looked upon me as the 'son' who would succeed him."

"But you preferred being a Detective?" said Emily, giving the word its full weight and fluttering her eyelashes in a way which I found infuriating.

'Looked upon me as a son'. Now I knew where I had heard the name. From Watson, as we wondered around the shipping area in Lower Manhattan admiring the way everything operated so smoothly. He had seen it on a horse-drawn van and began telling me all about the investigation into 'The Red Circle'.

"The one mentioned by Mr. Leverton when we met him at The Quay?" I asked. That meant there had been a genuine bit of sleuthing, not something Holmes dreamed up to meet their obligations to 'The Strand Magazine' while the two of them sat by the fire roasting chestnuts, or whatever else they did to while away the long winter evenings. With me sitting at home twiddling my thumbs.

"There was this very beautiful Italian woman," John had said. "My, she was a corker. She and her husband Gennaro Lucca had a small house in Brooklyn. But they were forced to flee to London because he had been told to murder old man Castalotte."

"And he didn't want to? I imagined those Italian desperadoes thought nothing of killing their own grandmothers and roasting them for dinner."

"We're not talking about the Mafia." Watson had sounded impatient for him, and I'd looked daggers. "Although," he'd continued unabashed, "the husband belonged to a secret society when he was young."

"The Red Circle!"

Watson had then gazed at me admiringly and said, "That's clever of you. The problem was, when the young couple first came to America they rescued this Fruit Merchant from some rowdies in that part of New York known as The Bowery. He was so grateful, he gave the husband a job and treated him like a son. Rather than kill him, they fled the Country. I made a pun, you know, for Holmes to use. You've already guessed the name of the Secret Society. When there was murder to be done members put their hands into a bag and drew out a disc. If the disc had a red circle on it (there was only one) then that man did the job. But to spice things up a bit after we discovered a dead body I suggested a very metaphorical sentence to Sherlock. He was really impressed with my 'his head encircled by a ghastly crimson halo of blood, lying in a broad wet circle'. Quite appropriate, we thought."

"And also quite disgusting," I'd said. After which we walked on in silence until we had both recovered our good humour and gone in search of some American ice-cream, which is almost as good as the Italian variety. I was wearing a green silk dress with yellow facings, and reminded John that Emily had gone on her boat trip in a white outfit with black pom-poms all down the front. I privately thought she looked like a pierrette. But the two men had been entranced.

"A symphony in black and white," the Pinkerton man had said, enthusiastically offering her his arm.

"Don't get too friendly," I'd hissed in her ear as they went off. "Remember you've a husband and children at home in 'The

Laurels'." Mr. St. Clair certainly had an arboreal taste in house names, what with that and 'The Cedars'. I wondered if he had read the peculiar tome which Holmes had been carrying when he disguised himself as an old bookseller. The one about tree worship, which he toted around for his own purposes along with a volume of Catullus.

"I can take care of myself," hissed Emily in her turn, glaring at me over her shoulder. A glare I pretended to ignore.

"I bet she can," John had said as we moved away from the harbour. "Take care of herself, that is."

Sitting contentedly in a quiet out of the way ice-cream parlour, and busy sampling the produce, he'd looked extremely chipper. I had reached across the table and given his free hand a little squeeze. "Even if this does turn out to be just a pleasure trip," I'd said, "I'm sure it will be a very pleasant one."

Which only goes to show that, in this life, one should never be too cocksure about anything.

Chapter Three

Old Mr. Castalotte's nephew said he would put his best man on the job and have him scour New York for news of Watson. But, in spite of her coquettish behaviour while in his office, as we left the building and walked hastily towards a cab rank Emily said she didn't trust Pinkerton's American Agency any further than she could throw it. Why, they'd even managed to lose one of their own employees! Instead we would drive back to the hotel, arrange for our rooms to be kept for us and go over the Brooklyn Bridge to Long Island, a place she had intended to visit all along and felt sure was where we would find John.

I didn't believe it. But I was desperate enough to try anything. Emily told me Long Island was shaped like a fish, its mouth towards Manhattan and its body stretched out, as Leverton had indicated, roughly one hundred and twenty miles to the Atlantic Ocean. I was somewhat surprised at such erudition coming from her. But there was more. The fish had two flukes to its tail, she said, enclosing a bay approximately thirty miles long and five or six miles wide. One fluke was known as the North Fork. The other was called The South Shore. And the stretch of water they encircled was the one which went by the name of Peconic Bay.

"My," I said to myself. "This woman must be really interested in the place to know that much about it." But I was puzzled nevertheless.

The trolley car took us across the Bridge and into the Railway Station on the Island and we caught the Greenport train to the North Fork. As we travelled towards the Bay, with one suitcase between us, I imagined all sorts of things. Watson dead and stuffed into a cupboard like poor old Cardinal Tosca, trussed-up and starving to death like the Gold King, maybe suffering from sudden loss of memory and wondering round like a benighted soul in a strange land. There seemed to be no end to the horrors I was experiencing. But Emily said she was sure my husband was safe. I wasn't to worry, just relax and enjoy the scenery. This proved impossible, of course. But there remained little time for reflection. After waiting for the engine to get up steam, the train moved very smartly out of the station – only stopping for a few minutes at some halts *en route* to pick up a number of people on their way to work.

To while away the journey Emily Fanshaw, who was easily bored, began to ask me some rather searching questions. The first one was, "Why did you let everyone think you were twenty seven on your first visit to Baker Street? No woman with an ounce of femininity would admit to being any older than she could get away with."

She was a fine one to talk about being feminine, what with always donning trousers and marching about with a boy's cap on her head.

"How did you manage to convince Holmes you were 'a dear little woman'?" I retorted, "with your 'keen look', and after leading him up the garden path before revealing, contrary to what Sherlock had just told you, that your husband was alive."

"That was one in the eye for him," she said with a laugh. "I had a fancy to make him half in love with me. Even your innocent husband asked Holmes why the investigations into Neville's disappearance weren't being carried on in London. But he was easily put off by a cock-and-bull story about important enquiries having to be conducted in Kent. Let us return to something else, however. Those pearls, for example. If the first one came to you in early May 1882, and you had *six,* then you must have presented yourself to those two men a year earlier than is often thought; and, when your employer's small daughter came upstairs with a letter for you, why did you say 'It was on this very day' that the pearls used to arrive when, in reality, it was two months later? You visited Baker Street at the beginning of July."

"'Stark insensibility, Madam.' As Doctor Johnson once said to a woman who asked him why he defined a word in a certain way."

"Who?"

"Samuel Johnson."

"Oh, is he a friend of yours?"

"A friend to the whole world," I said sarcastically, "who wrote an enormous Dictionary." For all her intelligence, Emily was just like Holmes. There were certain things she kept well away from her 'little attic of a brain'. "He also said that recalling a crime *committed in vain* was the most painful thing possible."

"That lets us out, since we haven't done anything of which to be ashamed," said Emily sententiously. "We solve crimes, not commit them. It may be less exciting, but..."

Here she looked at me quizzically and said, "To return to your somewhat murky history of what happened when you met Mr. Holmes. To make matters worse you were very precise about the date your father disappeared: 'December 3rd 1878 – nearly ten years ago'. But it could only have been eight and a half years at the most. If you were at your school in Edinburgh until you were seventeen, and then came down to London to the Langham Hotel, that would make you twenty-five, going on twenty-six when you went to Baker Street. Of course six is a nice even number of pearls to fit into a regular jewel case. Did you have the seventh hidden in your garter?"

"All water under the bridge," I said crossly, using one of my favourite expressions and thoroughly tired of this unnecessary grilling. "You seem to forget, I had no control over what went into that American Magazine. Any more than you would have done if you had been in my shoes."

"You've been to that house haven't you, 221B Baker Street?" said my tormentor, obviously forgetting what she had just said about my going there with a letter. "The business with the jack-knife sounded very peculiar."

"I expect that's why the housekeeper, who I later learned was called Mrs. Hudson, received such a high rent."

"To pay for a new mantelpiece? And I heard she was called Turner."

"Come now, Emily. You know as well as I do there was a fashion for putting a piece of cheap but stout wood on top of the marble and covering it with matching curtain material. Both easily replaced. As for the Hudson/Turner mix-up, well..."

"What about the bullet pocks on one of the sitting-room walls, the marksmanship spelling out the Queen's initials?"

"Pure embroidery," I said wearily. "In all senses of the word."

"I've sometimes wondered what happened to those highly valuable jewels," she said. "I read that your father's friend, Major Sholto, removed a chaplet from the Agra Treasure Chest before he hid the rest of the loot: and that his son committed the unbelievable vandalism of breaking off one of its 'very large lustrous pearls' at intervals to send to you after the man died. Obviously, since the old soldier had it by his bedside instead of in the box, the thing couldn't have gone into the Thames with the rest of the ill-gotten gains."

"Well, that's no affair of yours," I said, and stared resolutely out of the window. But, silent as I was, my brain still worked overtime. Describing Mrs. St. Clair in the twisted lip adventure as 'a little blonde woman clad in some sort of light mousseline de soie, with a touch of pink chiffon at her wrists', and not the tall, dark-haired hoyden she really was, must have been Watson's idea.

And she'd made sure to outline her figure against the light when she opened her front door to the two men, had even bent her body a little to disguise her height. Perhaps this was what gave John a false picture of the woman. And how she must have hated wearing all that fluffy stuff! I recalled a drawing of 'Miss Fanshaw' looking down at Holmes with one hand behind her back like a recalcitrant school girl. While he sat, in a very relaxed manner, deep in a basket chair and gazing at her with the air of a schoolmaster questioning a pupil. I thought at the time, from her very feminine stance before the great man, that there must be no limit to her duplicity.

It wasn't long before she was off on another tack, however. "Mr. Watson said, after Mr. Sherlock Holmes was supposed to have gone to his death at the Reichenbach Falls, that he would write fulsomely of the episode. But how could he? if he was aware that his friend wrote everything himself, then he must have known that friend was still very much alive and would be busy writing his own obituary! After all, the story did appear in 'The Strand Magazine' eventually. Unless you wrote it."

"That I didn't," I replied indignantly. "John said, when Mr. Sherlock Holmes revealed himself after coming round to our house with that agent fellow of his, 'I was absolutely certain you had gone over.' He was there at the Falls in person and, in spite of everything, had a great admiration for Holmes. The shock of his friend's supposed death caused my poor, ill-used husband to rise to the occasion; and I thought he managed to produce something quite creditable."

"How 'ill-used', if I may ask?"

"Letting John publish all that stuff. And then suddenly turning up disguised as an old bookseller peddling dirty books. Telling me to my face that he (Holmes) was never in that raging torrent after all. More's the pity."

"Yes," said Emily with a grin. "He deceived not only Mr. Watson but every city clerk in London. Remember all those black arm-bands we saw outside the Court-House?"

"I may have done and, on the other hand, I may not. After all, I did have much more important things to think of at the time. Just as I do now."

Really, she had no consideration for the state I was in; and it was patently obvious she wasn't to be stopped that easily. "You said when your husband went to Norway to find Sigerson he also met the King. Did you mean the King of Norway or the King of Sweden?"

"They weren't, they aren't, separate Kingdoms yet. Although I've heard that the people want them to be."

"Then you should have made everything crystal clear by calling him the King of Scandinavia, for whom Mr. Sherlock Holmes did do some sleuthing I believe. Or so he said, during all that business about the man he termed 'The Noble Bachelor' and his American wife."

"Only she wasn't his wife as it turned out."

"Did the editor pay you much?" asked Emily, abruptly changing the subject.

"What editor?"

"Of 'The Century Magazine'. I'm sure your husband begged you not to publish in 'The Strand.'"

"Enough." I wasn't in the mood to tell her what.

"And did your accounts ever come out in book form? It's a wonder nobody asked for their money back."

"I have sometimes thought so myself," I said. "Fortunately there was no-one to agree with us."

"Do you remember the lachrymose widow in Nantes, the one who wiped her eye on her white apron? You said the group of tiny houses where she lived resembled a beguine. But it's the person who is the beguine, not the place."

"Yes, yes. The group of houses is called a beguinage. It must have been too much gin," I interrupted with a yawn.

"Too much *what*?"

"Gin. As an aid to composition."

"A few footnotes might have helped: and everything such a muddle! It was almost impossible for the reader to work out just when our investigations had taken place."

"That's all part of the detecting process, and part of the..." I was about to say 'fun', but one look at her face made me change my mind. I sneezed diplomatically into my handkerchief and asked if she had ever read any of Watson's or, rather, Holmes' accounts of some of *their* investigations? "Most of which, I now know, came out of Mr. Holmes' own head. Chronology certainly didn't worry him. In fact, if he'd been too exact he would probably have been found out. People will spend years, and make a fortune writing books about it, trying to sort out when *those* investigations happened. If you're not happy with my writing, do it yourself! After all, you're just as much part of the Watson-Fanshaw Detective Agency as I am."

I said this as the train glided into Greenport Station: and I could have sworn I had said the King of Scandinavia when I wrote about Sigerson. However, there was no gainsaying a woman like Miss Fanshaw once she had the bit between her teeth.

48

Only one hotel of any consequence existed in Peconic Bay at that time so we were forced to go there and take pot-luck. Emily marched up to Reception and banged on the bell with her clenched fist. She hadn't enjoyed the journey any more than I had, and the last twenty miles had been made even more insufferable by her continual carping. When somebody did appear, she asked peremptorily if anyone could direct us to The Cave. The desk clerk looked at her as if she had taken leave of her senses. Yes, he said, there was the bay. There was the sea. And it was cliff country. But he hadn't heard that one cave was any more important than another. Perhaps if she found it she'd be kind enough to come back and tell him where it was.

Glaring into his face as if she would like to give him a thwack with her precious parasol, Mrs. St. Clair said in a loud voice, "But what about the Mystery, the Pinkerton Hero and all that?"

"Are you talking about the missing child?" asked the clerk, stopping Emily in her tracks. "The toddler who was stolen and then found by Mr. Leverton? Now I come to think of it, a cave was mentioned. But it couldn't have been a real cave."

"Real or not, have you any idea where it is?" demanded Emily crossly.

"Somewhere down on the North Shore, I think. A stone building that used to be a prison for drunks."

With that he walked off, with a cynical smile on his face.

Leaving our one case to be taken up to our room and saying we'd be back shortly, Emily and I ran towards the beach. Sure enough, there was a stone building standing on the edge of the sand. It looked old, run-down, uncared for and generally out of use. But a stout new door, which seemed as if it would be very difficult to open, occupied almost the whole of its front. Giving it, as well as stability, a decidedly menacing air. Emily went towards it, skirted carefully round the outside of the building and then, to my surprise, came back and banged on the door with all her strength.

The result of this activity amounted to precisely zero. I grabbed her by the arm and said I was going to walk along the beach to see if I could spot a likely aperture. If not, we'd read the newspapers. Mr. Leverton, if his deed had been truly heroic, must have featured in all of them, along with details of any cave.

"But," growled Emily, "where will we find the precious papers?" As far as she could tell, the noble deed hadn't happened yesterday – or even last week. It wasn't long, however, before I found an opening in the cliffs high enough to admit quite a tall person. At the same time Emily said she saw someone standing a hundred feet above us on the bluff. But, before I could look up, the figure had disappeared.

The inside of the cave, when we did get inside, presented a most amazing aspect. After a few yards the walls showed smooth and whitewashed. Some twenty feet or so further on, and with some bending and stretching on our part, an even more surprising thing happened. We came across a door identical to the one we had already seen at the stone building on the shore. But, as Mrs. St. Clair prepared to bang on this door as hard as she had done on the other, it opened so suddenly she would have fallen to the floor if an invisible presence hadn't grabbed her by the waist and hauled her inside.

Ten seconds later I felt someone grab me by the wrist. In spite of struggling, and screaming my head off, I found myself in her company. And in the company of the youth with the autograph book.

No longer boyish looking, he glared at us so ferociously I was reminded of an angry young bear I had once seen in Regent's Park Zoo. "I knew you were on that ship," he said. "But the passenger list mentioned a *Mr.* Watson. The best thing I could do was pretend to be a collector of autographs since I had to be sure of getting the right person."

"But why Watson?" I asked in a strangled voice.

"Black Gorgiano was my grandfather."

Emily and I looked at each other. We were both at a loss to know what he meant since I'd told her it wasn't John who killed the man. He'd simply accompanied Sherlock to the room where the corpse lay, and watched all that messing about with the lamp when Holmes lured Emilia Lucca out of her hiding place by letting her think it was her husband who was signalling to her.

But before we could say anything the young ruffian gestured fiercely to us to start walking. It wasn't a comfortable procession, with him bringing up the rear. But at least he didn't stick a gun in my back. As the dear-departed Professor James Moriarty had once done during a memorable march down a passage in that opium den 'The Bar of Gold' in Upper Swandam Lane.

It was one thing to demand we start walking, but the way seemed long and tedious. It became obvious as we progressed that we were moving even further underground. The noise of the waves, and the shriek of angry gulls quarrelling over rare scraps, reached us faintly at intervals before fading significantly away. Our journey had started in a small room hewn out of the rock, but now we had been traversing a long, winding corridor for what seemed an age. The faint sound of the sea suddenly grew louder. The birds screamed. And, just as I thought I could go no further, our captor stopped underneath a small trapdoor let clumsily into the roof of this miserable passage and signed to us to get ready to climb.

The area had increased in height. Stretching himself to his full six foot and standing on tiptoe, Gorgiano's grandson was only just able to knock at the rotting wood. He did this three times before the trap was opened and a rope ladder came rapidly down. Emily and I were then forced to clamber up this ladder but, short as it was, before she reached the top a pair of tattooed arms pulled her the rest of the way. They then did the same to me and we found ourselves in a well-lit room with comfortable armchairs and a number of small tables. Beautiful hangings adorned the walls. There were pictures by the greatest artists. Boxes of the best cigars were scattered around, and a tantalus containing the finest wines was well within reach. Several men of a swarthy appearance were lounging about reading newspapers or playing black-jack. But my eyes were riveted on two of them. One small, clean-shaven and hatchet-faced. The other larger and with a fine moustache. Mr. Leverton and John playing cards together at the biggest table: and for what seemed very high stakes. So much for pretending to put us off coming to Peconic Bay when he met us and took us to our hotel. The Pinkerton employee had assessed Emily's psychology very accurately. The best way of making her do something was to strongly advise her against it.

It struck me it was from Leverton that Emily had learned so much about the geography of Long Island. He'd cunningly reinforced her desire to go there during their jaunt to see the Statue of Liberty. I ran towards the card players. But the young man who had brought us to the place stopped me with an oath.

"This is Indian Country," he said. "Your husband's drugged up to the eye-balls. Thinks he's playing baccarat in some London Club, 'White's' I think it is, with The Earl of Euston. He certainly won't know you."

"Do you mind if I sit down?" said Emily weakly, suiting the action to the word and at the same time managing to give the young man a vicious poke with her parasol. "All this is a little beyond me. It has, I'm afraid, made me liable to swoon."

This from a woman who, I was sure, had never come anywhere near fainting in her whole life.

Looking as if he would like to throttle her, Black Gorgiano's grandson said, "We couldn't get Holmes because he's dead, and he's taken his arch-enemy with him. Now we're trying to put somebody in Moriarty's place." So they didn't know everything. But my John the wickedest man in the world? A 'Napoleon of Crime'? It wasn't possible. "Don't you believe it," said the little beast with relish. "The drugs make a person very suggestible, and they're already beginning to work. To start with, he's cheating like mad. Soon..."

A card-sharp? John H. Watson? The trial in London, where he'd been successfully defended by Sir Edward Carson, revealed he had some guilty secrets. But I knew he would never stoop to that. Never become, like Colonel Upwood in a case Sherlock investigated (or said he did) a cheat at cards in somewhere like the Nonpareil Club. It wouldn't fit with the image my husband liked to project of himself as an ex-army man of unimpeachable integrity. Nor was it in his very nature.

"Mr. Leverton, or to give him his real name Giuseppe Leverento," said the odious person I had once thought of as 'a boy', "recently pushed one of our stool-pigeons into the East River. But not before he'd persuaded him to hand over the Vatican cameos. That was," and here he bowed ironically to us both, "just before he met you two ladies off the ship and escorted you all to your hotel."

"And to think I was so pleased when he offered to take me to Liberty Island," growled Miss Fanshaw, throwing a dirty look over her shoulder. As I knew (to my cost) was her wont on occasions. "But what's all this about Vatican cameos?"

"Priceless works of art. Old as the hills. We had a 'plant' in Rome and, as soon as he'd stolen them, suggested he travel to the United States on an immigrant ship. All this took time, of course. But by then our friend Giuseppe here had come back from London and..."

"Just a moment," I said very severely. "Inspector Gregson introduced the so-called Leverton to Sherlock Holmes and John while he was in the Metropolis, and they were investigating the mystery Holmes called 'The Red Circle'. So why the charade with the autograph book?"

"I've already told you, I had to make sure I identified the correct person."

"Don't you ever listen you stupid little boy?" I demanded rather bravely. "That crook sitting there already knew my husband so he could confirm that the passenger he met off the ship was Watson."

"I double-check everything. Besides, it would have been stupid if he had gone to meet the wrong person and I didn't know. Might have ruined everything."

"You double-check. And double-cross too, by the sound of it," I said, thinking of the body fished out of the East River.

"You don't think we would pay good money to a down-and-out jewel thief if we could get something for nothing, do you?"

"From what you've just told me these weren't just any old cameos. It must have taken months of planning by an expert, and probably the greasing of a very large number of palms. There wasn't anything 'down-and-out' about the thief. Besides, murder isn't nothing."

"It is to me," said a merry voice from the card table – where Leverton was busy passing over the latest bundle of dollars won illegally by John. "You should see the notches on my gun. All it needed was a hefty push while the *spacone* had his back turned. That was after he delivered the goods of course," added the fake Pinkerton man, suddenly showing his teeth in a wolfish grin.

How such a person could ever have had enough interest in an opera singer to tell us about her was incredible. It suddenly struck me that, for two detectives, Emily and I hadn't been particularly prescient.

"Something a man should never do," said the boy with a grin. "Turn his back on one of this gang. I sent the *buffone* a message by Alfredo while he was in Rome to wear clothing with no marks, and to travel with forged papers. He'll not be traced to us."

Emily again said she felt faint and was directed to the kitchen where she was told to make coffee not only for herself but for everyone who wanted it. It seemed to my shattered nerves that she was absent for a long time. She emerged at last, however, and with a very sly look on her face. Coming over to me and bending close to my ear so that the others couldn't make out what was being said, she whispered that I wasn't to worry. She had everything under control. All I need do was try to keep up my spirits. I watched her and Alfredo hand round the cups – refused by a few of the men who preferred something stronger – and hoped for the best. It was a faint hope because I had already seen a look of suspicion on a certain face. A face more intelligent than all the rest of the motley crew put together, except perhaps Mr. Leverton's; and he turned out not to be particularly bright.

It seemed that, in spite of what we now knew about the gang and its hideout, we were to be released and sent back to our hotel. This was a facer. But it was also the signal for another uncomfortable trek down the very long tunnel, escorted by someone who certainly wasn't welcome, and a hurried exit from the cave with the stout door. "I suppose you know where we were," said Emily. "That trapdoor was the entrance to the stone house we investigated first."

"It couldn't be," I gasped, running to keep up with her. "With that tunnel underneath the whole lot would fall through the sand."

"I grant you there were many heavy artefacts, and it housed a number of people. It was also much bigger inside than it appeared to be when we first saw it. But, although it seemed to be on the sand, which is quite impacted anyway, it was much nearer the cliffs and fallen rocks than we thought; and it was obvious those villains went to a great deal of effort to shore up that passage so that they could come and go as they pleased."

A place that size meant there must have been an awful lot of drunks on Long Island at one time if the desk clerk in our hotel was to be believed. "What I don't understand," I said, "is how it, the tunnel I mean, got there in the first place."

"Neither do I understand it," said Emily, gathering up her skirts and moving faster than ever.

"English settlers hiding from hostile Indians perhaps. It was extremely old, and in any case had collapsed at a point just beyond the trapdoor. The main thing is that now we can go to the police and..."

"They can kill Watson."

"Kill Watson? Surely the whole idea is to make him into a second Moriarty, with them as his Lieutenants."

"What was the name of the man you told me about, the one you saw in Australia?"

"Do you mean J. Neil Gibson, the Gold King? Whose wife committed suicide at a place called Thor Bridge?"

"No, the other one."

"That old *shikari,* Colonel Sebastian Moran?"

"They would have him to deal with if he ever got wind of it. But although elevating Watson, if that's the right word, to the status of arch-villain would be a wonderful revenge for the murder of that little snake's grandfather, they'd forgo it rather than be caught."

By this time we had arrived at the hotel. Emily ordered dinner to be sent up to our room and, as soon as we reached it, lay down on her bed clad only in her chemise. I collapsed fully clothed into a chair and wondered how she could even think of eating anything. I was trying to figure out why the gang had let Emily and me go instead of killing us both and training Watson to be a second Moriarty all by themselves. John would be alone, and so presumably easier to manage.

"They have their methods," said Emily in an 'Ours not to Reason Why' kind of voice. But to me it was extremely important to know what was going on, and why we had been set free. But when I started to nag her about it she said, quite reasonably I thought after I had finished listening to her, that if my husband was going to be turned into a consummate villain, unsurpassed in the annals of crime, a wife and family would help to disguise the fact that this had happened. He would be wreaking havoc behind a facade if extreme respectability.

"After all I understand that the original Moriarty was a model of probity," she said. "Completely unsuspected by everybody but Holmes."

"But once John was back in the house and away from this gang he would surely return to normal?"

"He would never be away from those men. There would always be one or other of them in the house, if only to make sure he stayed drugged. Besides, if he became that much of a crook that he no longer needed the drugs he would keep you very much under his thumb. You'd be afraid to go against him for fear any harm came to the Nipper."

John hurt the Little Nipper? It sounded absolutely incredible as I listened.

And that would be the day when any man had me under his thumb. The plan seemed full of holes. But that didn't make the Gorgiano gang any less dangerous at the moment.

"Mrs. St. Clair," I said, suddenly recalling her long absence, "what exactly happened in that kitchen?"

"I let Alfredo make love to me."

"*What?*"

"You know. Nothing much. A little peck on the cheek. Holding my hand. That sort of thing."

Memories of theatre land and its casual prostitution came suddenly and unbidden into my mind. I had been a bit wild in my young days, before my marriage to John. But to hear this outwardly respectable matron going on like this took my breath away. "He was fair smitten," said Emily. "I had him eating out of my hand and he told me the whole plot. The first thing they did was get Leverton into Pinkerton's. They accomplished this by stealing a little boy who was sunning himself on the family porch of one of the houses in this part of the world. Don't look so alarmed, Muriel. Apparently the gang treated him well, even though they had to keep moving him from place to place. He rather enjoyed it by all accounts."

But I was thinking about the Little Nipper, and how I'd feel if I came out of the house and found him gone. Driven to distraction would be too mild a term for it.

"There was a terrible hue and cry," continued Emily, sitting up and resting her chin on her elbow. "But Leverton appeared after a day or two with the child in tow. Proving what a good detective he'd make because he said it was only after studying various clues that he'd managed to find the infant in a cave. The little darling was too young to give the police any information. Just said he'd met lots of new uncles, saw lots of lovely pictures and could he have some more ice-cream? Leverton got taken on by Pinkerton's American Agency without a reference (although I'm sure he could have produced a forged one if wanted), inveigled the Big Boss into sending him to London, met Inspector Gregson and told him he'd come over to arrest Black Gorgiano. In reality he had come to murder the Luccas."

I sat bolt upright in my chair. "This *is* all to do with the Red Circle then?" I said, remembering all John had said in that walk to find an ice-cream parlour.

"Is that what it's called?" asked Emily indifferently, having apparently clean forgotten all about mentioning the name when we talked about the scowrers during the Ricoletti investigation. "Apparently Gennaro Lucca tried to protect his wife from Gorgiano by hiding her in a house in Bloomsbury. 'A high, thin, yellow-brick edifice in Great Orme Street near the British Museum' by all accounts, while he went off to murder the blackguard. So of course he had to be killed himself. Watson would never have been involved if it hadn't been for the landlady consulting Sherlock Holmes."

I might have known it. He was well clear. But his interference meant my John was now in the grip of a gang of merciless villains intent on taking revenge on the entire world for an Italian desperado's well deserved death. "What did Alfredo tell you this lot did before they got their claws into Watson?" I said.

"And still do. Contract murders all over the globe. Going around in pairs stealing priceless works of art of all kinds to order. The paintings you and I saw on the walls are waiting for the time when they can be unloaded safely onto the people prepared to pay through the nose for them without going to the police."

"It seems to me they hardly need a Moriarty," I said coldly.

"To replace Black Gorgiano. He was the brains of the outfit. Without him the rest of them are at a loose end, unsure of the best way of going on. That's why there has been so much lounging around lately, drinking and playing black-jack."

"And that slimy little brute, who in my opinion would make a perfect Moriarty, is determined to get his own back over the murder of someone he calls his grandfather?" It was too much. I felt if there had been a cat around I would have kicked it. In fact, I did go as far as kicking a chair, at the same time as I swore like a fishwife.

Instead of showing any sympathy, Emily sat up straight on her bed, swung her feet onto the floor and grabbed a leg of chicken from the trolley which had been brought up and left outside the room by a busy waiter. "You are fast losing your celebrated aplomb and replacing it with a vicious temper," she said. "There isn't the slightest use taking it out on the furniture. It might only leave us a bill for malicious damage. Gorgiano's grandson would rather do his own thing than be in charge of the gang's operations. Besides, some of the older members don't like being told what to do by a callow youth."

"Not that callow," I said bitterly.

Chapter Four

The next day at breakfast, as Emily was tucking into bacon and eggs and I was toying with a dry bread roll, Mr. Leverton appeared to say he was ready to take ship to London. He would accompany all three of us, and continue to work on John with a cocktail of hallucinogenic drugs. We were to behave normally, and say nothing if we wanted to keep my husband alive.

At that moment the young man who had taken us through that horrible tunnel to the house near the strand strolled in with a glassy-eyed Watson. He was still full of the Vatican cameos. "Think of it," he crowed. "The Apotheosis of Creon."

"That's a big word for a small boy," I said sarcastically, at the same time ignoring his great height. "That is, unless you went to Harvard."

"No," he said, unabashed. "I'm a Yale man myself."

Thanks to Leverton's help, we were able to get back to Lower Manhattan with the minimum of fuss. Everybody knew him because of his supposed rescue of a child, having his name and photograph in all the papers and being taken on by Pinkerton's American Detective Agency. They applauded the way he now helped two ladies, and an obviously catatonic man, make the journey to the Quay. He was a real gentleman who had seen to their luggage, settled their accounts at both hotels and was more than ready to accompany them back to Britain.

I was surprised to see Emily treating such a crook exactly as she had before we knew how wicked he was. Instead of sitting staring stonily into space as I did, she was as sweet as ever. Did he need anything before we left the City? Could she perhaps procure him some cigars? How about a last cup of American coffee? Yes, he said. The coffee he'd had to drink at Scotland Yard was terrible, although the tea hadn't been too bad. So all four of us sat in a nearby diner waiting to be served; with Miss Fanshaw and Leverton making bright conversation and us silent as the grave. Watson because he was in a drug-induced dream, and me because I couldn't bring myself to speak.

Did the so-called Pinkerton detective take sugar? Yes, he did. She leaned over and began spooning it into his cup, while I sat fuming at such a blatant disregard for my finer feelings. But without warning the fake American suddenly said he felt ill. He needed to get some air. Walking unsteadily, he left the diner and collapsed dramatically into some long grass.

"Quick," said Emily, running like the wind and tearing off her petticoat. "Help me roll him into that longer greenery over there and cover him with this. It might be a good idea if you took off your petticoat too."

Terrified someone would see us, thankful we had been the only customers in the diner and that the owner was busy in the back kitchen, I quickly did as I was bid and then went to see if

Watson was all right. Emily followed. To my surprise she was laughing her head off and gasped, "They're not the only ones to know about drugs." It turned out she had put something in Mr. Leverton's coffee instead of sugar. When I asked her what it was, and where it came from, she put a finger to her twitching lips and said, "Mum's the word. The less you know about it the better."

"I'm not that silly," I thought to myself. It was quite likely she pinched some drug from that house on the strand and kept it on her person for future use. It reminded me of the occasion when she stole a single sheet of writing paper from one of the rooms while on a conducted tour of the Duke of Holdernessc's Stately Home on the off-chance it would come in handy one day. As it did. Which showed a remarkable degree of foresight.

Wringing my hands, I asked tremulously what we were going to do now. "Calm yourself, Muriel," she said. "Remember the essential qualities of the good detective and how resourceful you were with the man who had lost most of his fingers. The one thing we are not going to do is catch the boat to Liverpool. That snake outside, who is now literally in the grass, will be discovered soon and probably taken to hospital. But his friends will think he is on the high seas. That gives us time to make good our escape."

"Where to?" I asked.

She paused for a few minutes and then said, "Portugal? Spain? Morocco? Or how about Switzerland? I've heard the country has the most spectacular mountains: and anybody who *is* anybody is now making equally spectacular efforts to get there for their summer vacation. When they're not wanting to wait for the snow, that is."

"Wait for the snow?"

"Skiing is all the rage at the moment."

"Otherwise," I thought, "tourists are continually being hauled up the Rigi, the Pilatus and other mountains by little trains." Aloud I said, "What will we go to Switzerland with?" Neville St. Clair's 'birthday' money might not stretch that far.

"You remember Father Tomaso, the young priest you first met in my drawing-room? Come with me to the nearest telegraph office. I want to wire him for some money."

"How can you? The Tosca affair is over and done with."

"But the Vatican cameos investigation is still underway. I'm going to tell him we are involved, but need a considerable amount of cash to make any progress."

"And a considerable amount of nerve when he finds out we haven't got them."

"How so?" said Emily, lengthening her stride so that as usual I had difficulty in keeping up with her, burdened as I was with Watson. She patted the pocket of her dress and grinned almost as wolfishly as Leverento had done in that dreadful den where we'd been incarcerated for what had seemed an age. "Mum's the word," she said again. "Wait till we get on board ship and are heading for Cherbourg."

My dear friend and colleague finally went off to a telegraph office by herself. She came back jubilant, her face wreathed in triumphant smiles. She had waited for a while until Father Tomaso wired back, in answer to her message, to say he had complete confidence in the Watson-Fanshaw Detective Agency. More importantly, he was sending a draft for a considerable amount of money and said any extra would be made immediately available as necessary. The Vatican cameos were absolutely priceless and the new Pope was very anxious about them. He had ordered the *Chiaramonte* and the *Pio-Clemente* Museums to be more rigorously guarded, and fortified them against further daring depredations.

"A clear case of shutting the stable door after the horse has bolted," said Emily sourly. As promised, she showed me the cameos in the cramped cabin on the way to Cherbourg and I was so entranced I almost forgot to ask how she'd come by them. Two beautiful jewels (on which an intricate design was engraved in high relief) of immense value, and of outstandingly bright colour considering their great age, they gleamed invitingly on her outstretched palms. "I found them in an old

69

teapot under the sink in that Thieves' Kitchen," she said, punning away happily. "Since nobody in the place ever drank tea their hiding place was as safe as Fort Knox."

The journey to France was fraught with difficulty. Watson's behaviour was so peculiar, we had to lock him in our double cabin while I moved in with Emily. It was a most uncomfortable arrangement, and Mrs. St. Clair grumbled something shocking. We could hear John ambling around next door and saying over and over again, "I am the wickedest man in the world. Another Moriarty. My henchmen and I are going to rule over the Universe." The only comfort we had was in the dining-room or taking a brisk walk on deck. For safety's sake we arranged for Watson's meals to be brought to his cabin, with Emily or me on hand to snatch the tray from the waiter before he could see anything. After a few days of this, the man went away muttering that he'd never known someone be so seasick.

By the time we got to Paris from Cherbourg John appeared to be more normal. He hadn't had any of the mysterious drug for some time and no longer looked glassy-eyed. But neither did he remember anything after he went out to buy some tobacco. "That's just as well," I thought. Now that he seemed almost free of any narcotic I'd never be able to convince him he was being groomed to become a substitute for a dead Professor James Moriarty.

But now we were in the French Capital and Emily wanted to see the Mona Lisa. John said he was going to take a stroll along one of the boulevards and to be sure not to be late for our train to Geneva. "If that man's looking for 'Arcadia Mixture' again I'm going to murder him," said Miss Fanshaw, hitching up her skirts as if she was about to run after my husband with a stiletto.

We spent longer in the Louvre than we anticipated and had to hurry to the *Gare de Lyon* to catch our train. Watson was already at the station with our baggage. He looked hot and worried. But also very excited. When we asked what was wrong he burst out, "Auguste Poirot is here, all the way from Belgium." I had described him so accurately that, although John had never set eyes on the man, he was sure it was him.

"It's not that far, Belgium," said Mrs. St. Clair with a sneer.

"But it can only mean one thing," I said.

"Even two, perhaps three," said John. "He's chasing after that son of his, the one you told me wants to be a detective in spite of the fact that his father's a crook, he's taking a holiday or he may have got bored in retirement and returned to his old game of robbing banks."

"Why Paris, rather than Spa where he lives?" I asked.

"It's a much bigger place, and therefore easier to get away with whatever it is he may be up to than in a small place like Spa."

I had come clean with John and told him about my meeting with the little Belgian in the Savoy Hotel, and how he'd given me a map and instructions to go to Exeter Hall prior to blowing up the Houses of Parliament, and other buildings, on Moriarty's instructions. "That was where we two met, if you remember," I said to Emily.

"Yes," she said, "and you were silly enough to be still carrying a stick of dynamite in your bustle. You could have killed us both."

"The question is," I said, "are we going to stay and see what Auguste does get up to?"

"Paris is a big place. He could operate anywhere. One investigation is enough."

"What investigation is that?" asked Watson

"The one into the disappearance of the Vatican cameos," said Mrs. St. Clair.

"But you've already got them," I said, afraid Emily was going to defraud the whole Catholic Church, or at least the Vatican and the poor old Pope.

"Yes, but only as bargaining counters. An insurance against our lives. Once we've escaped from Gorgiano's grandson and his gang we can travel to Rome and give the cameos back."

"Meanwhile accepting money by pretending we're on their trail?"

"Well I did get on their trail," she said defiantly, "while I was endangering my reputation with that hideous Alfredo."

"Come on, Emily. You know it was pure accident finding the cameos in that old teapot."

"Not completely," she argued, stamping her foot. "Alfredo was dying to tell all about them, and where they were, in order to impress me. He dropped so many hints only a fool would have missed them."

"I bet he didn't expect you to pinch them. How did you manage it? That lot will kill him when they find out."

"Jolly good job. I wouldn't be surprised if he's committed more murders than Black Gorgiano himself, whose score I believe was at least fifty at the last count. I told him I couldn't find the coffee and whipped the cameos into my pocket while he was reaching up for it."

At that moment a call came for travellers to Geneva to board the train to Dijon and we walked hurriedly along the platform to our crowded compartment. Watson managed to get us two seats by the window and stood in the corridor until most of the other passengers left the train at Melun. We three then changed trains at Dijon, caught the next one to Geneva and relaxed for the rest of the journey.

For once Miss Fanshaw was very happy. We had got rid of Leverton and, as she had already pointed out, it would probably be some weeks before his confederates found he'd missed the voyage to Liverpool. If they then sent two or three bravos to London to deal with us it could take them some time to find out where we'd gone – if they ever did –and we would soon have plenty of money from Rome to cover our tracks. We also, said Emily, had all those dollars passed to Watson in the robbers' hideout to make him think he was winning at cards with Lord Euston, or perhaps Doctor Mortimer with whom he had once played écarté.

Then I nearly spoilt everything by suddenly beginning to worry about the Little Nipper. I asked her how she felt about her own two children. "There's nothing to connect 'Miss Fanshaw' of the Watson-Fanshaw Detective Agency with the Neville St. Clairs," she said. "So stop fussing about them and concentrate on getting as far away from that gang as we can. I was right to suggest your little boy stay with us. They'll never find him."

I could see Watson looked anything but reassured. He knew there was a connection between him, our Agency and Sherlock Holmes. The gang didn't know that Sherlock was alive. Would they go to Baker Street and beat our address out of Mrs. Hudson, the plump motherly woman I had met on my first visit to Baker Street? Although she'd promised to join Holmes in Sussex as his housekeeper and rent Number 221B out to her friend Mrs. Turner, who had sometimes helped her in her

74

domestic duties, she still had a lot of things to see to before finally leaving London. When we did return home (as we must eventually) would there be a whole lot of machete-waving murderers waiting for us on the doorstep?

"No, no," said Watson, sounding as if he was trying to convince himself as well as me. "They'll be in Naples, or more likely Posilippo, hunting for Gennaro and Emilia Lucca."

"Is that where those two came from originally?" asked Emily. "Do you think they'd be foolish enough to go back?"

"I know they didn't stay in London after Inspector Gregson agreed with Holmes that the husband shouldn't be charged with murder. But I seem to remember they returned to Brooklyn."

"Where they would be far too near the remainder of the Gorgiano gang to be safe. My guess is they are in Italy, or as far away from New York as they can get in another part of the United States. And under a false name."

"In any event," I said, "they're safer than I feel at the moment. It would never surprise me to see that horrible grandson waiting for us on the station at Geneva." Fortunately I was wrong in this surmise. But that doesn't mean we didn't have other things to worry us almost as much.

Watson talked volubly about the last time he was in Switzerland, travelling first-class at Holmes' expense to Lausanne because Sherlock said he couldn't leave London while somebody called 'Old Abrahams' was in terror of his life. "I told him I was feeling rather stale so he made that an excuse to send me off on a wild-goose chase. Even then he didn't really trust me, and turned up at a bad moment calling himself an *ouvrier*. He dashed out of a *cabaret* just in time to prevent me from being throttled by some huge black-bearded fellow recently back from the Transvaal, where he'd been doing a spot of gold prospecting."

"Workman, wine-shop," I said to Emily in an aside.

She glared at me and said, "When we were shadowing de Luc that time in Nantes I managed to learn quite a lot of French, thank you very much."

"Yes, yes," I said hastily. "I forgot."

"I bet you haven't forgotten your sore feet though!"

"I remember Holmes cabled me first about somebody's ear," went on John. "Thought it was his idea of a joke. But turned out I was wrong." He sighed, and looked disconsolately at his boots. "Some woman was going about the Continent insisting on taking valuable jewels around with her. Bound to attract crooks."

"Exactly like the Duchess of Loamshire. Determined on always wearing her diamonds," I said, and regretted it almost immediately. Mrs. St. Clair, who had been idly looking out of the train window, suddenly turned on Watson and said in a loud

76

angry voice, "Are they the same diamonds you persuaded me to lodge in your bank in Charing Cross? If so, it's very strange that I never saw them again."

Watson got up hastily and said he was going to see if there was a restaurant car on the train and, if so, would she like him to book a meal for us all? I turned to her and said, in the sort of voice I used when giving a mild reprimand to the Little Nipper, "Don't harass my husband. He's been through a terrible experience and is still recovering from it. We don't want a relapse."

She could see I was annoyed, and tried to put me in a better mood by talking about the Vatican cameos again. Just at that moment Watson came back into our carriage (which fortunately had stayed empty apart from ourselves) and said, "Vatican cameos? During one of our investigations Sherlock sent me off to Devon without him to enquire into the death of Sir Charles Baskerville..."

"He seems to have made a habit of it, sending you off somewhere," said Emily sarcastically. "What excuse did he give for not leaving London this time?"

"I can quote him directly," said John. "In his own words, 'I was exceedingly preoccupied by that little affair of the Vatican cameos, and in my anxiety to oblige the Pope I lost touch with several interesting English cases' – so there you are."

"And I bet that parasol there," said Miss Fanshaw, with a wave at her most treasured possession up in the luggage rack, "that he came down to Devon anyway."

"I'm afraid he did, and the reports he had asked me to send him were hardly worth the paper they were written on."

"Well he was destined never to set eyes on the cameos, unless they had been stolen on an earlier occasion. In which case the Pope is very careless. They're right here, sewn into my pocket. Mr. Leverton's friends stole them and I got them back."

Emily and I had decided if we needed to explain things to John we wouldn't say anything about his incarceration in the stone house on Long Island. Since one of his last memories before being taken there was of Leverton meeting us off the ship from Liverpool it seemed better not to mention the names of any other members of the Gorgiano gang, at least for the present. As it was, he seemed quite uninterested in why we had left America and, instead of going home, come to Switzerland. But he expressed some surprise on hearing that Leverton had such light-fingered acquaintances.

I reminded myself that we didn't know how John had got into the hands of such a murderous crew as The Red Circle in the first place. Emily's theory, that when he was hunting for his favourite brand of tobacco, the kind he always bought at Bradley's in London, Leverton spotted him and they went for a drink together in one of the many bars in Lower Manhattan, seemed more than plausible. Leverton, she said, was probably coming to see us anyway and would have found an excuse for getting Watson alone, taking him off and doctoring his drink. Meeting him in the street had made the whole thing that much easier for the gang.

But now John's amazement, when Emily told him about Leverton and that she had the Vatican cameos on her person, forced me to say something. "We've come to Geneva for a look at the scenery," I said, "before returning the cameos to Father Tomaso. You remember my telling you about him don't you, when Emily and I went to Rome?" It was weak, but the most I felt up to for the moment.

"And Moriarty fled over the roof of St. Peter's dressed as a cardinal. You know, Mary, I've had the weirdest feelings about Moriarty lately. Thought I was being trained to take his place!"

"What an idea," said Miss Fanshaw. "Quite ridiculous!"

What wasn't so funny was that we were fleeing from Black Gorgiano's cut-throats not only because she had stolen what they regarded as theirs, but because they also wanted revenge for the death of their leader. And, in the absence of anyone else, they were determined to wreak that revenge on us.

I decided to take a walk down the corridor to stretch my legs: and was amazed to see, sitting in a compartment all by himself, my little friend from the adventure at the Savoy Hotel. An adventure which had begun so long ago, before my other one in Ireland with Jane Marple's mother Ellen when we travelled on the Irish train together; and before I went to France with Emily to solve the mystery of the poisoned chocolates. I remembered John saying that he had spotted Auguste at the *Gare de Lyon*. When I made a sign to M. Poirot to draw back the door of the carriage so that I could come in and have a word with him, however, all I got was a blank stare. But he must recognise me. Hadn't he said before we parted in London and he hurried off to catch the boat-train to Dieppe that I was *tres jolie*? Said it somewhat erroneously really, since I knew I was no beauty. Even my own husband had remarked to 'his' readers that, when we first met on that momentous day in Baker Street, he thought my face 'had neither regularity of feature nor beauty of complexion.' It's true he apparently went on to remark that my expression was 'sweet and amiable' and my 'large blue eyes were singularly spiritual and sympathetic.'

But all this only showed was that he either didn't write a word himself, or my efforts in front of the pier glass in my room at Mrs. Forrester's (where I practiced being demure and womanly before rushing off to Baker Street at her insistence to consult Sherlock Holmes about my father's disappearance) had been singularly successful.

"But we went in a cab to the Savoy Hotel," I stammered, gazing at the little Belgian in astonishment. "You gave me a map and..."

He had risen to his feet and now made me a low bow. "I fear *Madame* is in error," he said politely. "I have not the pleasure of her acquaintance."

But there was no mistaking that dyed moustache, the egg-shaped head or those green eyes glinting at me under the heavy brows. It was useless to protest, however. M. Poirot would deny all knowledge of Moriarty, or that he had ever been one of his agents. He would say he had never given me the information I needed to help carry out one of the Professor's dreadful outrages.

He might even deny he had once been a bank robber, and declare that the young man who was training to be a detective was the son of some other M. Poirot. I could only smile, bow gracefully and go back to my seat in the train. Where I told John and Emily what had happened, and how surprised I was when Auguste pretended not to know me.

"What puzzles me," said Watson, "is how and why did he come to be on this train in the first place?"

"When you saw him in that French railway station and remarked that he had come all the way from Belgium," Emily said with a yawn, "you mentioned that he was either taking a holiday, chasing after his prig of a son or bored and planning a bank robbery."

"Well," I said, "as he's on this train it looks as if the holiday idea might be the right one. But why pretend that I was a perfect stranger?"

"We can't answer that at the moment," said John. "But one thing's for certain. He won't be robbing a bank in Paris."

"Ah," said Emily with a sudden burst of animation, "but is he planning to rob one in Geneva?"

She stood up and surveyed the reflection of herself in the glass which protected a photograph of the Cathédrale St-Pierre that hung over her seat, almost as if she was preparing to make a conquest of my little man down the corridor. Then she seemed to think better of it and fished in her travelling bag for a fashion magazine. Burying her long nose behind the cover, Miss Fanshaw said in a muffled voice, "We shall have to keep an eye on him after all."

"What with that, the Vatican cameos and the Gorgiano gang we're certainly going to be busy," I said to Watson. But then I saw he had tipped his bowler over his face and fallen fast asleep. It was Mrs. St. Clair who woke him up. While the train rattled on towards its destination, she suddenly shouted very loudly that some unmentionable thief of a Frenchman had crept into the carriage and stolen her parasol. A frantic five minutes ensued, with John crawling about the floor before we found it had dropped off the rack and rolled under the seat.

"I feel like wringing her neck over the blasted thing," muttered my husband uncharacteristically. He got up, pulled back the door of the carriage, stepped into the corridor and stood looking out of the window for a while to calm down. Just as he told me he had done when Holmes dismissed his favourite detectives as 'miserable bunglers'. Emily, meanwhile, continued reading her magazine, and I sat in my corner of the carriage trying to puzzle out why M. Poirot seemed so determined not to acknowledge me. I think we were all relieved when the train steamed into *Le Gare de Cornavin* and we could lose ourselves in the bustle and worry of seeing to luggage and finding a porter.

Having come from the *Gare de Lyon* in Paris we had first to go through the Customs House before entering the actual station and, while our luggage was being examined, Emily asked loudly and in her usual malicious manner if Watson had any drugs to declare or any tobacco. She then compounded the offence by sniggering like a street arab. "Keep a tight hold on what's sewn into your pocket," I hissed back at her, "or they'll never let us get out of the place."

When all the formalities were over and we caught a cab to a hotel, having sent Watson to walk the short distance to ascertain if there were any rooms vacant, we realised that we were in the

Pârquis area of the City and fifty metres from the Lake. Not only that, there were more interesting things in store. High ornate ceilings, open fireplaces, so-called 'period' features. In its own way the hotel was as good as the one at which John and I had stayed while we were in Ballarat.

Emily, of course, complained about her room. The bed was too high and the closets not roomy enough. There was a queer smell from the open fireplace. She wanted to go down to Lake Geneva at once, told us grandly it was also known as Lake Léman: and was only prevented from getting her own way by John telling her it would soon be dark. And, he said, surely she had noticed the delicious smells that were already coming from the hotel dining-room?

"I've also noticed a plump little man with an egg-shaped head and a waxed moustache prowling about the corridor," she said.

M. Poirot. I looked at John. Of course neither he nor Miss Fanshaw had actually met the man. As I said, Watson had only been going on my description of him at the *Gare de Lyon.* And now Emily might simply be trying to gain attention by repeating it, after listening to my husband's reprise while we were waiting for a train. I went out of the room to see for myself: and was very surprised when I came face to face with a much younger version of Auguste. Before I could say anything, he vanished through a door at the end of the corridor. All I was left with was the faint scent of eau-de-cologne, and a vague feeling of impending doom. But worse was to come.

It was when we were at dinner that I noticed Mrs. St. Clair had suddenly lost her normally somewhat robust appetite. She was looking across at two men by the window and completely ignoring the *rösti* on her plate. "That old man is the one you thought you knew, isn't it?" she said. "So the other one must be the detective, or at least training to be a detective."

"Considering what that little Belgian mentioned to you about his son when you met him in London," said John, "they seem to be getting on remarkably well together. The wine's flowing like water."

"Maybe," said Emily. "But they appear to be taking their conversation very seriously."

"Wine is a serious business on the Continent," said Watson facetiously. "There's none of the gut-rot stuff here. People like to know what they're drinking."

"I don't mean the wine," said Miss Fanshaw with a scowl. "They're talking as if they have something of great moment on their minds."

"Like a bank robbery," laughed John, busy tucking into his dinner.

"You don't normally tout a copper around with you in those circumstances," I said. "Not unless you've got a death wish."

"Death wish?" John put down his knife and fork with a clatter. "Whatever do you mean, 'death wish'?"

"You know, doing wrong but desperately hoping you'll be found out."

"My, but you're a dab hand at the psychology these days. Used to take an interest in it myself at one time. I remember Sherlock..."

"Bless Sherlock," I said, meaning just the opposite.

But Emily, sensing conflict (and having no desire to pour oil on troubled waters) asked sweetly, "What happened with Mr. Holmes?"

"We were on a case..."

"One of the very few," I said sarcastically. As I mentioned earlier, about some of their other activities which weren't in the investigating line, I knew they spent more time by the fire in 221B Baker Street than anywhere else except the race-course, Marcini's and the occasional concert. Probably reading more novels, and drinking whisky-and-soda instead of chasing after criminals.

"On a case," said John, pointedly ignoring my interruption, "involving a fellow who kept smashing plaster busts. 'The Six Napoleons' I think it was. I suggested to Holmes that whoever was doing it might be suffering from an *idée fixe*. He didn't agree with me, of course. Said my idea of monomania must be the wrong one. Even if a man hated Napoleon no amount of obsession would tell him where to find the images of the Great Emperor, the ones he was so fond of hammering to bits. Turned out Holmes was quite right," continued Watson unhappily. "We ended up buying one of the busts and..."

But Emily had lost interest and gone back to staring at the two Belgians. "Do you think they've found out about the Vatican cameos?" She asked. "Maybe Black Gorgiano's gang put them on our trail." She sounded rather worried for her. Even the resourceful Miss Fanshaw had been frightened by the horrible grandson; and I still trembled at the thought of that cave.

"Highly unlikely," said my husband decisively. "The Georgiano gang, as I know from the investigation I undertook with Holmes, is anything but law-abiding. They would have nothing voluntarily to do with any detectives. And if they did want dirty work done (assuming those two over there were willing to do it) why recruit anyone from Belgium when you have so many murderous thugs of your own hanging around?" In any case, and aside from all this hypothetical nonsense, the gang thinks we're in London."

"All the same, I don't like it," said Emily nervously fingering her parasol. Which she took everywhere, even into the dining-room. She watched the two men leave and then, with one swift movement, noiselessly followed them out.

"She's worried about their being on our corridor as much as anything else," I said to John.

"Then she shouldn't be. The young one has met his father here for a holiday and to keep an eye on him, stop him from any urge he may have to break into a bank."

"I just hope you are right," I said, preparing to go upstairs. In spite of what John had said, if the Long Island lot *had* somehow managed to get on to us, murderous thugs might not be needed yet. Far better to put two innocent-seeming foreigners on the trail of the cameos. Or, to be strictly accurate, one young man above reproach and busy making sure his old reprobate of a father continued to keep on the straight and narrow. There would be plenty of time for any butchery after the precious objects were returned to the gang. But it was certainly puzzling.

I spent that night tossing and turning, unable to settle to sleep. Hearing my watch tick away the minutes. Suddenly, in the half-light of early dawn, I peered over the top of the bed clothes and saw a round little figure busy rifling one of the closets. It then crept over to the bed and carefully insinuated a hand under my pillow. I held my breath so as not to scream: and thought of Mrs. Marple. Hadn't I done the same to her once while she was asleep? If only I could wake John with a dig in the ribs without letting this phantom realise I had my eye on it. But he was sleeping the sleep of the dead. So much so that I thought he might even be dead, and that the little fat figure had murdered him.

I sprang up with a shout. John turned over and started mumbling. The intruder hurriedly withdrew his hand. The light clicked on. And there stood Emily. She was fully dressed, with a colt revolver in her fist. "Leverton's," she said in answer to my stare. "I pinched it before we rolled him into the long grass." But she wasn't going to be allowed to use it. Before any of us could move, the door crashed open. A second little man scurried into the room and knocked the gun out of her hand. But instead of picking it up he grabbed my 'ghost' by the collar and, cursing volubly, propelled him towards the corridor.

"*C'est un chameau*," he said, "*espéce d' idiot!*"

By this time Watson was fully awake and in his dressing gown. He wanted to go after our unwelcome visitors at once. But we persuaded him to ring down for three stiff brandies while we decided what to do next.

"Obviously father and son," said Emily, "judging by their appearance. There couldn't be any two others looking like that."

"Auguste and his policeman offspring. "You were quite right, Emily. Poirot *pére* is obviously after the cameos. And Poirot *fils* is obviously trying to stop him."

Before she could say anything about this, or even make some sarcastic comment about my inaptitude, we heard a loud noise.

89

It was the sound of breaking glass. Miss Fanshaw, attempting to leave the bedroom in a hurry and hampered by her gown, growled, "Curse this bl..."

Fortunately the rest of the word were lost as she raced down the corridor, with us in hot pursuit. I was just in time to hear her mutter, "Oh, for a pair of trousers," before she arrived at the end of the passage and dived into a bedroom. By the time we reached it she had been trussed up like a chicken and a gag pushed into her mouth.

"Are there no other guests on this floor?" said my husband desperately to me as he prepared to put up a fight. The remains of a large glass bowl lay shattered on the bedroom floor, but the noise had attracted nobody but us three. And it was no use trying to get out of the mess we were in because Poirot *fils* (not Poirot *père*) had Emily's or, rather, Mr. Leverton's gun steadily trained on us. "We searched this woman's room from top to bottom," he said, with a gesture towards the recumbent figure on the floor struggling to release herself. "Then my father searched yours. I think one or other of you must have swallowed the Vatican cameos."

"There's no need to worry," said Watson heartily. "We were on our way to the Vatican to return them to the Pope's Press Secretary, Father Tomaso. These two women met him in Rome during..."

"Father Tomaso? What the hell gave you that idea, and who is he anyway?"

"A high-up cleric," said John, making the man sound like a trapeze artist.

"And why should I give the cameos to him?"

"Well, you're a detective aren't you? Or at least training to be one."

"*Sacré bleu*! I am a dutiful son, following in my father's footsteps and learning from him."

"Not learning enough," said the old man disgustedly. "If you had let this damned *Anglais* think you were a detective he would have handed over the cameos like a lamb and asked you to take them to Rome to save him the bother. As it is, we still don't know where they are."

Maybe that was the explanation for Emily still wearing her day dress. If she had hung it in the closet the young brute would probably have found what he was looking for quite easily.

"I would like you to release my friend," I said tartly. She was already red in the face with rage and likely to have a fit; and it couldn't have been comfortable on the floor in spite of the Aubusson carpet covering that part of it beyond where they had smashed the glass bowl. "After all, you have her gun. Then perhaps we can negotiate."

"Like hell," said Auguste.

But, rather to my surprise, the younger man did as I asked, almost without any hesitation. But when the gag was removed from her mouth Mrs. St. Clair let fall such a flood of bad language that the Belgian drew back with a start. *"Ma foi!,"* he said, nearly tripping over his boots, "The last time I heard words like that was on a prison hulk."

I hastily asked Watson to check if the brandies had arrived and been left in our room by a member of the night staff. Then turning to Auguste I said, "It may have suited you to pretend not to know me in the train from Paris, but I have a better memory than that. After we left the Savoy Hotel you said you were in a hurry to catch the boat train to Dieppe. You had to keep an eye on your son, a policeman who wanted to be a detective."

"That's Hercule. This is his twin brother, Achille."

I blinked, trying, and failing, to imagine Mrs. Poirot choosing such names for her new babies.

"Achille here is even cleverer than Hercule," said Auguste as proud as a peacock with its tail in full array. "He sometimes pretends to help his brother with police work, but he is normally extremely indolent and hardly stirs out of the house if he can help it. Except to aid me, of course. But that was in the old days before I retired."

"And now you've decided to come back into business?"

"Well, these jewels are priceless."

"You need not think the Gorgiano boys will give you even half what they are worth, and if you decide to cheat them and fence the jewels yourselves you'll have a job. To say nothing of no peace of mind for the rest of your life. Like the Canadian Mounted Police they always get their man."

"Gorgiano boys? I heard you and this woman discussing the cameos on the ship coming from New York to Cherbourg. Cabin walls are thin. Achille and I abandoned our other plans immediately."

"Much cleverer than his brother. Indolent. Never goes anywhere. That certainly reminds me of someone," murmured Watson who had returned to the room and, during the whole of the previous conversation, seemed extraordinarily abstracted. "Give me a minute and then I'll have it. Yes, by Jove. Sherlock's brother, Mycroft!"

"I do try to model myself on him in certain respects," said Achille with a modest smirk.

"And succeed only too well perhaps," I thought to myself. Although as far as physical appearance was concerned they were as unlike as chalk from cheese. And Sherlock's elder brother, I knew, was no crook.

Chapter Five

But Auguste was becoming restive. "We can't stay here all night talking," he said crossly. "One of them has the cameos." He saw John glance involuntarily at Emily and, pointing his silver-topped cane at her, said viciously, "That one."

"They're not in her room," said Achille. "So they must be on her person."

I recalled what Miss Fanshaw had said when we were in Whitechapel hunting for Leather Apron. Without her dressed in male attire and pretending to be my brother for our protection we'd be stripped naked, 'and not for any pleasurable reason I assure you'. No, for the clothes on our backs. Or, in this case, some stolen jewels.

"Give him the cameos, Emily," I said quietly. There was a hurried sound of ripped material as she tore open the pocket of her dress and passed the beautiful objects to the sham detective. Who put them into his pocket without a word and bundled us out of the room. I had some vague idea of asking the porter on duty downstairs to ring for the police. But Watson said that, as the Poirots still had the gun, this could result in a shoot-out. Which was why he'd done nothing when I sent him on that errand about the brandies. We would wait till the morning and then try to separate the pair in the foyer. That way he might be able to get a half-nelson on Achille while we two women

94

tackled Auguste. Still very dangerous with so many people milling around, but they might be able to come to our aid.

"What about that old service revolver of yours, and all those Eley cartridges?" I asked.

"I last saw it, and them, in my sock drawer at home," he said ruefully. "At least, it may have been my sock drawer. Or was it my..."

"For heaven's sake," hissed Emily. "I'm going to bed. But I doubt if I'll be able to sleep a wink. It's all been a complete waste of time and effort."

When we went down to breakfast, quite early and with Mrs. St. Clair still in a really foul mood, we found the place more than a little disturbed. Not only had the occupants of a certain room decamped without paying their bill, but they had relieved several guests of the wherewithal to pay theirs. A hotel window on the third floor was found wide open, and a short, silken ladder dangling from it was swaying in a light dawn breeze. By standing with both feet on the bottom rung, it was easy to swing over to the fire escape, run down the iron steps onto the pavement and then disappear in a maze of streets well away from the Lake.

"Half-way back to Paris by now," said John glumly.

But when we went to enquire at the station we were told that no-one even remotely like Poirot *père* or Poirot *fils* had boarded a train to the *Gare de Lyon*, or, rather, Dijon. "And," said Watson with a groan, "it's a sure thing two men looking like them couldn't possibly be missed."

"Even in disguise," I said. "If I had been here and seen them muffled up to the eyebrows and wearing hats and goggles I would still have recognised that mincing gait."

"But you weren't here," said Emily with a grunt, "and now nobody knows where they are."

"After lunch we'll go for a stroll by the Lake," said my husband in a placatory tone. "Some fresh air will help us collect our thoughts. If we can find a park, a walk among the flowers may also be beneficial." Out of the corner of my eye I could see Emily gripping the handle of her parasol at this high-flown purple-sounding nonsense. I hoped she was going to continue using it as an aid to elegance and not to give my husband an almighty dig in the ribs with it.

"I remember Sherlock going on about flowers once," said John. "Something vaguely theological, if I recollect it right: 'Our highest assurance of the goodness of Providence seems to me to rest in the flowers'. He was holding a red rose between his fingers at the time and said that it was an *extra*. I suppose he meant on top of what we *need* to support life. The smell and the colour of the thing were an embellishment of our existence. But that wasn't the end of the business because he went on to remark

'It is only goodness which gives extras, and so I say again that we have much to hope from the flowers'."

"Meanwhile," said Emily sourly, "everyone was simply dying for him to get on with the investigation, whatever it was."

"Well," said Watson, "some people were certainly miffed enough to question if it was the time and place for such strange behaviour when everyone was so worried about a missing Naval Treaty."

"If you ask me," I said, "it was a ploy to stop anyone asking awkward questions and finding out something for themselves. Before Holmes was ready to take them all by surprise with one of his staged grand finales. Or maybe he needed a few more words to fill a small space in 'The Strand Magazine'."

"You never did like Sherlock did you?" said Mrs. St. Clair. She adjusted her parasol and then lengthened her stride. So we were soon standing beside Lake Geneva and looking out across the water. The paddle steamers plying their trade between Switzerland and the French coast puffed softly on their way. "That's because exhaust steam from a marine triple-expansion engine is at a much lower pressure than a noisy railway locomotive," said John.

"You two," Emily hissed at me – she was becoming very good at hissing at yours truly –"are certainly well-suited. Always wanting to tell people things, both."

She was watching the flags fluttering from their staves aboard the paddle steamers and commenting on them in a loud voice. The Tricolour fluttered at the front of the vessels making their outward journey from our side of the Lake to the French coast, and the white cross on a red field for Switzerland hung at the back. "If we decided to take a tourist trip across the Lake," I said, "the steamer would probably hug the French coast and not allow us to land. Technically, we wouldn't have left Switzerland."

Mrs. St. Clair sighed heavily. "You never give up do you?" she said. "But I suppose one could disembark at Evian if one wished?"

"Provided you had your passport with you," said Watson. A small skiff had caught his eye and he was looking at it with a puzzled frown on his ingenuous face. "I don't suppose we put a telescope in our luggage, Mary?" he mumbled in an indistinct voice.

"If so, I haven't got it with me." Why on earth should my husband want a telescope?

"Here you are," said the completely unpredictable Emily Fanshaw, handing John a small monocular. "I object to that impossible affectation which makes a detective feel he has to crawl over the ground with a huge lens every time he's asked to investigate something. But, as the co-founder of a detective agency, I came to the conclusion some time ago that this might be useful."

"I could swear," said John looking keenly through the single eye-piece, "that those two in that vessel are our friends the Poirots." He swung round a little and then said, "Not only that, but they're landing in a small cove on the French coast."

"Let's hope they have their passports then," I said with a grin.

"That's their affair. The point is, why are they landing there? It's a bit hole-in-corner in my opinion. Not the behaviour of anyone who is not up to mischief. Otherwise they would have gone on to Evian, which is a much larger place with crowds of tourists interested in sampling the delights of the spa water." So a good place for those two villains to lose themselves in.

But "Surely not, with us looking on and able to spot them so easily from where we are," I said aloud, referring to their possible landing in a more populous part of France.

"It's the same as preparing to land somewhere smaller along the coast. I can see the skiff perfectly from here."

"I want nothing more to do with that horrible pair," growled Emily, who was no doubt remembering how narrowly she'd escaped a most degrading ordeal. "I only hope Gorgiano's grandson catches up with them instead of chasing after us and tears them to pieces. As far as I'm concerned they can keep the blessed cameos."

"A man's (or in this case a woman's) word is her bond," said Watson. "After what Miss Fanshaw told that parson in Rome we have got to get the cameos back."

At that moment there was an almighty crash of thunder and the rain came down in torrents. Dashing for cover, Emily tripped and nearly ruined the precious parasol. This discomposed her so much it was sometime before she could recover her breath and say anything. As it was, Watson cut her short. As soon as this storm is over we would catch a steamer to the French coast and follow them he said, referring to Auguste and Achille. The distance was relatively short and he could see some of the French resort's many buildings even through the gloom and without the spy-glass. With any luck we would soon catch up with the two Belgians.

"But if only this rain would stop!" I groaned.

"It will soon," said John knowledgeably. "I remember these sudden storms while in Lausanne. They do stop, almost as soon as they start. Look, there's a blue patch over there. Enough to patch a sailor's trousers."

When it became obvious that the storm was over, we embarked on one of the steamers for France. The French flag flew from the bowsprit (instead of the yard-arm, as is usual with sea-going vessels) and the Swiss flag dangled aft at the stern. After our disembarkation at Evian John hired a barouche to take us into the countryside. A long drive away from the port brought us to a bridge spanning a stream overhung by high mountains, which were densely covered by stout trees. A short time later we passed fields of vetch, and came upon two settlements not quite large enough to be called villages. I asked if the Poirots could possibly be nearby.

No, said Watson, who suddenly seemed to have become as prescient as Holmes. The two men had managed to get far ahead of us because of the storm and, he thought, were still some miles further on. After driving for another hour, he spotted an isolated building some distance from the road and surrounded by chestnut trees. Pulling the horses round, John guided them up a steep and rugged path, dismounted from the box and knocked hard at the door of a house which looked as if it was about to fall down. When a wizened little man answered, Watson said his delicate (!) wife had suddenly been taken ill and badly needed a glass of water, or even something stronger. So Miss Fanshaw wasn't the only one then to suggest such tactics when she wished to gain unauthorised access to a house? [1]

I descended carefully from our vehicle, with Emily making an effort to act solicitously towards me, leaned heavily on John's arm and followed what was obviously a very old (and somewhat decrepit) manservant down a gloomy passage into a

1. *The Sign of Fear*

none-too-clean kitchen; where I forced myself to drink a glass of tepid water. Meanwhile Watson had also defined the old man's status and asked cordially, "Is your master at home?"

"Why yes, *Monsieur*. As soon as *Madame* is ready I will take you to him."

Well, at those words *Madame* recovered pretty quickly I can tell you. Then all three of us followed the man out of the kitchen and towards a room where he said his boss always dined, "On the rare occasions when he is at home." The old servant stealthily opened the door. And there at the table (with the Vatican cameos in full view) sat none other than Auguste and Achille. Along with, of all people in this world, the late unlamented Professor James Moriarty.

"But you're dead," stammered John, as he had done on another occasion when Moriarty appeared so unexpectedly and said viciously that he would get his own back on us. I added that I too had seen with my own eyes the villain's unconscious body rolled into the river by Raffles, along with the body of the blonde-haired and ferocious Dane who (with the Lascar) helped to run the opium den in Upper Swandam Lane.

"On the contrary I am very much alive," said the Napoleon of Crime suavely, "and you are interrupting some extremely important business."

Watson stood for a moment looking puzzled. Then, scratching his head, he said, "But what was it exactly that happened in 'The Bar of Gold'?"

"As soon as I smelt the first whiff of chloroform coming from that sneak Bunny Mander's handkerchief, I held my breath as hard as possible. As result, I was still semi-conscious when I hit the water. Floating down-stream along with that completely unconscious idiot of a Dane, I remembered a wharf with some broken staves sticking out of the mud: with one of them leaning in a markedly mathematical manner towards the water. I stood on my companion's head and managed to achieve enough height to grab this stave and then pull myself onto the bank. Of course, the leverage I was striving at did for our foreign friend. My left foot pushed him right under. Nobody will ever again see him alive," added the Professor with relish.

So Sherlock's literary agent, Arthur what's-his-name, had been right after all when he said he would believe Moriarty was dead when he heard the body had been washed up at Gravesend.

"This Lazarus-like behaviour is most amazing," said Emily. "I'm told that the man has perished somewhere in Switzerland by falling over a ledge and plunging into some falls or other. Then the next I hear he has drowned in the Thames. Now I see him in front of me – *and* he has the cheek to be handling my property."

"Don't make me laugh," said Moriarty, looking as if the closest he ever came to such a condition was a malevolent cackle. "The cameos are no more yours than they are mine, or these two Belgians' here."

His normally pale face suddenly reddened, and the deep-set grey eyes blazed. Was he remembering when Emily and I prevented him from becoming the Successor to St. Peter and caused him to flee from Rome? It certainly seemed like it. I trembled at the thought of being stranded in this remote place, with one lone man and two women pitted against three arch-villains. Who would stop at nothing when it came to disposing of anything and anybody who stood in their way.

But, "Where's your fighting spirit?" muttered Miss Fanshaw. "If brawn's no use we'll have to use brains."

I was amazed to see her smile sweetly at the Professor and to hear her say cajolingly, "At least I intended to return them – the cameos – to the Pope."

"More fool you. What use could they be to an old priest? I doubt whether he's ever set eyes on them what with all the other stuff in that impregnable place." Moriarty caught himself up and said with a sardonic look on his aged face, "Well, almost impregnable."

Emily simpered again, this time even more winningly. I wondered what she thought she was up to. Unlike John, but very like Sherlock Holmes, Moriarty seemed impervious to feminine charm, if not to every kind of charm. And even more so to our feminine whiles. But stepping up to him she said softly, "All that about returning the cameos was so much eye-wash. We'll keep them and split the proceeds. That is, once you have found someone able to sell them." Her tone implied it needed a very clever man indeed to accomplish such a feat, and Moriarty was that man.

Hit in his weakest spot – appreciation of his acumen – the Professor, against all expectations, appeared to soften a little and we all sat round the table apparently in bargaining mood. Although I very much doubted if this so-called academic would allow any split to be in equal parts. Or the two Belgians either. I signalled to John to sit as near to the cameos as possible. Whatever Emily's plan, I was slowly evolving one of my own. Hadn't I come into the house under the pretence of feeling faint? And couldn't the performance be repeated? Putting my hand to my head, I began to groan softly, at the same time pressing my handkerchief into Watson's hand under cover of the tablecloth (but not before dear Miss F. had got a glimpse of it). Would he be able to guess what was wanted? I could see Emily signalling discreetly to him and exerting all her will to get him to do the necessary, at the same time as she was pressing her foot (a vain manoeuvre!) against Moriarty's whenever she got the chance.

With one final groan, I rose to my feet and staggered towards the door in such a way that everyone in the room was distracted for a moment. After a split second, John and Miss Fanshaw ran after me. We flew out of the house, knocking the poor bewildered old servant out of the way, jumped into the barouche (after hastily un-tethering the horses who had waited so patiently for us) and galloped off as if The Hound of the Baskervilles itself was on our tail.

We were not, however, silly enough to go back towards Evian. Instead, we hid behind a derelict barn some distance beyond that cursed house and waited. Would Moriarty guess what we had done and come after us immediately? Or would he, as he had at Victoria Station in the chase from London to Switzerland and the Reichenbach Falls, make a mistake? Either way, we couldn't stay where we were for very long. The barn was not a big one, and the horses were now restive. There was every chance we might be seen from the road in spite of all our precautions. The one thing that cheered us up was when Watson dug into his pocket, pulled out my handkerchief, opened it and revealed the Vatican cameos in all their splendour.

"Oh, well done!" breathed Emily. "You responded extremely well to my unspoken thoughts."

"I responded even better to my wife's handkerchief," said Watson. "I knew she hadn't passed it to me to blow my nose."

"But I was willing you what to do with it," she said with a frown.

"Not altogether. When it was revealed in *The Sign of Fear* that Sherlock and I had made up more investigations than we carried out, I was forced to admit that we got the material from somewhere. Mainly by reading hundreds of detective stories. There was one in particular which I really liked. It was about a crooked policeman who, called in to discover who had stolen some jewels, spotted them when no-one else was looking, dropped his handkerchief over the lot and snaffled the blighters himself!"

"Where did you read that?" I asked.

Watson thought for a moment and then said, "I've clean forgotten unfortunately."

"Now," I said, "with the Long Island lot, the Belgian crew and a mad professor after us we are really in the soup." In a foreign country, unwilling to go back to the Swiss hotel, unable to go home. The future looked extremely bleak.

No, said John. Emily and I *could* go home, and anything belonging to us in Geneva packed up ready to be sent for. As soon as he had arranged for that to be done and had paid our hotel bill He would go to Rome and restore the cameos to their rightful place in the Vatican Museum. As for the Gorgiano gang...

"You forget," I said, "that our name is known to them so they can easily find us out. Even in such a populous place as London, or in Rome."

Miss Fanshaw had been standing by most impatiently as I spoke. "But, as I told you on another occasion, mine isn't," she said, twirling her parasol; which she had managed to keep all through the agony of the chase away from Moriarty's hideout. "Miss Fanshaw may be famous, in my opinion deservedly so, but Mrs. Neville St. Clair is not. Neither is her address. Of course when we lived in Lee, before my husband's unfortunate brush with..."

"There she goes again," I thought bitterly, "harping on about her lack of cash and playing on her one-stringed lyre." Aloud I said, "But they're not knowing *you* won't help *us*."

"Why not? Your husband will be in Italy, and you will be living with me in Bayswater. As a nursery maid," she added maliciously.

Which is how I ended up for a short time as an unpaid attendant to my own son, with the upper servants looking down their noses at me and making snide comments about my lack of expertise. Since my first encounter with Bayswater, everything there had become increasingly opulent. Was Mr. St. Clair donning his red wig and ghastly make-up in another town? If so, he had better watch out if he didn't want Lestrade or Bradstreet on his trail.

But John couldn't remain in Italy for ever, and I dreaded the time when the Little Nipper and I would have to move out of 'The Laurels' and take our chances elsewhere. Just as I was working myself up into a fever about the whole situation, Emily slipped quietly into the nursery. For days she had been treating me as a not very competent servant or some kind of poor relation. But now her manner changed. "Muriel," she whispered, "Mr. Watson is in the drawing-room. You're to go to him directly." She made it sound like Elizabeth Bennet in *Pride and Prejudice* being ordered by her mother to receive Mr. Collins' addresses in the parlour at Longbourn.

Leaving Mrs. St. Clair to look after the Nipper, I ran down the stairs as fast as I could. When I opened the door of the drawing-room I saw John standing sturdily in front of the fireplace. He looked tired and rather dishevelled, but otherwise healthy. Giving me a weary smile he said, "You'll be pleased to know the cameos are back in the Vatican, and even happier to learn that I have another draft in my pocket from your Father Tomaso. I've actually been back in England for a day or two. But I've spent the time disposing of our own house and renting another one near Paddington Station. It's a district which, as you know, is very familiar to us both and I sometimes had railwaymen coming to consult me. The move and a false name, means we should all three be safe for a bit."

"What 'false name' do you suggest for us? Not Sacker, I hope."

"How about Stapleton or, perhaps, Vandeleur..."

"Too exotic, and bound to be noticed, if only by tradesmen – who are nevertheless great gossips. What do you say to Wiggins?"

Watson winced. "Would you be happy with a simple name like Wilson? That way we need not change our laundry marks, which would be something."

"Always supposing we can afford not to do our own washing."

"That's settled then. All you have to do now is collect the Little Nipper and all his belongings, pack your own valise, say farewell to Emily and give me time to whistle up a growler."

I asked him if he had had any difficulty in returning the cameos. Well, he said, there had been some trouble in establishing his identity, and more than a bit of bother proving he hadn't stolen the things and was returning them because of a bad conscience. But certain people, such as the wife of The Cavaliere de Santo Spirito, had come to his rescue. I blessed that evening in Rome when, feeling a little homesick during our investigation into the disappearance of Cardinal Tosca, I had described Watson to Father Tomaso's sister. But it surprised me that anyone should suspect an ingenuous person like John. A man who had practised only one deception in his whole life. Although I had to admit it was a big one. Surely his soldierly appearance, upright carriage and open countenance would prejudice everyone in his favour? I asked if he had experienced any danger from potential cut-throats while he was carrying the cameos.

"No. I had them well hidden. But at one point I did suspect some gangster had caught up with me."

Not Leverton the Pinkerton man? Or, as I should more rightly call him, Giuseppe Leverento. Due to his drugged state on Long Island, Watson would be unable to recall any other member of the Gorgiano gang except that two-timing crook who he had once met in London. And again before disappearing after going out of our New York hotel in search of some tobacco.

"It could have been him since he always kept his distance," agreed John. "But I thought the chap looked more intelligent, and quite a bit younger."

Black Gorgiano's grandson! The most ruthless of the whole lot. By the time I reached the new house in Paddington I was in a muck sweat ("A fine expression for a Lady to use," said Watson) and went into every room to make sure no-one was lurking around ready to knife us. I hated the place of course, and the lack of servants, after living in Kensington. But as John said, beggars (or, rather, fugitives) couldn't be choosers. But I felt that, if it went on for long, we would all three be penniless as well as runaways. And I wondered when, if at all, I would ever be able to resume my career as a woman detective to rival Sherlock Holmes.

To say nothing of keeping Mrs. St. Clair happy. She seemed obsessed with money, and the need to get back to Lee even though her parents, the retired brewer and his wife, had gone elsewhere. And it was highly unlikely that she would be able to purchase the same house.

Chapter Six

One day, when I was peering glumly out of the kitchen window, I saw a slim young man climbing over our back fence. Watson had gone to the races in disguise hoping to recoup some of his losses, and the Little Nipper was enjoying an afternoon sleep. Wild with terror, I rushed out of the house with a broom, prepared to use it to defend us both to the last drop of my blood. Before I could do so a voice said, "Calm down, my dear. It's only me, Emily."

"Then come into the house at once," I hissed. "Surely you remember that we'd decided there shouldn't be any traceable connection between you and me for the time being?"

"That's why I put on these togs, and disguised myself by sticking on this moustache."

"Well, take it off. It isn't any use, and it makes you look ridiculous." If the Gorgiano gang (to say nothing of Moriarty and the two Poirots) had somehow got wind of her and followed the stupid woman from her house to ours then moving to a new address was a waste of time and effort.

"But you don't think I was silly enough to come straight here do you?" said Miss Fanshaw. "I've been jumping on and off omnibuses, taking the Underground and riding in hansom cabs. Dodging about like a hunted weasel. And I walked the last half mile through the back alleys."

"Somewhat excessive," I thought. Paddington wasn't that far from Bayswater as the crow flies.

Emily settled herself in the kitchen, making herself as comfortable as possible and eyeing a large cake which was cooling on a rack by the window. "Do you know anything about cricket?" she asked brightly.

"I believe Sherlock Holmes' literary agent, Arthur, once bowled out W. G. Grace."

"There's hell on because somebody's pinched the Ashes. It sounds like a suitable job for us."

When John came home he was appalled. "I remember all the fuss in 1882," he said. "It happened about a year before I became involved with Holmes in that Speckled Band business. Australia beat the England team for the first time, and on its own ground at the Oval. 'The Sporting Times' wrote a satirical article saying it was the death of English cricket and that the body would be cremated and the ashes taken to Australia."

"And then what?" I asked.

"It's easy to see you two women don't read any news about sport and take little or no interest in cricket. The captain of the England side took his team to the Antipodes the following year. In, as a hysterical Press said, 'A quest to regain the ashes'. While there, a group of ladies from Melbourne presented him with an urn..."

"Containing the remains a dead kangaroo?" asked Emily eagerly.

"No," said John. "It's made of terracotta and is only six inches high. There was a rumour that it contained the ashes of a lady's veil – but it's much more likely to be the outer casing of a cricket ball, one of the bails or part of a stump."

"And there's an attempt to win it every year, when I suppose it goes either to Australia or stays in England?"

"It's not a trophy. In fact the captain seems to regard it as a personal gift and, as far as I know, keeps it somewhere in the family home. The last I heard, some people from Dublin gave him a hand-made red and gold bag to put it in."

"Did these strange Australian women have it specially constructed, the terracotta urn that is?"

"The jape probably originated at some wild party of other after the crucial Test. That would explain the story about the lady's veil. The so-called urn, I rather feel, is an old perfume jar."

"But kept in a house here in England," I said. "So we don't have to go chasing half across the world to recover it?" Which was something of a relief.

"Well, it's not exactly a palpable prize. One that's competed for," said John. "It's more a sort of symbol. Which probably explains why the captain (who, by the way, did redeem English

115

cricket after a very shaky start to the game) was given the thing in the first place and has been allowed to nurse the urn and not pass it over to the M.C.C."

"Who would have thought Colonials could have so much wit," observed Mrs. St. Clair condescendingly. "'We finally beat you after five years. One of your sporting papers wailed about the ashes of a dead tradition. Now you have won again and we are giving them back'. Very pretty."

"Have you any idea who could have stolen the urn?" I asked Watson. "It doesn't seem to have much monetary value and, given everyone knows what it represents, would be impossible to sell."

"A fanatical cricket-buff might buy it. But he could never show it off. But my guess is it's been stolen for a dare. By someone who knows about both the game and how to commit burglaries without being caught."

"And that is?"

"Well A. J. Raffles springs to mind, and he has the *entré* to many a country residence. He might do it just for the thrill, or simply to prove that he could."

"And that Bunny would encourage him," I said.

But Raffles? The man who had come to the house when John was poorly and threatened to kill Emily. And me too, if it came to that, if I didn't immediately give him her address. The

116

horseman who had earlier taken a pot-shot at us through the window of 'The Hammer and Pincers'.

"As a cricketer he's quite unique," said Watson. "A dangerous bat, a brilliant fielder and the very finest amateur slow bowler. Always carries his cricket-bag to Lords, and wears a Zingari blazer on those occasions. A blazer, I assure you both, to which he is fully entitled. He has, however, been known to remark that 'Cricket is a very good sport until you discover a better' and 'What's the satisfaction of taking a man's wicket when you want his spoons?'" [1]

As a result of this conversation Emily and I went, under cover of darkness and in a closed carriage, to Raffles' apartment in the Albany. Dodging the night porter, and avoiding the use of the lift, we lost no time in knocking discreetly at his door. Raffles opened it at once and we slid rapidly into a most elegant drawing-room. Bunny sat by the fire in his slippers and seemed somewhat discomposed at seeing two women entering the sanctum. Raffles ordered him to make coffee for four, and asked imperturbably to what did he owe the honour of this visit?

"We've come for the Ashes," I said. Capitalising the word, since Watson told me that was what everybody did these days. It seemed best to state our errand boldly, and at once.

"I can't deny that I've heard about the daring robbery," said

1. 'Gentlemen and Players' from *Raffles* by E. W. Hornung

117

Raffles suavely, at the same time grinning like a Cheshire cat. "But if I may paraphrase something you said to me on another occasion, Mrs. Watson, when it came to discussing the Duchess of Loamshire's diamond necklace, if I did know where the Ashes were why should I tell you?"

"Heard about the robbery?" growled Emily. "London is awash with the news. Lestrade, Gregson, Hopkins, even Mr. Mac (as Sherlock Holmes was fond of calling him), Bradstreet – the whole Yard is on the job."

"You've left out White Mason," said Raffles sweetly.

"They're not employing country bumpkins this time," said Miss Fanshaw imperviously.

"But what makes you think I've stolen the Ashes?" asked Raffles, peering vaguely round as if he was looking for something.

"Instinct," I said.

"Then that will help you to find them. Always supposing they are actually here. Take my keys, and permission to make a thorough search," said this amateur cracksman before strolling over to the fireplace and bending down to light a cigar.

It was highly unlikely that the urn would be hidden in any part of the building. But for form's sake Emily and I turned the place upside down, much to Bunny's indignation. She even went into the tiny service kitchen and repeated what she had done in the

Long Island cave – distracted his attention and looked in a teapot.

"You know, Emily," I said thoughtfully, as we returned to Paddington in the same way, and under the same conditions, as we left the area, "I'm not at all sure Raffles had anything at all to do with the theft of the Ashes. He steals for money, and usually when he's on his beam-ends. 'Vulgarly poor', as he has been known to put it."

"So inviting us to search was his idea of a joke? That perfume jar could have been in his pocket."

"Or Bunny's."

"We could hardly strip them both," said Miss Fanshaw regretfully. "Although I did look in their sock-drawers and went through their underwear. In fact I looked in some places no Lady should look."

"And all to no purpose."

"Well where do you suggest we take this investigation next? Not somewhere certain people get a kick out of pretending that they have stolen something when they haven't, I hope," said Emily.

By this time we had reached the house. Watson was in bed fast asleep, along with the Little Nipper who was dreaming away in his cot in the nursery. So I invited her in, and we sat companionably by the dying embers of the kitchen fire. "Look at

119

it this way," I said. "The captain of the cricket team which beat the Australians in 1883 keeps the so-called Ashes in a pot hidden in a bag at his Country Seat. What's the betting he also has many of his cricketing friends there for the weekend?"

"They would never steal it. They'd think it was sacrilege."

"There's no reason why any House Party should consist only of people who love the game. There could be some guests who have no respect for the so-called Ashes of English Cricket and would pinch them if they thought it was to their advantage. After all, it's pretty certain the man who regards himself as their owner would probably pay a fortune to get them back."

Emily shifted her sitting position and looked wistfully at the kitchen cupboard. She would soon be complaining that all this brainwork made her feel hungry. "So your idea is to get an invitation to one of these occasions and try to find out what happened?"

"It might be difficult, and even more so for three."

"You can count me out for the moment as Neville will be home next week. As long as we share the boodle after you've recovered the Ashes and pocketed a fat cheque."

"'Boodle'. Now that's a real Raffles word!"

Of course I promised she would get her cut, and spent the next few days figuring out how Watson and I could leave London without attracting the attention of all the villains I feared were after us. Wearing a black beard, false ringlets and disguising the Nipper as General Tom Thumb were three suggestions from John which I immediately rejected. I left him to wangle an invitation to the next House Party at the captain's through his connection with Sherlock Holmes and that ubiquitous agent, Arthur. Who was himself very well-known as a cricketer – with a bat almost as dangerous as that of A. J. Raffles.

One snag was, the captain of the cricket team which bested the Australians in that return match of long ago was away with his wife on a Caribbean cruise. "But that's no matter," said Watson, "since there's bound to be someone in charge."

I'm very glad to say we were lucky enough to get away from the Capital safely without going to some other extremes put forward by my dear husband. To save money, John and I packed the same clothes we had worn to the Loamshire's. The Nipper was still in short frocks so his luggage proved easy to manage. But, "Put a couple of his favourite toys in, and a few picture books," said John. "I bet he'll be bored stiff."

"What, with all those old dowagers drooling over him..."

"Typical mother," said my husband. "Everyone thinks her child is as wonderful as she does. Don't forget they've probably all got grandchildren."

This reminded me of a grandchild I would much rather forget, at least until we had solved this particular theft. But I managed to put the whole Gorgiano gang out of my mind, and listened to John burbling happily about some of the country houses he had visited with his dear friend, Sherlock. Stoke Moran, The Priory School, Baskerville Hall. The journey passed pleasantly enough, and we were soon being welcomed by our host and hostess ('Mr. and Mrs. Smith')   at the door of a most interesting mansion. Interesting, that is, to a female detective who hoped to make a great deal of money out of her visit.

"I wonder if Lestrade has been called in," said John.

"Don't you remember? All the resources of the Yard are concentrated in London at present."

"Well, they must have called in somebody local when they first discovered the Ashes were missing. Come to think of it though, our hosts look remarkably calm in the circumstances. It's a wonder they are able to party. When I mentioned this to the husband all he said was 'Life must go on.' Do you think he's pinched the urn himself, for the insurance money?"

This was a sobering thought since, if insurance money were involved, that would let Raffles in again. "Do you know any of the other guests?" I asked.

"Old Amhurst has been here for at least a week, with his disappointing son."

"How 'disappointing'?" I asked, sitting primly with my notebook poised.

122

"He's mad on cricket, but young Comstock barely made the second eleven at school."

"There are worse things than not being able to play cricket."

"Not for Amhurst. He's a fanatic."

"And no doubt makes his disappointment felt to this poor boy of his?"

"I'm afraid so," said John unhappily, with a glance over at the Nipper who was sleeping peacefully in a corner of our room, having been temporarily brought out of the nursery for a little cuddle. Which, said Watson, left no doubt about my origins.

"You forget," I said, "that I became motherless at a very early age, and there's not a lot of difference between a governess and a ward orderly in a military hospital. At least my father had steady employment as a soldier without having to go backwards and forwards to Ballarat."

"There's no need to exaggerate," said John crossly. "We only went once. And, although I admit that the trip couldn't be called an unqualified success, Dad made enough to let us continue at a good Board School instead of going out to work at ten, or even younger. Besides, you must know if you've any sense that I certainly wasn't implying you and I are so very different in our beginnings. After all, in some ways your years at that school in Scotland (and my years with Holmes) have given both of us a certain polish. I feel we could hold our own with almost anybody. But it might not do to give our humble origins away so easily."

"I don't feel my origins are all that humble," I said. "The daughter of an army officer..."

"In an Indian regiment," said John. "It's hardly The Brigade of Guards. Remember, people are such snobs. Especially in houses like this."

"You said we can hold our own if we're careful. And you are quite right," I added kindly, preparing to return the Nipper to the nursery for his bath. It's true Watson still stood in awe of some members of the aristocracy. But I had soon got the measure of *them* during my extra-mural adventures while working for Mrs. Forrester.

Later in the evening, when we were all assembled in the hall ready for the sound of the gong that would summon us to dinner, I had a chance to study Lord Amhurst's eldest son. He looked perfectly normal to me, and certainly not a disappointment to anybody. I determined to have a word with him as soon as the meal was over. Not about cricket. I had no intention of making his life more miserable on that score than it already was. Meanwhile John (sitting across the table to me) was enjoying the turbot and trying to make polite conversation with an old woman. Who if she wasn't using an ear trumpet definitely ought to have been.

I glanced at the man next to me. Tubby, shrewd, wearing tinted glasses, he had introduced himself as a detective. "Theophilus Barker by name, but most people call me Theo." Well, he didn't look like a Theo. So our hosts (or the two stand-ins for our hosts) were more democratic than the Duke and Duchess of Loamshire? Who had expected Lestrade to eat with the servants.

I asked my new acquaintance if he had been staying in the house long. Only since just after the disappearance of the Ashes, he said. "Mr. Smith was in a terrible state and showed me what had happened as soon as I arrived. Small as it was, the urn had pride of place in a cabinet in the drawing-room, along with some of the owner's cricketing trophies."

"A cabinet that was always locked?"

"Always, and Smith kept the key in his pocket at all times."

"So the perfume jar can only ever be seen through glass?"

"Our host for this weekend says the owner of the house is often asked by his guests to let them have a closer look at it, and he likes to take the thing from the cabinet to show it around. When he's not out of the country, that is. But on those occasions when he does remove it from the cabinet it never moves more than a foot or two away from its normal position."

"The captain keeps the urn in his palm, even when allowing his guests to see it better? After all, it is very small."

125

"Again, Smith informed me that some very special guests are allowed to handle the thing. For example, Lord Amhurst, who is cricket-crazy."

"So I understand. Did that happen this time?"

"No," said Mr. Barker, busily tucking into his fish. "I very much doubt if Smith would risk the responsibility of taking the urn out of the cabinet at any time while he is in charge, and the owner away."

"But the theft was discovered very soon after this Lord Amhurst's arrival in the house with his son? What happened to the red and gold bag?"

"That was still in the cabinet, where it's usually placed beside the urn. That way everyone can see the treasure even when the family is here alone."

"Any sign of a break-in?"

"If you mean a burglary, no."

"Do you suspect an inside job then? For example, what about the servants? Have there been any new ones engaged recently?"

"I'm working on it," said the detective through a mouthful of food.

"I imagine the cabinet was quite badly damaged?"

"Not a scratch."

This pointed to a key being used, which would exonerate a guest such as Lord Amhurst. Unless he had come prepared with one, which seemed very unlikely. He would have had to take a wax impression of the lock during an earlier visit and wouldn't know how to do it, even if he was willing to sully the family name by turning himself into a common criminal. Having a key to hand might also mean that Mr. Smith had stolen the urn. Or perhaps his valet, who could easily purloin the key and make a copy of it. But when I made this suggestion to Smith he was outraged. Ever since he had been in the house, he said, he had kept the key to the cabinet in his pocket or slept with it under his pillow: and his man was utterly trustworthy.

Knowing how easily I'd slipped my hand under Mrs. Marple's pillow without waking her when Watson and I broke into her house in our attempt to recover some stolen sovereigns, I was rather sceptical about the effectiveness of this stratagem: even though Auguste Poirot had been less successful with me in that bedroom in the hotel in Geneva, when I woke up while he was trying the same trick.

Leaving our host still somewhat ruffled, I went in search of the boy Comstock, and found him having a furtive cigarette in the Conservatory. He put it out as soon as he saw me, but I offered him one of mine and said I knew of a better place to smoke than this. One where he wouldn't run the risk of being found out. I could show it to him later. For the moment, however, I would like a little talk. He looked very uncomfortable at this and said he sincerely hoped it wasn't about cricket. Everyone was eagerly anticipating the match tomorrow except him. He would be forced to play by his father, and knew he would disgrace himself.

"Not at all," I said reassuringly. "I'll get Watson to bowl you a few overs after breakfast, well before the match begins."

"Fat lot of good that will do," he said moodily, obviously longing to resume the weed. "But thanks all the same."

"Do you know anything about the disappearance of the Ashes?" I asked.

Comstock was immediately on the defensive. "Certainly not. Why ever should I?"

"No reason at all," I said airily, "except that I'm going to ask everyone the same question."

"Don't you know there's already one detective in the house?" he said derisively.

"Yes," I said, "but I am the wife of Mr. Holmes' greatest friend. A person he worked with for many years. So I must have some advantages when it comes to solving crimes."

"Good grief," said young Comstock inelegantly. "A Female Sherlock!"

He went on to say that he hoped nobody would ever find that beastly perfume jar. There had been nothing but talk about the Test since that terrible defeat in 1882. It hadn't even stopped after the return match in 1883 and all that guff in Melbourne about burning a bail. His father wangled an invitation here every year simply so he could feast his eyes on the urn. It had blighted the young man's childhood and would probably blight his manhood as well. In fact, his whole life. Seeing how worked up my companion was becoming, I muttered a few soothing words and said I would speak to him again later.

"Yes," he said, "and tell me where to smoke in safety!"

Knowing John was enjoying himself in the billiard-room, I peeped into the nursery and then went towards the Library for a quiet recap. Fortunately the place was empty, although there was some evidence that a few guests had tried to read and then given it up. I took a piece of paper and a little gold pencil out of my evening bag and set about concentrating on a problem which, if I solved it, would satisfy Emily's lust for money and leave us with enough funds to put up a good fight against all our enemies, even including Moriarty in his present state of near penury.

I wrote down that I had visited Raffles and failed to find the perfume jar, and then added a note that his personality and his readiness to allow a search pointed to his not being the thief. But I added a rider that, if insurance money came into it, he may have been bluffing and, in fact, as guilty as the next man. But who was the next man? The easily angered Mr. Smith, if he knew the Ashes were insured, was even more suspect than old A. J. He was on the premises, and had a key to the cabinet. Even his name was against him. It was so ordinary that it might not be his real one. But would the captain choose anyone who wasn't absolutely copper-bottomed to guard his most treasured possession while he was away?

What about Lord Amhurst? He didn't have a key, but... And if not the next man, how about the next woman? I recalled everyone I had seen in the dining-room that evening and decided that none of the female guests had it in them to rifle a cabinet. Would the wife pinch the urn? She might if she had regularly overspent her dress allowance. But how to dispose of the thing? Especially for as much money as she might need.

I considered it not unlikely that Mrs. Smith would know all there was to know about somebody like Old Abrahams who, according to Holmes had once been 'in terror of his life', or indeed any of the other London pawnbrokers and fences. What about young Comstock, however? He quite obviously loathed not only cricket but any mention of the perfume jar. I had promised to get John to coach him for the all important match. A match which was the sole reason for this hospitable weekend. But first that boy and I would have another little talk.

The next morning I caught the lad sneaking off to the Conservatory for a pre-breakfast drag and hissed, "Not that way.

Come up to my sitting-room."

"But where's your husband?" he stammered.

"Helping to put up the nets."

"But surely that's the servants' job?".

"By your own account you've visited this place often enough to know that the captain likes to do it himself, with a little help from some of his male guests. But, of course, a servant or two will be there to lend a hand if necessary, since I'm sure Mr. Smith is nowhere near as expert at the task. Now, what would you like to drink?" I had judged it best to treat him as a fully-grown man, and had ready a bottle of the whisky Watson insisted on bringing with him in case of a sudden thirst in the middle of the night.

"Anything that goes with a fag," said this charming youth. He then went on to berate the Smiths as 'nobodies'. "*Parvenus* who'd do anything for free board and lodging."

I couldn't help reflecting that surely everyone else here (except perhaps me, John and Mr. Barker who all had a job to do) was exactly the same? But Comstock certainly sharpened my suspicions of our present hosts. However, when I mentioned these to him he started up in horror and dropped his cigarette. Which I only just saved from burning the carpet.

"No, no," he said hoarsely, and burst into tears.

In spite of my affection for the Little Nipper, I wouldn't call myself a particularly motherly person. But now I asked young Comstock his name and let him weep on my shoulder for a full five minutes. When I judged the storm was over I said, "James, you must tell me what this is all about. Otherwise..."

"I took the bloody thing," he said.

"Why? You must have known all the trouble that would cause. To say nothing of all the talk."

"Yes," he said. "There's been plenty of talk. But I thought it would stop me having to come down here every year and play that rotten game."

"Did you throw it in the river, or dump it in the compost? Or have you destroyed it altogether?" It probably wouldn't do him any good. His father would make him go to some other Country House during the Cricketing Season. He probably did already, as well as forcing him to come to this one.

"I dare not," said Comstock sheepishly. "it's been in my pocket every day and under my pillow every night. I've been mortally afraid one of those valeting johnnies who lay out one's clothes morning and evening would find it."

I had to smile to myself at the idea of such a precious object going from pillow to pillow, first Smith's and then his. The state of my protégé's nerves meant he would probably wake up at the slightest movement towards his bed. But I suddenly remembered it was the *key* Mr. Smith rested his old grey head on every night and carried in his pocket by day. The urn stayed in a cabinet, next to its little red and gold bag. I asked James how he had got hold of it, the key that is.

"Didn't touch it. Used a betty."

Just like Mrs. Marple's lover, Angelo, on the Irish train! It was all the same with these toffs. Some of them, especially the younger ones, knew as much about crime as the so-called 'undeserving poor'. The only difference was, if they were caught all they'd get was a slap on the wrist and a pi-jaw.

"You needn't be afraid to give the urn to me," I said. "I'll take it and see it gets back to base." A cable had been sent to the first port of call of the cruise ship and the owner of the Ashes was already on his way home.

"But how will you explain things?" asked the boy. "I don't want you, or any of the Watson family, to get into trouble."

"I'll manage," I said, and went to see how the men were progressing putting up the nets. Halfway across the lawn I came upon Lord Amhurst, with an ancient bat before him, practising his stroke. I grabbed him unceremoniously by the arm and said in no uncertain terms that forcing his son to play a game he loathed would only lead to disgrace and chagrin. I hinted at crimes of the deepest dye, and said it would have to stop if he wanted his family name to remain untarnished. By the time I finished, the poor man didn't know what to think and would have gone off to accuse his heir of committing blue murder if I hadn't pulled him back and said, "Send James to the Transvaal and the gold fields. It will be the making of him, and probably ensure you a tranquil and prosperous old age."

My next task was to find Barker, slip a fiver into his hand and tell him the investigation was over. "Same old story," he said resignedly. "Engaged to look into something, and then I find someone else is on the job. Only last time it was my old friend and rival Sherlock Holmes."

"The retired colourman again." I thought to myself with a shudder.

Smiling sympathetically at Theophilus, I went off to tackle Smith, gave him the urn and suggested he keep in out of sight in a secret cupboard, at least until his friend got home. In spite of all his probing I refused to tell him how I'd come by it, said it should be enough for him that I'd got it back, and advised him to be more vigilant in future. After that, it was time for a good lunch and a stroll out to see the match. The last one that James and I hoped he would ever play in.

It seemed like real cricketing weather, bright sunlight interspersed with sudden short but light showers, during which we women raised our umbrellas in a riot of colour which matched our best summer dresses and some chatted lazily about other matches they had seen, other players and other times.

Some weeks before, our host would have written to the secretary of the nearest village team to see if it could raise a side, and maybe invited one or two of the best men to play in the same eleven as his guests. He would also have suggested that other village teams within a certain radius should be approached to see if they had any good players.

It was a two innings match and Watson acquitted himself well at the wicket. But not so well at the bat. And so, surprisingly, did James. Had his father already told him this was to be his last match? Soon it was all over. We women furled our umbrellas for the final time. The men from the village went towards the kitchens laughing and joking – ready for a hearty and well-earned supper. Those who had played in the same team as the guests collected their ten shillings. The gentlemen, with their ladies, went slowly upstairs to dress for dinner. Everything seemed very English. And as far away from the Gorgiano gang, the Poirots and Moriarty as it was possible to get.

There was a note from Emily when we arrived home asking how we had got on, although it was in all the papers that the Ashes had been recovered. Watson wondered if, like Holmes, we should let the officers of the law take the credit. I said that I had already slipped a fiver to Barker but that it might be as well to tell the press that Theophilus had been the benefactor of the whole cricketing fraternity, and not The Watson-Fanshaw

Detective Agency – 'the Proprietors at the moment being somewhere overseas'. After all, we were desperate to remain incognito, weren't we, and ready to forfeit any useful publicity the investigation could have brought us?

Emily, disguised as usual as a young man, but without the novelty-shop moustache, came round to say how awkward it all was. How could we detect if we had to lie low? John said that we could perhaps follow the practice of his great friend, Sherlock. "As he said to Lestrade on one occasion, when that gentleman was barking up the wrong tree and thought everybody at the Yard would find out he'd nearly caused the wrong man to be hanged, 'Instead of being ruined, my good sir, you will find that your reputation has been enormously advanced. Just make a few alterations in that report which you were writing, and they will understand how hard it is to throw dust in the eyes of Inspector Lestrade'. That self-important copper asked, 'And you don't want your own name to appear?' Holmes said, 'Not at all. The work is its own reward'. Rather fine, I thought."

"And quite untypical," I snapped. "That man loves praise as much as anybody." But it wasn't a question of who got the credit for what. We were unable to put our noses outside the door without running the risk of being recognised. The cheque I expected for recovering the Ashes (a very large one when it did arrive) had been delayed, and I had already made several futile trips to a small post office (*not* the one in Wigmore Street) to see if it had come *poste restante*. Rather unexpectedly, I had already collected a small cheque from Mr. Smith (who was no doubt weak with relief after having such a thing happen on his watch) in the same way. But I still felt cross enough to criticise Sherlock.

Emily said that, at the moment, it might be better if she undertook an investigation by herself. Just as she had done in the Ricoletti affair which, she flattered herself, had been very successful: at least monetarily, even if most of the people concerned in it had either been murdered, imprisoned or hanged. Two days later I learned she had gone, of all places, to Afghanistan. By troopship: and would be away for at least ten weeks.

"Does her husband know?" asked Watson in amazement, knocking his pipe out on the fender.

"She probably told him she was taking the children and their governess on a visit to that retired brewer."

"Her father? Won't he give her away?"

"Not he. She can wrap him round her little finger. Her mother too, if it comes to that."

"But what about the governess?"

"In her pocket," I said shortly.

"It's quite a journey," said John who, although he'd never been there, had made sure he knew all about it. "A stop at Malta, then on to Karachi, by train to Sibi (the hottest place in all India) up the Bolan Pass to Quetta, on to Charman and through the Kojak Pass into Afghanistan. Even then she'll be a long way from Kandahar."

"She says she's travelling to Kabul."

"Then the ship will still call at Karachi for the men to disembark before going on to Bombay. From Bombay..."

"All right," I said peevishly. "A sweaty train, and then a journey by *dak* (if she's lucky) up the Grand Trunk Road to Peshawar and over the Khyber Pass to the Capital. She's the one who is making the trip not us, and a pretty gruelling trip it seems to be so I hope she succeeds in it."

"You haven't yet told me the reason for her going to Afghanistan."

"The Amir has lost his favourite horse and wants her to find it."

"I can't remember if Afghans marry more than one woman at a time. But he's taking more trouble than if he'd lost his favourite wife."

"Horses are more important in that country," I said, preparing to give the Little Nipper his tea.

138

Chapter Seven

Emily came home very excited. She sat in our tiny sitting-room, with a flushed face and happy smile, telling us all about the wonderful time she'd had on the way to India, after she got there and when she went up to Kabul. "The officers, my dears, so attentive, so helpful. And the Amir! The handsomest man I ever saw in my life."

"But did you find his horse?"

"Naturally. And on the way here I went into Thomas Cook's, changed a bag of Afghan rupees into sovereigns and deposited them in our account with Cox and Company."

"How on earth did you discover the quadruped?" asked John.

"The same way one would discover an elephant," she said cryptically. "I found out that the Amir's son and heir coveted the animal. I reasoned that if he had stolen it he would hide it up in the hills. All we'd have to do then was persuade one of his servants to bring it back. But the boy, really a man and a very good-looking one at that, simply hid the nag among a lot of others near the market place."

"I see," said Watson. If you want to hide an elephant you put it among a herd of other elephants. But how did you decide which was the right horse?"

"I looked for the most magnificent animal and then, to make quite sure, spoke a few words in pushtu, including the special ones the Amir uses when he wants to pet his favourite. The stallion detached himself from the rest of the group immediately and galloped over. I had taken a groom with me so everything concluded in quite a satisfactory manner. But my most exciting news has nothing to do with any of that," said Miss Fanshaw, putting her hands in her trouser pockets, crossing her legs and looking at us triumphantly, a smile playing about her rosy lips.

John responded at once. "Something more exciting than a visit to a Crowned Head?" he enquired, obviously remembering how thrilled he had been to catch a glimpse of a Royal Coat of Arms on the side of Sir James Damery's carriage at the conclusion of the Gruner case. So thrilled that he 'gasped with surprise', went back upstairs to Holmes' room 'bursting with my great news' – and immediately met with one of Sherlock's put downs. Before poor Watson could finish his sentence and reveal who was the real owner of the vehicle the Great Detective held up 'a restraining hand' and said, 'It is a loyal friend and a chivalrous gentleman. Let that now and forever be enough for us.' So once again John was denied his moment of glory, and everything became as usual between the two.

Emily took her handkerchief out of her pocket, blew her nose and then slowly put the large square of fine linen back in its place. She loved an audience, and was a mistress of suspense.

"You remember I took the children to Margate with their governess before going abroad..."

"Yes, yes," we said together somewhat impatiently.

"Well when I went down by train to fetch them home I decided to let them play on the sand for one last time; and while doing so I saw a woman with no powder on her nose."

"Obviously a Lady," said John approvingly, "and not a painted hussy."

"My dear man," said Emily, "we all paint these days. A little lip rouge, some of Madam Rachel's powder. It's a tribute to our art that you haven't noticed. However, it was the first thing *that I noticed* and it made me suspicious. She was young enough to care about her looks, had a good figure (though not much of a bust) wasn't wearing a wedding ring and, apart from that shiny nose, would have had no difficulty in attracting a young man. Instead she was sitting all alone in the shade, with her parasol up protecting her complexion from the sun. And in such a way, it was impossible to accurately judge her expression."

"Sherlock Holmes thought women were inscrutable," said Watson. Their most trivial actions appear to speak volumes but may simply depend on a hair-pin or a pair of curling tongs. The fact that he could never understand what he called the fair sex irked him. He said during one of our investigations that it was my department."

"Did you speak to the woman?" I asked, anxious to get back to the subject in hand.

"I gave her good-day, and the children smiled at her. To tell the truth, I thought she might have some sorrow, or perhaps an illness."

"All because of her bare nose," said John.

"Not entirely," said Emily crossly. "I was intrigued to know what she was thinking."

"Probably about the time of the next train and whether she could afford to stay by the sea for a little longer."

"It's strange you should say that because she was on our train later. The children's governess pointed her out to me."

"Does she wear powder?"

"Who?"

"The governess."

"It would be beneath me to notice. But she is addicted to caraway seeds. Nibbles them all the time and drives us to distraction by dropping them on the carpets."

"Was she in the same carriage as you four," I asked, again wanting to get back to the woman.

"No. I think she travelled third class," said Emily vaguely. "Anyway, I didn't see her myself until we were at the ticket barrier, when she hurried away very quickly indeed and I thought I'd lost sight of her."

"End of story then," I said, wondering why all this was more exciting than finding the Amir of Afghanistan's horse and earning all those rupees for us both.

"No it isn't. I told the governess to take the children home and then went after the parasol."

"But haven't you already got one?" asked Watson, trying vainly to keep a straight face.

"I've already told you, I was curious why an attractive young woman should be so careless as to go about with a distinctly shiny nose, and to sit with her back to the light so that one couldn't easily fathom her expression. Some instinct told me that the two things were linked."

I distinctly heard Watson say, "Well, what utter rot," and rose hurriedly to make the tea. When I came back from the kitchen the two of them were having a violent altercation, with Watson waving his arms about wildly and Emily beginning to shout. "Be quiet," I said, "or you'll wake the Nipper."

"Can I help it if you have an insufferable husband?" muttered Mrs. St. Clair. "He seems to think there's no such thing as a woman's intuition."

"It ought at least to be backed up by common sense," said John irritably.

"It was," said Emily. "By following her onto an omnibus and alighting when she did, I was able to find out where she lived."

"And?"

"Well, it was a start."

"Emily," I said, "this is fast becoming intolerably tedious. For heaven's sake drink, your tea."

"I am drinking it," said Mrs. St. Clair suiting the action to the word and grabbing a biscuit. "It's just that you're so damned impatient."

"I've heard of dragging things out for effect," I said, "but I swear I'll crown you if you don't get on with it."

"I wonder if it's anything to do with this latest robbery at Coutts' Bank," remarked John, reaching for a folded newspaper. "A young woman cashed a very large cheque which turned out to be dud, and she hasn't been seen since. Of course, the Bank has her name and address but when Gregson went there with a warrant for her arrest all he found was a nervous young man who said he knew nothing of the woman or of the audacious crime."

"A false name and a false address. It's not like Coutts to be so careless," I said, collecting up the tea things and carrying them to the sink.

"Apparently she was a known client of the Bank and had made small deposits and withdrawals for at least a year."

"Well I can't go looking for every woman in London who defrauds a bank, even if it is Coutts'," said Emily impatiently.

144

"True," said Watson in a conciliatory tone. "But you may have found this one's address by accident."

"Better tell us what it is Emily," I said, "and put us out of our misery."

As soon as she had done so, Watson said he was going in disguise to Scotland Yard to ask his friend Lestrade if that was the same as the one given to Coutts' by a possibly shiny-nosed female. As soon as he left the room Emily, rapidly running through most of Sherlock's disguises, asked me with a sneer whether my husband intended to pass himself off as an old woman who couldn't control her umbrella, a decrepit bookseller, a groom, a plumber in search of a fiancée or simply shave off his moustache.

"He's too proud of it to do that," I said. "But he may pretend to be an expert in Chinese porcelain, as he did in the investigation carried out for an illustrious client. Either that, or the black beard business."

Half-an-hour later, just as Mrs. St. Clair said she ought to be getting home to 'The Laurels', John burst into the room with a look of triumph on his face. He had discarded his disguise in the bathroom (so Emily would never know what it was!) and beamed genially at us in much the same way as I imagined he looked when he first saw Wiggins and the rest of Sherlock's task-force (The Baker Street Irregulars) that day in 221B when

Holmes asked the young street arabs to search for *The Aurora*. "I told you so," he said. "We are on the right track."

Knowing how much John like sleuthing away from Sherlock, on the rare occasions he was allowed to do so (and when they were detecting and not sitting by the fire making it all up), I was very pleased with his efforts. Unlike Holmes, I didn't immediately belittle them and point out just how deficient they were. True, he hadn't done much – and always enjoyed his little chats with Lestrade in spite of saying the policeman got on his nerves. But he'd acted on a hunch, one which turned out to be absolutely right. All that remained now was for The Watson-Fanshaw Agency to follow it through. And therein lay the difficulty. Amateur disguises wouldn't deceive anyone for very long. They were also irksome, and cramped one's style. After all, we couldn't pretend to the acting talent Holmes was said to have had. Or that belonging to Neville St. Clair either.

On the other hand, John and I and the Little Nipper had been forced to move to an anonymous address to avoid the unwelcome attentions of the Gorgiano gang, the Poirots – father and son – and, above all, Professor James Moriarty. Emily was doubling for me. But there was a limit to what she could do alone. In spite of her success in the Ricoletti rampage; and her successful chase after the man with the aluminium crutch. John, although he had never been in the army, had developed many of the characteristics of an officer and a gentleman and said he hated 'this shady business'. He had half-a-mind to go back to Kensington, use my share of the Amir's gold to buy another house and 'brazen it out'.

"If it wasn't for you and our little boy," he said, "that is exactly what I would do."

After my husband's spirited outburst, I went round to the house in Bayswater with the hood of my cloak pulled right down over my eyes and a scarf covering the rest of my face. As soon as I arrived I stared down the servants, looked the governess straight in the eye and gave her two small charges some mint toffees. Soon after that, I found Emily in the drawing-room having a heart to heart talk with her husband. She was dressed in a very fetching outfit of green and gold, with the skirt just short enough to afford everyone a tantalising glimpse of a shapely ankle, and with the narrow bustle she usually favoured. As soon as a lackey showed me in, Neville St. Clair excused himself, gave his better half a peck on the cheek and said he was sorry but he had to catch a train and had very little time in which to do it.

Of course I couldn't ask her what kind of conversation the two were engaged in when I made my entrance. Neither could I ask him where he was going. But Emily made me welcome and called hurriedly for some tea. I explained how tired John and I were of the 'hole-in-corner' behaviour forced on us by having to hide from so many enemies, and how Watson had threatened to go back to Kensington. But all she said was it reminded her of when he had used the same expression about the Poirots, after seeing they didn't intend landing at Evian but were somewhat craftily disembarking from their hired skiff somewhere else along the French coast.

After a while, however, she began to speak more kindly about our difficulties, but nevertheless said, "All the same, don't you think, my dear Muriel, that I ought to finish the investigation into that powder-less woman from Margate before you and Mr. Watson do anything rash? It would be such a pity if something went wrong after his brilliant flash of inspiration."

She certainly knew how to get round me by flattering John. It made a change from Holmes telling him to his face that 'he was not in himself luminous' but could, in certain circumstances, be 'a conductor of light'. "I'll see what Watson says but, the mood he's in at the moment, I don't hold out much hope."

"That's right. And don't worry."

It was all very well for her to say 'don't worry'. She was as safe as houses. As for my husband, he proved unusually intractable. "The three of us or nothing," he said. "When all is said and done, it's The *Watson*-Fanshaw Agency. And you must admit you and I were a great help to one another in Ballarat."

"If you've worked out a plan of campaign, by all means let me have it," I said.

"The first thing to do is get the girl Millie back for a while. That way the Nipper will be well looked after, and I'm sure we can teach her to be discreet. The only thing is, the child will have to take his airings in the back garden and not a public park."

Feeling my heart about to plunge into my boots, I sat down heavily and asked John to bring a glass of brandy. I recalled that one group out for our blood knew all about kidnapping a child. But this time he wouldn't be returned to his mother. Not alive, that is. And what an exquisite revenge for Black Gorgiano's grandson!

"Then once the Nipper is settled," said Watson, after he had handed me the brandy and stood by while I drank it, "we must make a rota so that the house – the one Emily found – can be watched. If necessary all round the clock." Seeing my face he added hurriedly, "I, of course, will do the night watch." It sounded like a painting by Rembrandt.

"She – the thief – may never come back to it."

"Didn't Mrs. St. Clair mention a young man? He may know something, even though he told the police he didn't."

The watches began, and for some time our various disguises worked. Worked, that is, in that nobody accosted us, stabbed us or tried to garrotte us. Emily, of course, was free to come and go as she pleased since, although her face might be familiar, none of the crooks knew her real name and so would find it more difficult to track her down and perhaps murder her on the quiet. Although anyone with the slightest gift of observation would wonder why the same woman kept appearing in the same place so often, going into all kinds of nearby shops and buying such a varied number of items – at the same time as she hovered close to the doorway instead of sitting sedately by the counter waiting for her purchases to be wrapped up. "And," said Watson, "she could easily be followed if anyone from the cave did recognise her."

He fulfilled his obligations like the brick he was, but I saw little of him during this very trying time. On duty at night and asleep by day, we were almost strangers to each other. The whole business became so nerve-racking I almost wished there could be a confrontation. To add to the tension, all the while we were watching the house so assiduously it remained quiet – with nobody going in or out. But one afternoon, when it was my turn to be on duty, the door opened and a young man walked down the path and out of the front gate.

I almost dropped the apples I was busy buying from a coster's barrow and ran home as fast as I could. Shaking a gently snoring John in much the same way as Sherlock Holmes had done on one occasion when they were conducting an investigation into the Abbey Grange I said breathlessly, "The young man, the one from the house we are watching, I saw him today and..."

John opened one eye, turned on his side and went back to sleep. But I was determined to make him listen. I shook him so hard he sat up in bed and asked anxiously, "Is there a fire?"

"A young man came out of that house. I recognised him."

"Did he have powder on his nose?" mumbled my husband, falling back on the pillow and threatening to drop off again.

"I recognised him," I said exasperatedly. "The old Duke of Loamshire's Secretary." The man who I had run away from to find Watson and warn him to keep out of the way or he might have to resume the role of doctor until the Duchess's own physician arrived in the house.

A startled John became fully awake at last. "The one who said he didn't care to stay to serve the new Duke but wanted to branch out on his own?" he said."I thought he'd gone to America, or big-game hunting in South Africa. Instead..."

"He's in a poor part of London in a mean little house."

Watson got carefully out of bed and put his feet expertly into the famous slippers. "Then he can't be involved in any robberies, at Coutts' or anywhere else. Otherwise we'd see him living in The Albany or Whitehaven Mansions." Or somewhere else equally fashionable.

"I must say he does seem to have come down in the world for such a suave and efficient operator." The young man had struck me, when I first met him, as someone who relished the good things of life – with a very sound idea of how to get them.

"Does this mean we have to start looking somewhere else?"

"It's possible. But I would like to have one last crack at it. Emily will be there tomorrow morning. I'll join her and see what turns up."

It reminded me once again of the occasion in Nantes when we both spent so much time walking up and down outside the old widow's house waiting for de Luc to put on what we had vainly hoped would be an early appearance. But Emily became increasingly impatient and finally said that, come what may, she was going to knock at the door of the London house. Whatever the outcome, it couldn't be worse than all this hanging about.

The door was opened not, as I had expected it to be, by the old Duke of Loamshire's former Amanuensis, but a worried looking young woman in the latest seaside rig. Tight blue skirt with a narrow black belt, red and white shirt-waister with leg-o'-mutton sleeves and a bow at the neck, she only needed a natty straw boater to finish the outfit off. Emily whispered to me that the girl looked ill. Pale, with dark circles under her eyes. She nevertheless made an effort to seem animated, and definitely had a light dusting of Madam Rachel's powder on her nose! Miss Fanshaw apologised profusely for coming to the wrong house and we went down the path together.

"Is that the woman you met in Margate?" I asked as we hurried home.

"Difficult to say. I didn't get a really good look at her because of the parasol, and we were together for only a few minutes." It was poor old Cardinal Tosca all over again, the priest she met on the *Corso* and couldn't be sure of after he disappeared.

"There's so much in all this that reminds me of 'The Stockbroker's Clerk'," said Watson when we told him our tale. Having no room for a study in the mean little lodgings we were forced to occupy for the present, he had to keep his battered tin despatch box in the garden shed. He hurriedly changed his slippers for boots and went out in the rain, returning later with some torn pages of an old newspaper. "Here we are," he said. "*The Evening Standard.* Listen while I read what it says about a daring raid in the City of London: 'There can be no doubt that Beddington obtained entrance by pretending he had left something behind him, and having murdered the watchman, rapidly rifled the large safe'."

Beddington, explained Watson, blowing his nose hard as the dust tickled his nostrils, was a notorious forger after a huge amount of American railway bonds. His brother usually worked

153

with him. But he couldn't do so on this occasion because he was busy keeping a young clerk hanging about in Birmingham.

"Why?" asked Emily.

It took my husband some time to answer this but at last he said, "The youth worked for a London firm, which Sherlock called a 'financial house', and was lured to the Midlands by the promise of a better job. It was this clerk the first Beddington replaced, after studying and then copying a sample of his handwriting."

"Impossible," said Miss Fanshaw. "Everyone would know it wasn't the same fellow."

"True," said Watson, scratching his head. "But I seem to remember the first young man, although he had been engaged, hadn't actually started work yet and was encouraged by the man in Birmingham to write and resign his post."

"A letter that never got there?"

"Of course it didn't. It was the sample of writing I mentioned earlier, sent by one Beddington to the other."

"So the case was about impersonation as well as robbery." I said. "Do you think it's the same here?"

"But who is impersonating whom?"

"The seaside-loving sister with no powder on her nose the sick sister *with* powder on her nose." I suddenly stopped short and said, "But there's a youth involved. Could he be imitating his

154

sick sister?" At that thought I turned to Emily and said, "Is there any possibility that the person you met in Margate was really a man?"

"The parasol, being in the shade, the expression on the face..."

"I agree. That would all make it hard to tell." And it would also be quite difficult for any man to assume the demure look of a well brought up Victorian Miss. Besides, the former Duke of Loamshire's Secretary, although under thirty-five could hardly be described as a youth.

"I'm afraid I'm 'out of my depths' as I once told Holmes," said Watson. "Where does this stuff, the powder, come in?"

"I'll tell you where," I said, all my detecting instincts coming to the fore. "If I'm right and we do have a brother imitating a sister, rather than a woman imitating another woman, then it is of the greatest importance. A man, especially one with a slight youthful-seeming figure, could borrow his sister's clothes and even her hat. Possibly her shoes too, although I don't think that's likely. But," and here I again turned to Mrs. St. Clair, "unless he was like your husband he would completely forget the face powder."

"I'm not sure what you're getting at exactly," said Emily, bridling. "But I'm certain it's something objectionable."

"No, no." I said hastily. "I simply mean that, with Mr. St. Clair's knowledge and expertise in the use of paint and powder

155

when he acted on the stage, it isn't something *he* would be likely to forget."

"Since you're so clever, what was this person doing in Margate?"

"He obviously wasn't used to playing the part of a woman. A week in a seaside resort where there are always plenty of people would accustom him to it, and give him some idea whether or not he could carry it off. After all, even with all that you've said, it wasn't only the shiny nose but also something about the expression which intrigued you."

"Where was the poor sick sister all this time?"

"Possibly down there with him and confined to the house."

"And when my children's governess saw 'her' at the station prior to going back home he had her in his carpet bag?"

"She has you there," said Watson. "I think myself that invalids are sent to Margate for the sea air and encouraged to take walks or rides along the sea front. The poor girl might as well have been 'confined to the house' in London if she was never allowed to go out."

"Maybe she was, with an old servant to look after her while her brother told her he was going away for a week for a break from nursing."

"Old servant," said Miss Fanshaw derisively, "in a district like that!"

"You forget, apart from everything we've been discussing so far, things are definitely not what they seem. Someone who has been Secretary to a Duke for a number of years will have plenty of money and be well able to entice an old biddy into looking after his sister for a few days. Besides, although the girl looked pale, she may not have been that sick, and perhaps preferred to be in London by herself."

"If this Duke's Secretary is that well-off, why did he need to pass dud cheques?" asked Watson.

"Maybe because he gambled too much on the nags," said Emily spitefully. "Or had a very nasty, demanding mistress."

"It's much more likely he's been gambling on the Stock Exchange, or is trying to raise the wind for an expedition to Antarctica."

This was something which had been very much in the news. But it would have had to be a very substantial cheque to answer for either purpose; and if the young person was in the habit of making only 'small deposits and withdrawals' somebody ought to have been mightily suspicious. Maybe the bank was losing its grip?

"Probably said a rich relative had popped off suddenly and left her the money."

"Surely," I said, "If one is passing a dud cheque one takes the cash and scarpers before the bank finds out?"

"You would certainly think so," said Emily. "If the police go to the house again and the same girl answers the door to them as did to us, Lestrade and his cohorts won't be fooled by a dusting of powder into thinking, not without some more substantial proof, that she's an innocent bystander."

"I badly need a recap of all this," said poor Watson. "The young man, the old Duke of Loamshire's Secretary, went down to Margate with, or perhaps without, his sister. Nevertheless at some point he dressed in her clothes. But unfortunately didn't have her expertise in the face-powder department. The purpose of his trip was to see if he could pass as a woman. Having decided from this experience that he could, but not realising how much his nose shone, he then returned to London and robbed Coutts' Bank of a considerable sum of money. He either told his sister what he'd done, or he didn't tell his sister what he had done. However, he made two mistakes. One was meeting a suspicious Miss Fanshaw, and the other was not leaving England as soon as he could with the cash. To be seen by Lestrade, Gregson or one of the other Scotland Yard Inspectors and then by you, Mary, at the same address as one of Coutts' clients who had just presented a cheque which bounced would need more than simply saying one knew nothing about the matter. In my opinion that was extremely weak, and certainly would not have deceived Holmes."

158

Having delivered himself of all that, Watson mopped his brow and looked rather pleased with himself. "A masterly summing-up," I said kindly. "I suppose he had a woman in the house to disguise his own comings and goings, sometimes as a girl and sometimes in his own *persona*. But the cash must be somewhere else. It would be as foolish as not leaving London at once to keep it in the house. In case the police came back."

"Stashed in an old sock and stuck up the chimney," said Emily.

"I doubt it. My guess is he has already invested it in some enterprise. Imagine, if he only *could* be the first to mount an expedition to Antarctica it would be the making of him. He said, when the young Lord St. Vincent succeeded to the title, that he wanted something more exciting to do than continuing to be a peer's dogsbody."

"You can both go round tomorrow and nab him," said Watson decisively.

"No," I said, "You'll go tonight and do the nabbing. It's no job for delicate females."

"Show me where these two mythical creatures are," said John, "and I might just do it."

He was gone for such a long time that I became really worried. What if my husband, the father of my child, had bumped into Moriarty or one of the Poirots? Worse still, suppose one of the Black Gorgiano gang waylaid him in a noisome alley? Emily had gone home, and by the time John did come in I was a nervous wreck. "The birds have already flown," he said.

The same as Mrs. Marple and her lover, Angelo, after we had recovered the Curragh sovereigns and the police went down to arrest the pair. Only to find the house empty and up for sale and their house agent nowhere to be found.

"There was one surprise," said Watson. "I found out the couple who had been living in the house are twins. That would certainly make it easier for the man to imitate his sister. Apparently they went down to Margate together but she came home after two or three days. Then he arrived at the house, went into Coutts, did the necessary – and they both bunked off. There was no old servant looking after anybody, or anything remotely like it. Neither do I believe the girl was confined to her room when she went to the seaside. My guess is that she and her brother went about quite openly (and in their own togs) until her return to Town."

"It's obvious you think she was in the swindle too. But I think you're wrong. Otherwise there would be no need for such an elaborate charade. She could have gone into the bank as herself to cash the cheque and that would have been it. Think of all the difficulties over a signature."

160

"If you are right, and the woman did have nothing to do with it, then the brother no doubt practised writing her name, as well as how to move about in women's clothes. A twin might find forging his sibling's signature very easy since the handwriting would, or could, be very similar."

"And now they've gone to ground, just like Ellen and Angelo. But at least we recovered the loot on that occasion." I was determined we would do so again. But, as it transpired, that little adventure would have to wait, and turned out to be futile as far as recovering any cash was concerned. So one down for the Watson-Fanshaw Detective Agency, worst luck. Meanwhile, Miss Fanshaw came round to say she had almost bumped into James Moriarty recently in the Haymarket. The Haymarket! What memories that evoked. When I had first set eyes on a bent old man with deep-set grey eyes who suggested I become one of his minions and help blow up the Houses of Parliament.

"And where Moriarty is, can the Poirots be far behind?" asked Emily, echoing the words of a famous poem. "Fortunately he didn't see me and I came straight here to acquaint you both with the good news."

It turned out she was quite right about the Poirots. The next day John spotted them on Paddington Station. Then to my horror a week later, when out buying a few necessities, I saw Black Gorgiano's grandson coming out of a district messenger's office. Our enemies, although they might not know yet exactly where we lived, were nevertheless rapidly closing in on us.

"There's nothing for it," said Emily, hurriedly calling at the house again, this time in her masculine garb. "I fear it will have to be the circus."

I had sent a ragged little street arab round to 'The Laurels' with a note to tell her about my almost bumping into the Italian-American, impressing on the child (with a welcome sixpence) that he wasn't on any account to speak to a living soul: and to tell her at once if he thought he'd been followed.

Miss Fanshaw was in less danger than we were because no-one as yet had guessed her real name. But all four villains had seen her in the flesh, and were not above scouring the whole of London until they finally found it out. It was becoming increasingly obvious that something drastic had to be done to relieve our situation. And done quickly.

Chapter Eight

But, "The circus?" said John, after Emily had left in her usual manner by climbing over the back garden wall. "Whatever is she talking about?"

"Well she can't mean Piccadilly or Holborn Circus. Or even The Elephant and Castle. It must be the real thing, and possibly on The Common." Which was notorious for its showmen. I had heard about 'Lord' George Sanger, the world's greatest fairground proprietor. He wasn't a Lord, of course, but had started calling himself so after Buffalo Bill began putting 'The Honourable William Cody' on his publicity posters. But there could be no denying Sanger looked the part, in his top hat and frock coat, and the name stuck.

But there could also be no doubt that circuses and the fairgrounds associated with them were extremely dangerous places. Nearly seventy years earlier a man had been literally kicked to death at Stalybridge by miners using their iron-shod clogs. Men, and women, in cities up and down the country were known to come out of the stews as soon as the 'respectable' patrons had left the fairgrounds and wreak havoc with the stalls and sometimes the circus animals. Ruffians of both sexes, mad with cheap and adulterated drink, broke open cages with picks and shovels. It was even said two elephants escaped when their pantechnicon was overturned by a ferocious group of half-starved slum-dwellers indulging in mob violence for its own sake.

One of the worst offenders was 'Carrotty Kate', an enormous red-headed and half-naked shrew who periodically came out of the aptly named Bull Paunch Alley in Bath and incited her followers to wreck the booths in any fair unfortunate enough to come within their orbit. Even the so-called circus 'freaks' were occasionally infected by what went on around them as it got later and later and no constables arrived to restore order. On one memorable occasion an American billed as 'The Living Skeleton' tried to murder a professional 'Fat Man' by knocking him on the head with a tent-peg.

I guessed things had improved since then, even if such places were still highly undesirable. But, said Mrs. St. Clair, suddenly arriving on the doorstep in her best outfit, the Nipper must be left with Millie and we three go parading in the Haymarket, through the Burlington and Lowther Arcades, and along the Strand. Places where any of the villains might spot us.

"Not on your life," I said. What if that horrible boy from the Long Island cave had already discovered where the Watson family lived and knocked on the door while we were out? It didn't bear thinking about.

"Have it your own way," said Miss Fanshaw, twirling her parasol. "But somehow we have to lure them to a performance."

"It would be much better," said Watson gravely, "if I did the luring and you women were left out of it."

"And even more so," I said to Emily, "if we had the remotest idea what your plan really is."

"Just get that little snake of a grandson inside the circus tent along with those two Belgians and Professor Moriarty. Then you'll see."

"So, if we stroll about in the late afternoon and are lucky enough to be spotted," said John, "then all we do is drive over to The Common and buy our tickets. The crooks are bound to follow. Is that it?"

"Lucky isn't the word I would use," I said.

"Neither would I," said Miss Fanshaw. "And, as a matter of fact, I'd rather you two kept out of the tent."

"Are you quite sure she didn't take a stick of dynamite away from Exeter Hall when all you so-called members of The Women's Franchise League met for instructions on how to blow up half the historic buildings in London?" asked Watson after she'd left. "But surely even Emily can't be planning to murder so many of the inhabitants of Wandsworth."

After this conversation there followed a frustrating few days when, once Millie and the Nipper had been left safely at 'The Laurels', we walked round parts of London where we thought Moriarty might be. But without any success. This was hardly surprising in a City of four million inhabitants. Miss Fanshaw began to worry that the circus might pack up and go, since none of them stayed in one place for very long. However, in spite of my and John's qualms about the plan, I was relieved one afternoon when I realised I had been spotted by Achille. The next day we three repaired to the place. To see all our pursuers dodging into a nearby divan. John immediately whistled for a hansom. Emily and I climbed in. He followed; and we had the satisfaction of seeing our pursuers come hurriedly out of their hiding place, call for a growler and bowl merrily after us.

The circus tent was almost full when we arrived. But, carefully obeying Emily's instructions, Watson and I didn't go in. Instead we said we'd wander round the fairground stalls. Emily, however, did go in, carrying a parcel under her arm. On the way to a shooting gallery I told John a story which I had heard from Mrs. Marple on the train to Dundalk, about some performing bulls.

"Not here, I hope?"

"Somewhere in Ireland. Apparently they were the star attraction. But all they did was step clumsily on and off something. There was very nearly a riot. She told me another story too. A young and, by the looks of them, very poor couple paid to guess whether a coiled leather belt would or would not unravel. Apparently you stick your finger or a pencil into one of the   coils, the man in charge of the booth pulls the end of the belt, and if it unravels you've no prize and lost your stake."

"It sounds incredibly complicated to me. Worse than the thimble riggers. Who, by the way, are over to our left."

"There was a happy ending, however. A little English woman dashed forward, put the pencil in the proper place, won the money and ran after the young couple with the soft. Which was an absolute fortune to them, of course. The men argued like mad that the woman was making a mistake. But she stood her ground."

"And got out of the place alive? I wonder she wasn't waylaid somewhere and strangled."

By this time we had reached the gallery, where I was pleased to see Watson acquit himself very well and win a large fluffy teddy bear for the Nipper. I bought some gingerbread for Millie at another stall, we dodged the drinking booths (where people were already becoming riotous), John refused to go into The Bearded Lady's tent – and I said that on no account would I visit The World's Most Tattooed Man.

We carefully ignored anything vaguely resembling fawney dropping. Where an innocent-seeming boy would accost a person and say he'd found a gold ring on the ground and was it valuable? The man or woman spoken to wouldn't be able to tell for sure in the half-light. But, with any luck, ring and money changed hands. The boy vanished, and the dupe was left with something completely worthless.

After a while we grew tired of all the noise and gravitated towards the circus tent. Greatly daring, John lifted the edge of the back flap. And just as quickly dropped it. Propelling me towards a quieter spot he gasped, "Mary, *Mr.* St. Clair is in there. Prancing about in his red wig as a white-face."

A Joey. In make-up devised by the famous clown Joseph Grimaldi and used ever since. A man of such pathos that one of his most famous songs, 'An Oyster Crossed in Love', was said to reduce his audience to tears. Since he was usually accompanied by a large cardboard oyster continually opening and closing its mouth, my guess was they were tears of laughter. However, the idea of Neville St. Clair playing the part of a clown was so intriguing I felt I must see for myself.

"Take a quick squint through one of the eye-holes," whispered John, not keen to lift the tent flap twice.

Well, there the man was, in his baggy clown's trousers and large 'Toddles' boots, holding the audience spell-bound. While Emily Fanshaw shinned up the tent pole in trousers and shirt and with a man's cap on her head, completely unnoticed by everyone but me – and perhaps John when, overcome with curiosity, he went against his own advice and carefully lifted the tent flap again.

"They probably think 'he's' something to do with managing the tent," said John when I told him. "If Emily registers on their consciousness at all, with all this malarkey going on."

"But," I hissed, "did you see who was sitting on the front bench? Moriarty, the Poirots and Black Gorgiano's grandson!"

Thunderous applause signalled the end of the show, and people began to pour out of the tent laughing and wiping their eyes on their sleeves. Just as I judged it nearly empty, and was preparing to defend myself against any dirty work on the part of our British, Belgian and American friends, John suddenly shouted, "Stand back!"

The tent had started to fall. Not suddenly, but with the grace of a ballerina performing 'The Dying Swan'. It gathered momentum as it reached nearer the ground, and finally fell with a resounding thud. Auguste and Achille were knocked unconscious and taken to hospital. Black Gorgiano's grandson was killed. We heard later that the members of his gang who had crossed the Atlantic to help him find us fled back to Long Island completely demoralised by the loss of their temporary leader. These didn't include Leverton, who had decided to branch out on his own and thought that anyway he would be too easily recognised by Scotland Yard if he came to London. Neither was the notorious Alfredo one of the elite bunch of cut-throats. He'd been murdered in Naples.

But where was Moriarty? Come to that, where were the St. Clairs?

John and I had retired hurriedly towards the shooting gallery when a sudden suppressed burst of triumphant laughter made us once more run to the back of the fallen tent. Emily and her husband were sprawled most inelegantly on the grass. But at least they were safe.

"We persuaded the rest of the circus crew to enjoy themselves in the drinking booths towards the end of the performance," said Miss Fanshaw. "I even gave them some money to do so. I knew Neville could hold the audience enthralled long enough for me to climb up and loosen those ties in such a way that it would be some time before everything collapsed. After all, we never intended to injure or kill any of the innocent nincompoops living in this part of the world."

Perhaps not, although they almost had. But, I wondered, how did our two friends get out?

Mr. St. Clair said rather pompously that of course they knew what was going to happen. "So I gradually worked my way towards the back of the ring (where my wife was already waiting in the shadows), saw that everyone except the members of that murderous bunch had left, hopped over the said edge at the last minute and, just as the tent gave a final shudder, crawled out from under it."

"Mind you," said Emily, "it was a close thing. if I hadn't already got out just in front of him, and supported part of the canvas on my aching shoulders for as long as was necessary, Neville might never have made it."

John, who had been standing apart for some time deep on thought, suddenly said, "Now that the danger has passed why don't we all go home to change and then meet up for dinner at Marcini's? I remember telling you once it was one of the places Holmes liked to frequent in the days before he left Town. Although he would insist on going to hear some opera or other afterwards. Or there's Goldoni's, of course. I recall Sherlock asking me to turn up there one evening with some very queer..."

"There's still Moriarty," interrupted Miss Fanshaw brusquely.

"Yes. I wonder what happened to him?"

"He can't do that much harm all by his little self," I said, thereby underestimating the man, "and I could do with a night out after the strain of the last few weeks."

I asked Mrs. St. Clair over dinner when her husband had become involved in our troubles. She said it was on the day I saw her in the drawing-room having a heart-to-heart talk with Neville. "I told him the whole story of the Watson-Fanshaw Detective Agency, and the way we were being persecuted by so many villains. He said we obviously needed all the help we could get."

"Too right," said Mr. St. Clair through a mouthful of asparagus. "And now, Watson, I expect you'll be moving back to Kensington?"

"Can't wait," said my husband, tucking into his food with equal vigour.

"Do you think we'll have any more bother with those two Belgians?" I asked Emily's husband.

"No. I went round to the hospital and was told they're being sent straight back to Spa as soon as they have recovered enough to leave England. Let's hope they are well on their way by next week. Meanwhile both of them are too anesthetised to cause anybody any trouble. Although the doctors tell me the old man is quite good at cursing, for all that he's unconscious."

Emily, who had been busy studying the menu trying to decide between *paté de fois gras* and what her husband was having, said suddenly, "Muriel, you know such a lot of things. Have you ever heard of Wilson, a canary trainer?"

"I've never taken much interest in canaries," I said. "I think birds should be left to fly freely, not blinded and put in cages."

"Blinded?"

"Some of them are. The dreadful wretches who own them occasionally do that. They think it makes the poor little creatures sing better. The sellers can then expect a higher price from those who want to buy the birds."

"Well, this man is said to be 'notorious'. But I don't think it's for that."

I was later to find out what it was for. But meanwhile John and I had to get on with once more moving house. Our former residence, of course, was sold so it meant some serious hunting in the area to try to secure another. Should I ask John about the pearls that had come to me over the years, before I was married? There were, I supposed, still one or two left. We had money from John's time in the cave on Long Island, as well as from the Vatican. There had been small payments from Mr. Smith and the family of the man who died from lead poisoning, as well as a large one from the captain who kept the Ashes in a cabinet at home.

But our junketings about Europe in an effort to evade certain people, and my enforced idleness during the weeks we'd had to spend in Paddington, had made serious inroads in our finances. In the end I persuaded John not to buy but to *rent* a commodious property, one where the servants came with it, fixed up an office in the same way Emily and I had done before and sent her a note with our new address. Apart from our investigation into what was going on in Long Island, the return of the cameos to the Vatican, the recovery of the Ashes and, to a certain extent, the partial solving of the mystery of the man in Margate (we still had to recover the money), the activities surrounding The

Watson-Fanshaw Detective Agency had become somewhat perfunctory. It was high time we both got back to serious sleuthing.

So you can guess how happy I was to receive a message offering Emily and me some work. I invited her to come round right away. Looking critically at the new office, she nodded approvingly. It wasn't quite up to the standard of a New York Agency. For example, Mr. Castalotte's. But she certainly thought it would do. And yes, it should be a great help now that her husband knew all about our enterprise.

"We don't have to make all those excuses anymore," I said. "Or wait until he goes off on one of his nef..." I had very nearly said 'nefarious escapades' and hurriedly changed it to "business trips." But I knew by the gleam in her eye that she guessed what I had meant to say. I wondered how long it would be before I'd have to pay for the slip.

I rose from my office chair and opened the desk to show her the request. "We can forget about the canary trainer for the moment, however notorious he is," I said. "Somebody wants us to find The Holy Grail for him."

"I don't even know what it is," said Miss Fanshaw emphatically.

"Neither do a great many people," I said as I opened my notebook. "And I'm rather puzzled what my correspondent

174

thinks it is. The Cup Christ used at the Last Supper, King Arthur's favourite drinking vessel, a plate, a saucer or maybe some kind of a bowl? The stone which sheltered the angels who didn't take sides in the great battle between God and Lucifer, and which fell from Heaven about the same time as he did? The Pre-Raphaelites were very keen on it. Dante Gabriel Rossetti painted Janey Morris as 'The Lady of the Sanct Graal' holding some kind of cup."

"All Rossetti's women look the same to me," said Emily, "and *where* does this man think this Holy Grail is? Provence, Calabria, Nova Scotia, Maryland, Minnisota – Wales?"

"They've each got their share of Grail crackpots. He's extremely unclear on the first point, but says he thinks that (whatever it may be) it's in or near his castle on the West Coast of Scotland. But if it is Christ's Cup someone has done a lot of research trying to prove that's buried underneath a Chapel near Edinburgh, along with a bundle of papers. The point is, are you prepared to drop everything and come up to the Highlands with me?" Now that had a familiar ring. I sounded positively Sherlockian.

"Yes," she said. "After all, it's our job. But give me time to do a little shopping in Cork Street."

"There's to be no parading around in a man's kilt," I said severely. "Don't forget, they wear nothing underneath."

Even Emily looked shocked at the thought of going without her underwear and said she had no intention of buying a kilt.

"What is it then?" I asked suspiciously.

"I'll tell you later."

It reminded me of the Vatican cameos, which she refused to discuss until we were on our way to Cherbourg. Had they gone missing yet again?

"No," she said. "Whatever makes you think so?"

"Well they do have rather a habit of wondering about," I said, locking up the desk.

"But that can have nothing to do my going to Cork Street."

We managed to catch the ten a.m. train from King's Cross which, after a luncheon stop at York, took us on to Edinburgh in time for dinner at six-thirty. Emily complained of tiredness, and said on no account was she going any further without a rest. It was impossible to do any detecting the way she felt.

That meant a night spent in The North British Hotel. I sincerely hoped she wasn't going to make a fuss about the room, especially as much fuss as she had already made about our midday meal. She called it a 'snack', but I felt it could have felled a fair-sized horse. I left half of my share on the plate and wondered how, with such an appetite, she could keep her figure.

"It's difficult for shorter people to eat and still keep slim," said Mrs. St. Clair graciously, as if all that extra height was the

176

result of personal cleverness. "And really, Muriel, you will need to keep up your strength."

I felt I could do this without looking like an india-rubber ball, and was glad when she fell asleep almost immediately that night instead of suggesting a foray into the City slums. However, having slept so well, my dear friend arose quite happy and we went on to Alford, changing first at Aberdeen. The Forth Bridge was now in operation so we didn't have to experience the discomfort and delay of a ferry, or the long diversion by way of Perth. A major consideration when travelling with such an impatient person as Emily Fanshaw in tow.

When we got to the final stop of our journey and walked sedately out of the railway station in front of a perspiring porter wheeling our luggage along on a sack barrow, we discovered that The MacQuiver of that Ilk had sent a comfortable conveyance for us. A welcome change after all those hours on a train. But the journey to his castle proved long and tedious in the extreme.

"Of that Ilk?" asked Miss Fanshaw, raising an eloquent eyebrow.

"Too complicated to explain," I said. "Something to do with owning land, being Head of the Clan. A Chief of Chiefs."

"The Sinclairs are a clan you know. They were originally French, when the name was rendered St. Clair, in the same way as ours. Neville is descended from a knight who was with Robert Bruce. The Watsons don't have their own clan. They're only part of someone else's."

"A Sept," I said briefly. "But John has the right to wear the Buchanan tartan. Then I remembered he wasn't a Watson by birth and hastily changed the subject.

We arrived at our destination at last, stiff, weary and ready for some Highland hospitality. But first we had to meet our host. A huge, bearded Highlander led us along a passage hung with a tartan of a particularly virulent sort, and we were shown into a room with cloth-covered walls of the same pattern. The tartan here was looped back in places to show an antlered deer-head or two, along with paintings of some kind. But this did nothing to improve the overwhelming effect of so much bogus Scottishness. The MacQuiver sat with his back to us, in front of a roaring fire, and appeared to be quietly smoking a hookah. Bottles of Tokay alternating with Chianti stood on a small side-table well within reach, and two glasses containing the dregs of both wines stood on the hearth.

I looked at the high domed head of the man in the chair and at the wisps of reddish hair, which only served to accentuate his baldness, round the edge of that dome. Surely...

He turned his armchair round and I found myself looking into the prematurely aged features of Mr. Thaddeus Sholto. "We meet again dear lady," he said in his high piping treble. "But when my brother Bartholomew, and a few other close relatives, died I became the Laird of these parts. Very cold parts," he added, turning the chair round and putting his feet back on the fender.

I recalled the journey near the beginning of the 'The Sign of Four' when I went in a four-wheeler with Holmes and the man who was destined to become my husband to what Sherlock described in his account of the case (passing it off as John's, of course) as not very fashionable regions and 'a questionable and forbidding neighbourhood.' Forgetting how long I had worked for Mrs. Forrester in that part of London known as Camberwell, Holmes began to show off his knowledge of the Capital.

"Rochester Row. Now Vincent Square. Now we come out on the Vauxhall Bridge Road. We are making for the Surrey side, apparently. Yes, I thought so. Now we are on the bridge. You can get a glimpse of the river..."

Well, we had already seen the Thames for ourselves. But Sherlock wasn't to be put off. "Wandsworth Road. Priory Road. Larkhill Lane. Stockwell Place. Robert Street. Cold-harbour Lane." He joyously rattled them all off. But we still had some way to go, past garishly illuminated public houses, rows of two-storied villas – and what Holmes called interminable lines of new, staring brick building, tentacles thrown out into the country by a giant city – before reaching the mean little house to where Thaddeus Sholto had taken himself after leaving the family home, Pondicherry Lodge, in South Norwood.

I looked round the room we were now in. The luxurious deep-piled carpet which had made me feel I was walking on moss wasn't there. It had been replaced by the ubiquitous (and, it seemed, inevitable) tartan. The rich glossy curtains were gone. No wonderful tapestries draped the walls. There were no oriental vases. The model of a dove which hung on an almost invisible gold thread from the ceiling had disappeared. It could no longer dispense a suspect oriental perfume with each turn of its beautiful silver body. The hookah seemed to be almost the only souvenir of his home in London that The MacQuiver had carried with him to the Western Isles. Looking closer at what was on the wall, I saw that he still had the same pictures: a Corot, the questionable Salvador Rosa and that modern Bouguereau. But even the Hindu servant, the Khidmutkar, had vanished. In his place was this very handsome Highlander.

"Poor Mr. Holmes is no more," said Thaddeus, proving news travelled slowly in the Highlands, "but where is your husband? It is very kind of him to bring you to see me. Quite like old times, when Holmes came with you both to my London residence. He wanted, if I remember rightly , to find out why I had been sending those pearls from the Agra Treasure to you so

180

regularly. I must be patient, however. No doubt Dr. Watson is in the lobby providing himself with freshly warmed socks. It's always best to change into dry socks after a journey. To keep away colds, you know."

I didn't much care for his mentioning the Agra Treasure, and especially the pearls, in front of Mrs. St. Clair. She had already shown far too much interest in them in the train to Peconic Bay.

"Watson is in London looking after the Little Nipper," I said.

"The Little Nipper," said Thaddeus nervously. "Who is that?"

"Hamish Hopley Holmes Watson," I said. "Our son and heir."

I didn't tell him what a row there had been over 'Holmes'.

"But the Watson-Fanshaw Detective Agency? I've no idea who Fanshaw might be, but it was the name Watson which persuaded me to send that letter."

"That's us," said Emily coldly and with a vicious glance at me. "I am Miss Fanshaw."

"But," stammered the Laird, "two ladies...I hardly think you will be equal to the task."

"It's us or nobody at the moment," I said.

It ended with The MacQuiver being taken into his private apartments by the Highland servant, to be prepared for the hazardous process of going out into the open air. After what seemed an age, he reappeared in the full Highland rig thought necessary for day wear. Kilt, a jacket and waistcoat of tweed with horn buttons, plain knitted hose kept up to the knee with garters, and an Inverness cape in place of the fringed plaid. The *sgian* (or *skean*) *-dubh*, showing its hilt, rested very correctly inside that part of the stocking covering his outer right leg and he wore a stout pair of brogues. Gone were the extra-long be-frogged top coat with the astrakhan collar and cuffs, and the rabbit-skin cap with lappets covering the ears. But the former Mr. Sholto insisted on some kind of bonnet. When the Highlander asked which one, The Glengarry or The Balmoral, The MacQuiver settled for the latter, a broad, blue affair, but said it was to be sure to have his personal crest pinned to it. Even so, it was too small for his head.

In my first letter to John I told him that, when we went into the castle grounds, there were heaps of newly dug earth everywhere. His reply, which came by return of post, assured me that everything was going well. He and the girl Millie (as well as the Nipper) were coping beautifully and I wasn't to worry at all. Enough to convince any wife that things might be going very badly indeed, and there would be any number of crises for her to attend to as soon as she managed to get back home.

He asked if the mounds of earth reminded me of the time we held hands in the gardens of Pondicherry Lodge, when I had remarked on the heaps of rubbish and said what a strange place it was. He had replied that the scene 'looked as if all the moles in England had been let loose in it' and told me how reminiscent it was of his time in Ballarat at the gold diggings. Well, he was right. Like the two Sholto brothers in their anxiety to find the Agra Treasure, someone in the castle was searching for something, and had organised an army of retainers to help them do it. That someone could, I thought at the time, only be Thaddeus. Memories of digging frantically in the Norwood garden with Bartholomew had caused him to follow the same procedure when he became The MacQuiver of that Ilk. But by the look of it he'd been singularly unsuccessful in his quest so far.

After a short time, however, we had to go back inside. Thaddeus felt the cold very easily and in any case was anxious to show us the magnificent Ballroom. He planned to give a great dance there very soon. Emily looked at me triumphantly and mouthed the words 'Cork Street'. The festivities, said our host, were to be in our honour and he would invite everyone who was anyone for miles around: Mackillicuddy of the Reeks perhaps, and even a Belted Earl or two.

Of course, he had been looking forward very much indeed to introducing his neighbours to Dr. John H. Watson, the friend and colleague of the Great Detective Sherlock Holmes. But one couldn't have everything.

That evening, after an informal meal in the dining-room at which there were only seven courses and as many servants, Emily and I retired to a sumptuous bedroom. Our cases had been unpacked by the Laird's servants, of course, and most of their contents hung up in two commodious garderobes. (It's funny how one slips into using medieval words in a castle). In addition to this, our night attire lay ready on the single beds. But I saw with surprise that two magnificent sashes had been placed carefully over a clothes horse. One was bright, very bright: red and green with a thin blue stripe – the Sinclair tartan, and the other was the Buchanan – a garish mixture of red, orange, yellow, and green with a slightly wider blue stripe. Were they for us to wear at this Ball? I'd look like a walking rainbow.

"Don't be silly," said Mrs. St. Clair in her role of respectable matron. "You'll have your evening frock, which I trust is a chaste white, and the sashes will be fastened on, and worn over, the right shoulder to show we have married into the Clan. That is," she added hastily, "unless Morstan is a Scottish name and you have the right to a different tartan."

"It's of no consequence," I said, remembering the name Sacker. "I'm not a Scot as far as I know. Even if I were, I would probably be expected to wear my husband's tartan." And in my circumstances Buchanan would do as well as anything. I asked her if that was why she had been in Cork Street. Yes, she said, where a famous warehouse supplied everything from scarves to kilts in every tartan. I congratulated her on another example of her remarkable foresight and climbed wearily into bed.

The MacQuiver hadn't dressed for dinner that evening. Instead he wore a green smoking jacket with tartan trews, and leather pumps. Neither had we two women bothered to change. Emily said she was too tired; and I needed to keep her in countenance. It was a different matter on the night of the Ball. Every light in the castle blazed. Anything that could be polished was polished. Carpets were cleaned with cold tea-leaves. A magnificent specimen ran through the *porte cochère* to the hall door. Guests were driven up the long, sweeping drive and under this edifice so that, in the event of rain or heavy snow, they could step out of their carriages and enter the castle with their finery and their dancing shoes perfectly dry.

"Only it isn't a proper castle," said Emily. "One swallow doesn't make a summer, and it needs more than a couple of turrets to make this place look like a medieval stronghold."

"It's good enough for me," I said. "Elegant, commodious and in fine setting."

"Yes, and with a bitterly cold wind wafting towards us from the sea."

"Bitterly cold winds don't waft. They go through you like a knife."

The Macquiver appeared in full Highland Dress for the evening, wearing an open velvet doublet with lozenge-shaped silver buttons, a bright red waistcoat with lace jabot, hose matching his kilt, a silver-mounted sporran and low-cut leather dancing shoes. He had fastened his plaid to a narrow shoulder with a silver brooch bearing his crest and was adorned with sword belt, claymore, powder horn and pistols. Rather too much, I felt, although he would remove the plaid if he wished to dance. The idea of such a funny little man dancing, over-burdened as he was with all that finery, caused me to smile behind my fan. But I hadn't much time for jollity. Emily was tugging at my elbow and said, "That woman over there has her sash fastened on the *left* shoulder."

"She must be the wife of a Clan Chief," I said soothingly. The last thing we needed was an embarrassing scene.

"But what about that young person opposite? The sash is over her right shoulder. But instead of hanging loose It's fastened in a bow on the left hip."

"Married out of the clan," I said briefly.

"I wonder when we can go into supper," said Miss Fanshaw.

I was led into the supper room by The MacQuiver himself after several hours of strenuous dancing. I was right in thinking that Thaddeus refrained from joining in any of the reels. "I'm afraid, Mrs. Watson, it is inclined to over-heat the blood, which of course can lead to all kinds of distressing disorders. As it is, I have already been obliged to leave the room once or twice to seek relief and comfort from my hookah. I apologise most humbly at having to forgo the very great pleasure of taking you, the guest of honour, and your charming assistant for a turn round the floor but..."

My charming assistant! I could just see Emily's face if she heard that. "Miss Fanshaw and I have an equal partnership in our Detective Agency," I said kindly.

"Of course, of course," stammered The MacQuiver, who seemed mortally afraid of offending anybody. "You know I have a strong sense of justice. More so than my father or brother. Even Mr. Holmes said I had acted well after he heard the account of my behaviour over the pearls – which I arranged to have delivered to you when you were still in a state of single blessedness. As I am now. When you were still Miss Morstan. But unlike Miss Fanshaw who, I believe, has never met Sherlock Holmes, you were in a position to learn from him, and of course to benefit from what your husband must have learned as well."

I refrained from disillusioning the poor man by not saying I probably saw almost as little of Holmes as he did after the investigation into 'The Sign of Four' finished. I also didn't mention that one of the things my husband would have garnered from Sherlock was how to develop further an already considerable imagination – rather than any expertise in solving crimes that actually happened. And I decided not to tell the Laird that Mrs. St. Clair had met Holmes. If she found out, she would be wasting time complaining to him about her loss of income instead of getting on with any investigation. But Thaddeus was still fussing as we went towards the laden tables, telling me not to eat this, to be careful with that. "A very little salmon, dear lady. From our own river, but you may find it somewhat too rich."

All at once his attention was caught by a young man who had slipped quietly into the space beside him and was about to whisper in his ear. The MacQuiver was too disturbed by what he heard to excuse himself and the two hurried out of the supper room, with the Laird skipping agitatedly along in an effort to match his companion's easy stride. But not before I had spotted a familiar face. Walking as rapidly round the tables as the enormous crush there would allow, I found Emily talking to one of the handsomest men in the room, telling him all about our trip to Long Island and making his Highland hair stand on end with her graphic account of what went on there. I noticed his plate was still piled with food, and that hers was nearly empty. However, there was no time to chaff her about that.

"Come into the hall at once," I hissed.

"An assignation under the antlers?" Smiling sweetly at her young man, Emily excused herself (but not before offering him her card so that he could claim the first strathspey of the second part of the evening) and followed me out of the overcrowded supper place.

"You know," I said as soon as we found a quiet corner, "that the man from Margate and the old Duke of Loamshire's Secretary are one and the same person? Well he's here, and has collared The MacQuiver."

"I saw him," she said, "when I went up to the nearest table for some more food. He's the illegitimate son of The Duke of Holdernesse. James Wilder by name."

"How can you possibly know that?"

"He passed through the house just as Neville and I were about to begin our Stately Home Tour. I told you all about it when we were trying to think of a way of getting legitimately into de Luc's house during that investigation in Nantes."

"But the illegitimacy?"

"Not official of course. The Duke of Holdernesse apparently passed him off as an employee as much as he could, although the Duchess wasn't deceived. And when she left her husband and went to live in France it was pretty obvious why. Common gossip, in fact. She'd put up with the situation for some time but..."

"Was it ever resolved?"

"Well, you ought to know more about that than me since your husband and Mr. Sherlock Holmes were both heavily involved."

In my next letter to Watson I asked why he hadn't reported that James Wilder was one and the same with the personage with no powder on his/her nose. The answer again came back by return of post. Nobody (man, woman or child), said John, had come out of that house while he was watching it: and James Wilder had been sent to Australia. It was true he did know the young man because Holmes had been called in to investigate a kidnapping from an educational establishment called The Priory School, but he was as surprised as anyone to hear the news. Especially as I had told him that the man from Margate also resembled the old Duke of Loamshire's Secretary.

"Not resembled, *is*," I thought to myself as I carefully folded the letter and put it in my pocket. Had James Wilder gone to Australia after relinquishing his post as Secretary to one Duke, returned to work in the same capacity for another Duke and ended up living in a mean house in London and passing dud cheques, before suddenly turning up in Scotland as yet a third person's Secretary? It certainly needed explaining, and I wondered how soon I could tackle the young man. I was sure he hadn't noticed me in the supper room. He'd been too anxious to carry off The MacQuiver.

190

The following day, knowing Emily was busy swotting up clan lore with her handsome Highlander of the evening before who had managed to wangle a bed for the night solely on her account, I went in search of Thaddeus to ask him about his Secretary. I found the Laird sitting with his feet in a bowl of hot water before a blazing fire and swathed in blankets. "Come not near, my dear Mrs. Watson," he said piteously. "I have caught a most terrible cold."

Welcoming his guests and, worse still, seeing them off after the Ball had, in spite of the *porte cochère*, proved too much for him. "Night air of any sort is always calamitous. But after all the excitement of watching the dancing, and making sure everyone had enough to eat and was thoroughly enjoying themselves, I was in a state of collapse. Fit for nothing except drinking a hot toddy and staggering off to bed. I couldn't even bear to listen to what James had to tell me."

I pricked up my ears. "James?" I asked. "Mr. Wilding, who used to work for the old Duke of Loamshire, and The Duke of..."

The MacQuiver sneezed three times in quick succession and gave a deprecating cough. "You must mean James Hamilton Oscar de Wilde, he said. "A similar-sounding name, I grant you. But I hardly think a man who has worked for two such exalted personages as the Duke of Loamshire, and still more the Duke of Holdernesse, would come to bury himself in the wilds of Hibernia for such as me. There isn't much here to interest anybody. I imagine he must really be on his uppers to have come so far north."

"Uppers or not, I would be grateful if I could have a word with Mr. de Wilde – in private."

"If you would be so good as to touch that bell over there," said Thaddeus with a piteous wipe of his nose, "my Highlander will find him and bring him to you. It is next to impossible for me to move away from this fire at present and, as for your communing with my new Secretary *in camera,* there is a small room off the hall which you can use." The little man shifted in his chair and said wistfully, "I understand it came in handy for romantic assignations at the dances held here in the old days. But that was before my time of course."

I was determined there wouldn't be anything romantic about my meeting with James Wilder and went in search of Emily. It was high time she stopped her dalliance and did something for The Watson-Fanshaw Detective Agency.

"But it wasn't dalliance," she said. "I've found out there's no tradition of a Grail here, holy or otherwise."

So who had put such an idea in the MacQuiver's head, and caused him to dig up so much of his demesne? "It's a good thing most of the destruction is behind this so-called castle," said

Emily. "If the local gentry (and all those other parasites for miles around) hadn't been so eager to get into this place they might have seen it all and consigned their new Laird to a lunatic asylum."

Which would be a cruel and unnecessary procedure. The MacQuiver was eccentric. He thought too often and for too long about his mainly imaginary illnesses. But he had a kind heart, and a sensitive conscience. He'd had no need to send me pearls, no need help what he had called 'a wronged woman'.

I reflected gravely on what might have happened to me if Thaddeus hadn't taken it into his head to get in touch with a lonely governess. I had no fortune. I wasn't particularly attractive to look at. With little chance of marriage in what was a very competitive market, I might have withered away into old age and extreme penury; with only memories of other people's children to keep me company. Instead I had a good husband and child. As well as more satisfying work than teaching subjects to pupils who had no wish to learn them.

Not for the first time, I blessed the impulse which had sent me hot-foot to Baker Street.

Chapter Nine

When I reached the little room off the hall, after telling Mrs. St. Clair to continue keeping her ears and eyes open, The MacQuiver's Secretary had already arrived and was standing by a small window looking out onto the carriage drive. As soon as he turned round to face me as I came through the door I saw that he had a most superior look on his handsome face. This, however, vanished as soon as he realised who I was. He went as white as a sheet and stammered, "The wife of Doctor Watson!"

"We met," I said, at the Country Seat of the Duke and Duchess of Loamshire. You said then that the Duke was a good employer, 'allowing for the natural high-handed manner of the aristocracy' but that the Duchess was 'a little highly strung'. One thing you didn't say was that, although you had been a Duke's Secretary for ten years, it wasn't always the same Duke." Leaving him to digest this for a minute or two, I walked across to a basket chair on the other side of the room and fired my next salvo from a sitting position. "Neither did you tell me the first Duke was your father."

"Why should I? It was no business of anyone but me, and certainly not the business of a couple of *parvenus* out for a free weekend. Exactly the same situation as at the old Duke of Loam -shires'."

"I'll ignore that," I said.

"And was it my fault that there were diamonds stolen, and a murder investigation? That only gave you and your husband an opportunity to stay longer – and for a whole lot of flat-foots to invade the house."

"Judging by what you've been up to since, it's a wonder you weren't accused of murder and stealing diamonds. In fact..."

"You think the wrong people got the blame? Well they didn't. If my father had treated me as he should have done I wouldn't have needed to be anywhere near the place. After all, I am the rightful heir to the Dukedom of Holdernesse."

"Not if you were born on the wrong side of the blanket," I said tartly.

"If my poor mother had been less high-minded she would have married the Duke instead of refusing to do so because she thought it would harm his career. Then, let me tell you, I *would* have eventually become the Seventh Duke, Baron Beverley, Earl of Carston, Lord Lieutenant of the County with two hundred and fifty thousand acres of land and mineral rights in Lancashire and Wales. I'd have a London House in Carlton Terrace, a real castle in Bangor and not a trumpery place like this one; and be Lord of the Admiralty and a Secretary of State in the Cabinet."

"Not unless you had your father's brains, and your sister must have inherited the high-mindedness of your other parent rather than you," I said. "That is, if there was really any high-mindedness to inherit."

"I don't know how you discovered all this," said James Wilder through set teeth. "But I see no reason why you should insult my dear mother."

"Then let me enlighten you. We'll pass over your time with the Loamshires and our meeting when you were careful not to give me your name, although I expect you were using a false one, and go immediately to when my friend and colleague discovered you in Margate dressed as a woman. We'll discuss how you imitated a girl we later discovered was your twin, and succeeded in cashing a dud cheque at Coutts' Bank. By the way, was she implicated?"

"No, said the young man explosively. "She knew nothing at all about it."

"And where is she now?"

Instead of answering immediately he said, "My mother concealed the fact that she had given birth to twins and when she died I went to live with the Duke, while my sister was taken to Montana to be brought up by an aunt."

"She's an American then?"

"Almost a Canadian, if it depended solely on geography. But of course both our parents were born in Britain."

"But your sister has left England?"

Again he didn't answer directly but said, "After all that business at The Priory School, when Sherlock Holmes insisted I be sent away to Australia, I managed to jump ship. Wishing to hide the fact that I was nowhere near the Antipodes, I buried myself in the country with those frightful people the Loamshires."

Seeing my raised eyebrows, Mr. Wilder went on, "He may have been a Duke – but the title only goes back to 1801. And she had been some sort of chorus girl at one of the most notorious casinos in London. I took myself off as quickly as I could after the murder. But, with no money, all I could afford to rent was that sordid little house in Bethnal Green."

"Surely the Duke of Loamshire paid you well, and your father must have settled an allowance on you, or how were you to live when you got to Australia?"

"Work in the goldmines, I expect. But all my money had been gambled away on girls, as well as horses, and I've had more than enough truck with money-lenders to last me a lifetime."

People who bled others white by advancing money at exorbitant rates of interest and were none too fussy about the kind of methods they used if the victim failed to pay up. He had been unable to collect The Duke of Holdernesse's allowance, of course. I felt sure it must have been very generous. So perhaps the thought of all that cash building up in a Ballarat bank caused him to decide to rob Coutts. And the bank in Victoria would probably get in touch with Carlton Terrace before very long to ask what was going on. Then the fat would really be in the fire and Mr. Wilder a hunted man over two Continents.

No, he said. Never mind the bank in Australia. It wasn't that which made him defraud Coutts. Since I already knew so much, he might as well tell me he needed the money for a sure-fire enterprise. "Otherwise why would I be here dancing attendance on the poor old bird who calls himself, quite appropriately I feel, The MacQuiver of that Ilk?"

"I think you'll find that, far from being an old bird, you and he are much of an age." I had to admit he was wearing considerably better, however. But I was no nearer knowing how his twin sister fitted into all this.

"I wrote giving her my new address and she decided to come over for a year. Of course, she had charge of all the finances. That is, charge of what little money we had."

"Because you were already such a notorious bilker you couldn't get a reference to open a bank account of your own."

"If you like to put it that way," he said evenly.

The upshot of all this, as I already knew, was that he dressed himself in his sister's clothes, imitated her signature and got money under false pretences. "She went home to Montana to get married, I bought myself a fine set of new clothes and answered an advertisement for a Gentleman's Secretary. After all, I had plenty of experience."

"But why this particular gentleman?" I asked. "This is a very remote spot and The MacQuiver, although his heart's in the right place, isn't a very attractive employer. I imagine he can be quite peevish, especially when he imagines he's ill."

"Which is nearly all the time."

But I felt sorry for Thaddeus and repeated severely, "Why this particular gentleman?"

"That's my secret," sneered James Wilder. "What I would like to know is how you found out about Margate."

"And that's mine," I said, sweeping regally from the room.

"So you didn't tell him about the powder on his nose," said Emily, "or, rather, the absence of it." She sounded disappointed. After all, it had been due to her intuition that we had found out so much about Wilder.

"Never mind that now. We really have to get to the bottom of why he's here and what ideas the Laird has about where he thinks we'll find the Grail."

"Then you had better start detecting."

"I thought we were in this together?"

"Yes," she said. "But don't forget, my dear, that I am only the 'charming assistant'!"

"I was taught that it is very bad form to eavesdrop on a private conversation," I said.

"Only a *parvenu* would have such scruples. How do you think the police find out anything. Or even your precious Sherlock Holmes?"

"That's the one thing he isn't as far as I'm concerned," I retorted indignantly. "Precious is not a word I would use about him, except perhaps in a derogatory sense."

"I'm told your husband admired him."

"It doesn't mean that I have to. And, believe me, even John's patience was sorely tried at times."

"Especially when his favourite detectives were called into question, I remember."

"That's the last time I tell you anything in a French railway carriage, Miss Fanshaw."

"Neville would have punched the great detective on the nose as soon as look at him after that."

White with temper, I marched over the chequered marble floor of the hall and out of the castle into the garden. Taking a few minutes to cool down, I carefully studied the work there and quickly came to the conclusion that somebody had put the diggers, presumably directed by The MacQuiver, completely on the wrong track – and that somebody could only be his own Secretary.

I saw nothing of Emily for the rest of the day and wondered if she had gone off with a ghillie to explore the surrounding countryside. The Laird was not one for grouse shooting, but he kept up a large establishment for the look of the thing. Even though he was highly unlikely ever to be seen with the guns.

When I went upstairs that evening Emily was already in bed, with her hair in curl papers, sitting up reading a magazine and eating chocolates. "Shall I tell you what the latest is?" she asked. "Feather boas! We'll be well out of fashion when we return to London."

"They're easily bought, and hopefully we will have money in our pockets."

"Have you made any progress with the investigation?" she said sweetly.

"More so than you have by the look of it. That Secretary of his has convinced Sholto the Grail is a solid object somewhere underground. But I have a notion it must be something more delicate, if only I could think what."

"Paper, a drawing, some kind of medieval manuscript?"

"That's an idea. I suggest that tomorrow we make a thorough search of those turrets you abjure so violently."

"One can achieve as much, or more, lying in bed as crawling about on one's hands and knees in the damp grass," said Emily, shutting the box of chocolates, throwing the magazine on the floor and preparing for sleep. "And it's decidedly more comfortable than peering through lenses at stale tobacco ash or other even less desirable muck."

But when we climbed up to one of the turrets the next day we could hear someone ferreting about inside. Emily, now quite her old bossy self, told me to look through the key hole while she stood guard in case anyone should interrupt. Was it likely I asked, since the stairs were so grimy it was obvious nobody ever ventured this far. Certainly not The Macquiver. It would make him dizzy, he'd be terrified of germs and it would need far more than half-an-hour with a hookah to convince him he'd ever recover.

"Nobody up here?" said Miss Fanshaw scornfully, "when you can hear a noise inside that room and see those footprints in the dust? A fine detective you've turned out to be, Sexton, if they eluded your eagle eye."

I could see she still smarted over the label 'charming assistant'. So much so that she called me by the name of a detective whose adventures were written up *for children* by a large number of different hacks grinding away in Grub Street. It reminded me of when Watson said that slave-driver friend of his found blood marks on the stairs in Oberstein's house. Blood marks which were missed by John and therefore made much more of by his oh so clever mentor.

"Well," said my dear friend, "can you see anything through that hole?"

"No," I said, "It's as black as pitch."

She bent down impatiently. "Someone with the mind and morals of a rattlesnake has blocked it up. That means whoever is in there is definitely up to no good."

"Unless the Laird ordered all keyholes to be blocked up because of the draught."

"I don't think the Western Isles agree with you, Muriel. You'd be better off in Edinburgh, or back in London with that dozy husband of yours. It doesn't strike me that The MacQuiver would ever go to bed without ordering everything to be locked and bolted twice over, making damn sure himself that this was done every night. People of his temperament are even more terrified of burglars than the rest of us. Blocked up keyholes would make everything very difficult for the staff. The continual blocking and unblocking all day when it came to locking and unlocking doors would drive them into Bedlam. Besides, you've already said nobody normally comes up here. Sholto probably doesn't even know these doors have locks."

Any more of this and I'd be in a madhouse myself. "I'm off to look into one of the other turrets," I said, picking up my skirts with a flourish and preparing to move off in a rush. "Follow me at your leisure."

However, we drew a blank at every turret except the one where I had missed the footprints; and Mrs. St. Clair was behaving like a great baby. Pretending to be a princess entombed in a tower and saying over and over again, "Rapunzel, Rapunzel, let down your hair."

"You can't be entombed in a tower," I said crossly. "You can only be imprisoned. And all this skipping about doesn't suit you. You're much too tall to act like some kind of sprite. And too old," I added, feeling I must do something to keep my end up after the detective jibe.

But we drew a blank. One of the turrets was empty, apart from thick layers of dust and a number of ancient candle ends and other bits and pieces of junk. We found nothing in the second turret except more dust, and a few shreds of what looked like bone: and the third was full of bat droppings because a hole in the wall hadn't been boarded up. Emily said with relish that the bone proved someone had once been locked in the place and probably starved to death. After being tortured, of course.

"Then why do you keep on about this not being a real castle? Locking your enemies up, then torturing them and/or starving them to death, are medieval ideas and I don't see even a trace of a rack or the thumbscrews."

"What about the erring wife, or even wives? They are around all the time according to most husbands."

"Stop letting your imagination run away with you. A dog probably got in here at some time."

"And couldn't get out again. But then there would be a lot more bones."

"And stop being so daft. It sneaked in here, gnawed the bone in peace and then went looking for another one."

"Why aren't we going back to the first turret?" said Miss Fanshaw. "The one with the blocked-up keyhole?"

"We are. As soon as you've come to your senses."

We found it locked and silent. But whatever had been blocking our view was no longer there. "It was probably a key," said Emily, "and if you can't recognise the butt end of a key when you see one..."

"Anymore than you," I said. "Perhaps we should both stop calling ourselves detectives."

Neither of us had heard the door open. Or the sound of footsteps descending the winding stairs. But then we had been at some distance away. "If you notice, these hinges have been well-oiled. They aren't rusted like the others. This door has been made to open and close quite smoothly," I said, looking carefully at each part.

"Oh, well done," said Mrs. St. Clair enthusiastically. "That means somebody comes here regularly and isn't partial to anyone knowing about it. But it's a puzzle who it could be."

"Not really. One of The Duke of Holdernesse's by-blows, The Duke of Loamshire's aberrant Secretary, the man from Margate who likes to masquerade as a woman. He has many aliases, but my guess is it's The MacQuiver's most recent employee. The one who calls himself James Hamilton Oscar de Wilde."

"It's his office."

"Then why keep it locked?"

"So that he can work in peace."

"What at?"

"How should I know?" said Emily exasperatedly. "Letters, estate bills, The MacQuiver's Memoirs."

"All the same, I'd like to see what is in there."

"And so you shall, just as soon as I can get the key."

Having quite a lot of faith in Emily's resourcefulness, as well as her daring, I was surprised when she told me later that she had been unable to get what we wanted from James Wilder. "He guards it like the crown jewels. I saw the lout making his way to the turret a few moments ago. I suggest we go there too."

The door was again locked, however. "We need an 'outsider' she said.

"A what?"

"Something to grip the butt of the key and twirl it so the door can be opened."

"With him in there? He'd simply show us out."

Emily looked as crestfallen as she had done when we discovered the very first piece of detection offered to The Watson-Fanshaw Agency was a request to find a lost dog. "Wait until tomorrow when the Secretary has to go into town for yet another prescription for his boss. Then we'll see if we can't get in."

She appeared the next morning in a shirt and a pair of trews of a very loud tartan – all yellow, red and orange. Fortunately we were alone. She had told the servants that once the food was placed on the sideboard they wouldn't be wanted anymore. The Secretary, as she said, had had to go into town: and Thaddeus sent a note to ask if we would excuse him. He had suffered such dreadful nightmares he couldn't possibly face any food.

"Do you think he's being drugged?" asked my sole companion in the breakfast room. "Like Mr. Watson in the Long Island cave?"

"No. And wherever did you get those dreadful trousers? Come to think of it, why did you get those dreadful trousers?"

"I went into a man's room and took them out of the garderobe."

I put down my coffee cup with a clatter and looked at her wide-eyed."You, a supposedly respectable wife and mother, a pillar of society, went into a gentleman's bedroom and pinched his-his- *nether garments?*"

"Not a gentleman's room. A servant, merely. Mind you, he came in unexpectedly and I had to dive for cover."

"Where to?"

"Under the bed. If he had stayed much longer I would have given myself away by sneezing. The dust was so thick."

"The Laird has some slovenly retainers then?"

"I don't see why a man shouldn't leave dust under his own bed if he wants to. Or anywhere else if he has a mind and is allowed to do so. There were two beds in the room but I didn't think to look under the other one. It would be a lark if the floor there was as clean as a whistle. Think of the rows it could cause! As to why I am wearing trousers, it's because I intend to climb out onto those phoney battlements and get into that turret through a window at the back. And I don't think it could be done easily in a dress."

"And I don't think it could be done easily at all."

"I'm determined to try. Although James Wilder is out of the way for the time being I'll wager any money he has taken the key with him after locking that door again."

"Then it won't matter if you lose your balance on those battlements and crack your skull on the stones of the courtyard below, since whatever you do in the climbing line I won't be able to get in and you won't be able to get out. Except by the way you came, of course."

"That's the idea: for me to have a thorough search and carry away anything I can find which might possibly be termed a Holy Grail."

"And risk your life even more by prancing about at such a height while carrying something which could be heavy."

"I never prance," said Mrs. St. Clair. "It isn't done. And do you have a better idea?"

"Haven't you ever heard of twirls, pick-locks, bettys?" I can use those with the best of them thanks to the time I spent with Mrs. Marple, who said her lover Angelo used them to open a safe on a crowded train. She described the method so exactly I felt..."

"Can you do it with the fingers?" interrupted Emily eagerly. "Mine are very nimble. Before I left school I won prizes for fine cross-stitch. Samplers and such."

I had to smile to myself at the idea of her indulging in such a lady-like pastime as sewing a sampler. But then I remembered how two-faced she could be. It was probably done to deceive her teachers: and she made a present of it to the headmistress when she left. A headmistress who was still showing it off to all her new pupils.

"We need a steel rod, thin but strong, with a hook at one end."

"Then we had better set about getting it, " said Miss Fanshaw with spirit.

But to our great surprise there was no need to do so. The MacQuiver's Secretary, with a nasty glint in his eye, suddenly asked us one afternoon if we would like to see what he called the Muniment Room. "He's removed whatever we're after and taken it somewhere else," said Emily.

"It will be worth taking him up on his offer, however."

"You think he may have left a few clues behind?"

"Anything is possible. Besides, having climbed up those stairs a couple of times for nothing I would welcome the chance of a conducted tour of that young man's domain."

"It's a pity you didn't appreciate my offer of getting into the room from the battlements."

"And not being able to get out again. Suppose James Wilder came in and found you rooting among the Laird's accounts and whatnot. Where would you be then? He'd accuse you of I don't know what."

"It would take more than a young man to frighten me," said Miss Fanshaw.

"But think of the risk you were prepared to take climbing out of windows high enough for you to be very dead indeed if you fell!" I said.

"Risks are in my blood," said Mrs. St. Clair. "My father's a retired brewer. By the way, would you like to know what I've done with those trews?"

"Returned them to their rightful owner I hope. Before you get any more ideas about wearing them."

"I put them in the laundry basket."

"Then let's hope the colours don't run."

"And that the young man has a second pair of trousers!"

When we eventually went into the Secretary's office we found it as neat and tidy as a bride's trousseau. Letters which had already been answered were on a spike, and correspondence still to be dealt with placed in a neat pile on a desk. As far as we could make out the Laird's accounts were in perfect order. Bills already settled were neatly docketed, outstanding ones clearly marked with the date they fell due, cheques (Mr. de Wilde even showed us those) were properly endorsed. It all looked highly suspicious.

Because, said Emily as we walked down the turret stairs in high dudgeon with our faces set leaving the young man to get on with his work, he had no call to show us anything. The room was his kingdom. He was very efficient. The MacQuiver obviously trusted him completely It would certainly need all our expertise as co-partners in the Watson-Fanshaw Detective Agency to find out what was going on, and how to get to the bottom of it.

"I'll see you in the Library," I said, sailing away from her as I had done after my first meeting with James Wilder in the little room across the hall after the MacQuiver had ordered his Highland servant to bring him to me.

It was back-breaking work. Taking down every book. Blowing the dust off. Riffling through the pages. We hadn't finished half of it before having to lock up, go upstairs and dress for dinner.

Thaddeus Sholto seemed in surprisingly good form when we went into the dining-room. Two tartan-clad footmen stood by the sideboard, another guarded the door, yet a third stood behind The MacQuiver's chair, and two or three Highlanders stood by to serve us as soon as they knew what we wanted to eat. The butler appeared in a black jacket and kilt, and yet more footmen stood guard by each window to close it at the slightest hint of a draught.

"Please do not be worried about the possibility of becoming over-heated," said the Laird. "At the slightest sign of anything so debilitating the windows will be opened at once. But of course," he added hurriedly, "one must beware of the smallest suggestion of anything approaching cold."

It did his eyes good, he went on, to see such kind and pretty faces at his table: and such beautiful dresses. He was a great admirer of Indian muslin, although his dear mother had much favoured bombazine. At dinner time he normally liked to wear a cross between the Highland dress deemed fit for day wear and that which was considered essential for formal occasions. "But without the sword belt, the claymore and the powder horn." However, he trusted the ladies would excuse his wearing just his kilt and doublet at present. As a person who had been confined to bed for some days, they would (he felt sure) make every excuse for him, and have every sympathy for his unfortunate constitution.

The Secretary came in while all this was going on and took his place at the end of the table. Where, to my great surprise, he started to regale us all with jokes, puns, quips, rather risqué stories and a series of quite clever limericks. Thaddeus was beside himself with laughing, his high treble making him sound like a neighing horse; and it was as much as the footmen could do to keep their faces straight. Even the dour Highlanders serving the food were hard put to it not to spill the soup.

"To think I regarded him as a haughty young prig as well as a crook," I said. "He has The Macquiver in stitches. I don't suppose he's enjoyed himself so much for years."

"It's easy to see what he's really up to however," hissed Emily. "Any more evenings like this and the Laird will be eating out of his hand. He won't believe a word against his Secretary."

"Be that as it may, it's back to the Library for us even if we have to stay there all night to finish the job."

But it was not to be. Thaddeus asked me very politely if I would be so good as to join him in what he called his inner sanctum. He needed, he said, to have a serious talk. Once I was settled in his room and he had satisfied himself the hookah was in good order he suddenly said, "Do you think, my dear Mrs. Watson, that it's possible for such a thing as The Holy Grail to really be here?"

Not wishing to upset him, and thinking about my fee, I temporised. "It could be anywhere," I said. "Perhaps Scotland is as good a place as any."

"Not Scotland. Here in this house. My men have been digging in the grounds to no avail. It reminds me of what Bartholomew and I did to the gardens of Pondicherry Lodge, when he urged me to dig as if my life depended on it. Not that I've done any digging myself on this particular occasion," added the Laird disconsolately.

"Well, you won't have any Andaman Islanders coming to look for treasure this time," I said cheerfully.

In spite of being so merry over dinner, this joke did not go down at all well with my host. I suddenly recalled that his brother had been killed by a dart from an Islander's blowpipe and said hastily, "One of the big problems is that we have no clear idea of what the Grail really is."

"James is quite convinced it's a goblet of some kind and encourages me to keep on digging."

"Would you be very disappointed if it wasn't?"

Thaddeus took a puff at his hookah and said, "I think I might be. A goblet would look so well on a stand in front of that Corot. Or next to the Vernet I have upstairs."

"Whatever it is, and if it's here," I said soothingly, "Miss Fanshaw and I will do our very best to find it."

That night, before we went to sleep, Emily asked me if The MacQuiver was barking up the wrong tree. "The Scots are Celts, aren't they? So are the Irish. And the Welsh. I found that out in the Library while you were hobnobbing with the aristocracy."

"I'd hardly call it that," I said. "The Laird was quite chipper when I first entered his room. He even asked me to join him in having a glass of Tokay. But by the time I left he had become somewhat subdued. That could be, of course, because of a tactless remark I made."

"Never mind that. The Holy Grail also has Celtic connections. So it could be in Ireland or Wales as much as here."

"What do you suggest, packing up and going to Ballybunion?"

"There's no need to be funny. It was just an idea, that's all. I read a book in the Library called, let me see, the Mabin something." She suddenly jumped out of bed, ran to the dressing-table and grabbed a piece of paper. "*The Mabinogion*, that's it. About a young knight called Peredur."

"The 'Per' means bowl or drinking vessel," I said, surprised she hadn't already found that out from the book.

"He travelled to The Castle of Wonders and met The Fisher Lord. This was a well-lit place. But when the 'Graal' was brought in it extinguished all light by its own brilliance."

"This is all quite, quite fascinating. But I'm tired, and I don't see how it helps poor old Thaddeus."

"That's it," said Emily. "Fall asleep as soon as I uncover something."

The next day I asked the Laird if he could detain his Secretary on some pretext and keep him busy for a while. I intended to search James Wilder's bedroom and hoped his door wasn't locked. When I later told Miss Fanshaw what I had done she said indignantly that I criticised her for entering a *servant's* room while I...

"That was because of a silly idea you had to get into the Muniment Room. This was in a good cause. When I opened the door I saw a large portrait on the dressing table of the Duke of Holdernesse with the words 'My Dear Father' written on it, I assume by Wilder. On the opposite side of the room, as far away from the Duke as possible and in a far less ornate frame, was a much smaller picture of a woman who I took to be the Secretary's mother. She greatly resembled her son and had a sweet, winning face with quite a lot of character in it. In fact it was like looking at a 'James Hamilton Oscar Wilde' who hadn't gone to the bad."

"This is 'all quite, quite fascinating'" said Emily with a yawn. "But..."

"I searched everywhere without success and was just about to give up when I spotted some spills on the mantelpiece."

"So Wilder is a smoker. Did you ever see such detection!"

"Hidden behind the spills was a narrow tube with a cartoon in it which, after I'd had a good squint, I put back where I found it and left there."

"Perhaps he likes a laugh before he goes to sleep. But surely it would be easier to have a copy of *Punch* on his bedside table."

"This," I said, "was 'The Holy Grail' of the art world. A preliminary drawing by none other than Leonardo da Vinci for a painting which has been lost for centuries. I'm now going to ask The Macquiver to call the police and have them search his Secretary's bedroom. Before arresting him and carrying him off to prison in Aberdeen."

"I told you he'd removed something from his office. He'll say he was saving it from the damp or something."

"Then why keep it rolled up in a tube in his bedroom? Thaddeus knows quite a lot about art. He would have better ideas for preserving the cartoon than that."

The Secretary was absent from the room when I went to speak to the Laird, who said he'd sent him to the Muniment Room on some pretext but that he would be back shortly. "It was quite difficult to retain him for so long, my dear. He seemed very fidgety, like a cat on hot bricks."

Did this mean that he intended to leave the castle this very day with the loot? "Call the police at once," I said. "I want him nabbed just as soon as he comes back into this room."

That's if he did come back.

But, as we learned later, it transpired that Miss Fanshaw turned up trumps. Going into James Wilder's bedroom to see the cartoon for herself, she surprised him in the act of putting the tube into a stout valise. "He had all the signs of doing a bunk and pushed me aside like an old shoe. But I put my foot out and sent him flying. Fortunately the cops (are Scottish police called cops?) arrived at that moment and took him away."

"To await the decision of the Area Procurator Fiscal whether or not to charge him," said Thaddeus sadly.

"Area Procurator Fiscal?" asked Emily.

"Responsible for the Western Isles. It's not a Capital Charge, stealing art works, so we won't have to wait for the Lord Advocate to come to a decision whether or not to prosecute."

"I bet you any money," Emily whispered to me, "that he wriggles out of it."

"What if he does? The MacQuiver has the drawing, and I'm going to persuade him to take it down to London to show Lord Leighton at The Royal Academy. It will cause a sensation. The

Laird will leave it there on permanent loan and be famous as a benefactor of world art for the rest of his life."

The former Mr. Sholto, dressed in what he called his 'travelling attire', the long coat which buttoned up to the neck and the rabbit skin hat, hired a Special and we embarked for the Capital. There were four of us in a First-Class Compartment, including the Highlander who acted as the Laird's valet and almost his keeper, with the rest of the household (from the butler down to the boy who turned the spit in the kitchen) making merry somewhere else in the train. They were later to cause a riot at a rugby ground near Blackheath owned by Mr. Fletcher Robinson.

"The MacQuiver had an annoying way of putting his hand in front of his mouth," said Emily after we said goodbye to them all and Thaddeus promised to put a substantial cheque in the post for us. He would do this, he said, as soon as the excitement of visiting The Royal Academy was over and he'd been safely returned to his castle in Scotland. And perhaps after the search for a new Secretary, less heinous than James Wilder, had yielded positive results.

"Let's hope he won't be too long about doing it," said Mrs. St. Clair sourly. "After my being at the back of beyond for so long, suffering that terrible climate and putting up with the man's irritating habit."

219

"He's self-conscious about his teeth," I said soothingly. A very visible line of yellow and irregular stumps. I'd noticed myself how often the Laird tried to hide them.

"A man that ugly has no business worrying so much about just one of his many defects," said Miss Fanshaw, "and getting on his guests' nerves."

When our hansom dropped Emily at 'The Laurels' and then took me home to Kensington, John met me on the doorstep in a considerable state of excitement. Everything was fine, he said. There was nothing whatever to worry about but did I remember Miss Fanshaw's mention of Wilson the canary trainer before I'd gone off to Scotland? The name, he said, had been familiar to him. Although it was difficult to recall from where, since he had met so many Wilsons when working with Holmes.

"There was a Wilson in our investigations into 'The Red-Headed League', 'The Hound of the Baskervilles', 'The Dancing Men', 'The Golden Pince-Nez', and three or four of them in 'The Valley of Fear'. Wilson Kemp, a particularly vile specimen of humanity , turned up when we were trying to sort out Mr. Melas's little problem..."

"If it's to be another investigation by the Watson-Fanshaw Agency, and not by that arch-imposter and impersonator Sherlock Holmes, I would like to take my coat off and have a cup of tea first."

"Well, you need not trouble yourself about figuring out why the canary trainer is so notorious. Millie and I, and to a certain extent the Nipper, have already solved that conundrum."

Millie?

"Yes," said John. "She noticed that whenever the Nipper needed his nappy changed he made a funny little noise. She described it as being between a sigh and a little squeak."

"I trust that the canary trainer didn't..."

"No," said John, "But it gave me a clue. I went round to see him and asked about the julking contests."

"The what?"

"Singing competitions. You see, Wilson was particularly good at teaching canaries airs, or 'toys' as they are often called. It meant he always won. Which wasn't fair on the rest of them."

"Who first called him notorious?"

"Sherlock, during our investigation into Black Peter. I've just remembered."

The man with the harpoon?"

"The very same, and a really vicious brute."

I studied this information carefully. It didn't seem to me that what the canary trainer did justified the appellation 'notorious'. Mr. Sherlock Holmes had quite possibly become extremely bored with all that writing and put in an outré line or two to keep himself amused.

"The canary trainer," I said, "where does he keep these birds?"

"Search me," said John, shrugging his shoulders. "His shop is more like Old Abrahams' than Sherman's."

"Whistle for a growler. I'd like to see Sherman again."

When I reached Pinchin Lane and went into the shop Sherman said, "What is it this time, pearl pendants or solid gold statues?"

"Canaries," I said. "Live ones."

"My main business is stuffing dead ones so that their owners can feel they still have the dear little blighters with them."

"Wilson..."

Sherman started back, his face white. "Don't class me with him," he said angrily. "That cove deals with an entirely different kind of canary." Then, seeing the puzzled look on my face he went on, "Housebreakers and their women."

"Tell me about them," I said.

Cracksmen in a small way carried a jemmy or one or two bettys, he said. Tools that could easily be secreted about their persons. But men who went in for burglary in a big way often had a full kit. This could include a very strong sheath knife, something called an American auger with a number of drills, a brace and bit, a rope, a jack and a spot lantern. The list was endless. And different tools were needed for different jobs. Carrying a kit like that under the clothes was impossible. It was much too heavy. And if a man was stopped by the police and searched it would be obvious what he was up to. "So they employ a woman, or several women, to go by different routes to the lay and hand over the tools there – as well as sometimes carry off the loot. Although that can be rather risky."

"Why are they called canaries?

"Because, in a manner of speaking, they can 'sing out' if there's trouble."

"And they have to be trained to do this?"

"Yes. Taught to dress properly even if not very smartly. To look respectable, and as if butter wouldn't melt in their mouths. Quite an effort for some of the judys, I can tell you."

Well I knew all about that, having practised in front of the pier glass at Mrs. Forrester's before my first visit to Baker Street. "And Wilson has the reputation of being able to teach these women?" I asked.

"Yes. They have to learn to walk in a lady-like manner, to speak softly and not to swear. But I couldn't tell you what method he uses, the stick or the carrot."

Thanking Sherman profusely, and promising to come back soon to sample his unclaimed pledges, I went on an omnibus to Bayswater and called at 'The Laurels'. Emily was just about to sit down to a cup of tea and asked me to join her in the drawing-room. I explained all about Wilson and asked if she would like to be one of the 'canaries'. I would be the other, I said, with John as the 'housebreaker'.

"Then I ought to be the 'crow', the look-out, and not the 'canary'."

"That's usually a man's job, so Sherman told me."

"So what?" she said brusquely. It was obvious she wanted the chance to put on trousers again.

"Only don't look too smart," I said. "Respectable coster, or a man who has seen better days and is reduced to handing out tracts is what we're after. So that no-one would ever suspect him John is getting his duds from one of Wiggins' contacts. Has Mr. St. Clair still got his old Hugh Boone rags, the one's he wore when he pretended to be a street beggar?"

"Yes, but they don't get much use these days. Thanks to your friend, Sherlock Holmes."

"He's no friend of mine, I assure you. Even though I believe he's an excellent actor."

"I think we should co-opt Neville," said Mrs. St. Clair. "I'm certain he's a better actor than Mr. Watson." She had a point. Mr. clever-dick Holmes had once said to my husband that he sometimes withheld information from him because he would be sure to give the game away, if only facially.

It ended with all four of us going to Wilson's shop; with Emily sporting a dowdy dress she had acquired by sending one of her female servants to a pawnshop. Wearing something of her own, she said, would have aroused the canary trainer's suspicions by looking too expensive. And perhaps it was the presence of her husband which made her change her mind about wearing trousers. As for me, I thought we could give the game away (as the two of us had done in Whitechapel when hunting for Leather Apron) by seeming too healthy. But the canary trainer accepted us without a qualm. Although he did say training more than one woman at a time was a tall order. I said the gear was too heavy for me to carry (in a covered basket) all by myself. I needed Emily's help. Besides, that way the lay could be approached by four different routes rather than three. With the men coming on it from north and south, and we women approaching it east and west.

"My," he said, "but you're a sharp one. How long have I got to train you in, you brazen hussy?"

John had stepped forward with his fist clenched on hearing this, and I was afraid that if he floored the canary trainer with a well aimed punch all our plans would come to nothing. But I managed to tread on his toe before he could say anything and the moment passed without further incident. In any case, it wouldn't, I thought, do a lot of harm for Wilson to see how belligerent Watson could be when roused, and how ready to defend us if necessary.

"How long have I got?" repeated the canary trainer.

"As long as it tikes," replied Mr. St. Clair in a surly voice. "And mind you git it right."

Three days later we were ready. Wilson said he had never met such quick learners. Unlike the men, our faces were scrubbed clean, our hair neat and tidy and our skirts the right length. Not above the ankle, which would have given us away immediately as women of low repute, and padded out by our usual number of petticoats. Our demeanour, said Wilson, was good enough to get us an invite to Buckingham Palace. The best bit of handiwork he'd done yet. It almost made him want to consider retirement.

"You'll retire all right," I thought, "as a guest of Her Majesty in one of our many prisons."

When the day for cracking the crib arrived we all four had details of our differing routes. Miss Fanshaw and I carried baskets containing certain things, none of which had anything to do with housebreaking; but were eminently respectable goods for the poor to be carrying about should we be stopped for any reason.

"It looks as if we're going on errands of mercy," said Emily before she set off. "To people as poor as ourselves," I answered. But we had thought it best to carry out the charade to the end as if it was the real thing.

So, after we had both arrived at the 'crime scene' and been relieved of our burdens, Watson and St. Clair broke into what was basically an empty house with a few valuable bits and pieces lying about. To keep up the pretence in case any genuine members of The Fraternity should be about, I walked past the window and coughed in the way Wilson had taught me, to warn the men inside to be careful not to come out yet. Emily came by a little later and did the same, and then fluttered her handkerchief discreetly to show that the coast was now clear.

In next to no time after that the men exited furtively with the swag, and Lestrade's men appeared as if from nowhere to 'arrest' them. Meanwhile Gregson was already halfway to Wilson's shop to take him into custody. "Altogether a most successful conclusion," said Mr. St. Clair in his pompous way. "Let's hope we can look forward to a substantial reward from the Public Purse. I'm sure we're all very relieved to see such a thing as 'a plague spot removed from the East End of London' as somebody said once."

"That somebody was Sherlock," said John. "You screamed blue murder at the time, if I remember right."

" It's always a mistake to rake up the past," said Neville St. Clair.

Chapter Ten

Our journey to Baden-Baden (Miss Fanshaw's and mine) took place almost by accident. An English woman had died in one of the hotels, and the German authorities thought it best if two of her compatriots came out from London to investigate the matter. They were anxious to hush things up at the height of the season.

"I would have thought the best way to do that was by looking into the matter themselves," said Emily, "and not to invite strangers in."

"What, with Lestrade breathing down their necks and saying how incompetent all foreigners are?" We had already had trouble persuading the Scotland Yard man to let us investigate the matter. And had only succeeded by promising he would get all the credit – if any credit was to be got by the British police – so long as we were the ones who were paid.

"I'm not surprised the woman, whoever she is, popped off. Most people who come to the Spa are already on their last legs."

"Far from it. Many of them are in the best of health, and only looking for a bit of cosseting."

"Hypochondriacs to a man," said Mrs. St. Clair. "Or, in this case, a woman."

"The weapon and its position in the body both appear to rule out suicide or accident, and she certainly didn't die of natural causes."

Rooms had already be reserved for us in the hotel where the tragedy took place. The manager met us in our suite and looked lugubriously at our luggage. It was terrible, he groaned, that such a catastrophe should take place in one of the finest *Gasthofs* in Baden-Baden. His heavy jowls quivered at the thought, and he seemed ready to burst into tears. Such a thing was unheard of in a long and laudable history.

"They all say that," said Miss Fanshaw as we went towards the mortuary to view the body.

"She's quite young," I said. "More or less our age. With a good figure, apart from that gaping wound in the chest caused by the knife."

"Are there any other bodies we should look at while we're here?" asked Emily eagerly. "For comparison, you know."

"Certainly not," I said, hurrying her out.

When we returned to the hotel I was amazed to see Kate Witney standing in the vestibule. She had been the leader of a gang of girls who terrorised me as a child at school in Edinburgh. I arrived there from India after my mother died and so seemed sufficiently strange to be made fun of. And Kate urged everyone to make the most of what she called their heaven-sent opportunities. Many years later, she come to the house to ask Watson if he would fetch her husband out of the opium den in Upper Swandam Lane. Now she said that, although herself in the best of health, Isa Witney still suffered from the effects of his drug habit. "Though he hasn't been seen in 'The Bar of Gold' for some time."

"Good for him," said Miss Fanshaw heartily. "Coming to Baden-Baden is much better."

"But almost as expensive," said Mrs. Witney.

Although I disliked her as much as ever, I thought the two women looked well together. Both tall, slim and with almost identical parasols, which emphasised an innate elegance. Their hair similarly styled, and almost the same colour, they could have passed as sisters. But I suspected that, for all her lack of general knowledge (which I sometimes thought was rather a pose) Emily was the more intelligent. She was certainly the more caustic. Kate Witney, as I knew to my cost, was all sugar on top and bitter as gall underneath.

"Have you come here to lose weight, Mary?" she asked sweetly.

"No," I said. "Watson likes me as I am."

She sniggered, and Emily snorted with laughter. "All right," I thought to myself, "if the two of them mean to gang up on me, I can take care of myself. I am here to solve a murder mystery. To let my judgement be clouded by such childish behaviour would be a serious breach of professional ethics." When Kate Witney left the hotel to visit the baths (in order to see how her dear Isa was getting on) I was surprised, however, to see a change in my colleague's manner.

"What a fright," said Miss Fanshaw. "I feel some dodging may be in order. We want none of that 'We British must stick together' stuff."

So there had been a little jealousy in the air after all. "You both looked extremely smart, standing together complete with parasols. Tall, slim, elegant..."

"Never mind, Muriel," said Mrs. St. Clair, looking down at me kindly, "Good things come in small packages."

"And one never knows when Mrs. Witney may come in useful," I said. "Or even old man Witney."

The body of the dead woman had been found in bed by a chambermaid. "Who probably screamed the place down," growled Emily.

I couldn't say I blamed her when all she'd come in for was to deliver the early morning cup of tea and pull the curtains. "I would like to check the dead woman's name," I said to the manager, even though I had seen it on the wall above the slab in the mortuary, "and how long she has been staying in Baden-Baden." He went into a little office and brought out the clerk, who marched to the Reception Desk and fumbled with the Hotel Register. Turning the pages so slowly I thought Emily would give him a thump with her parasol, while I and the manager were also ready to burst with impatience, he finally said, *"Frau Doktor*. No, that can't be right. Lady Frances Carfax..."

"Wie kann einer nur so dumm sein?" said Miss Fanshaw with a long sigh, leaving me wondering how she came to know so much German. Foreign languages didn't seem to be her forté. Hadn't she complimented me, somewhat sarcastically I'd thought, on my grasp of the French language when we were together in Nantes?

"She was here two months ago," shouted the manager, his mind still on Lady Frances.

"Here we are," said the clerk without batting an eyelid, *"Fraulein* Agnes Greenfly."

"Greeenfield," said Emily, who had also been squinting down at the page of names and addresses. "Late of 3, Bunbury Mansions, Weston-super-Mare."

I felt the 'late' a little unnecessary, seeing that Miss Greenfield was barely cold. But at least we had made sure that the name in the Hotel Register was the same as the name in the mortuary. "And hopefully the same as the one on the police reports," said Miss Fanshaw. Then, "Have the relatives been informed?" she asked officiously, glaring at the clerk as though he was personally responsible for seeing that they had been.

"We are not aware the woman had any relatives," murmured the manager sadly. "She gave no name of any next of kin." He turned sharply to the clerk who nodded in agreement. "Consular officials..."

I guessed there would be difficulties when it came to repatriating the body. But first we were here to try to find out why there was a body.

"Did Miss Greenfield have any friends?" I asked.

"Many friends. She was a most charming lady."

"And how long did you say she'd been staying here?"

"I didn't say." The manager glared ferociously at the clerk in his turn, who went back to the Hotel Register and, after a great deal of fumbling with his glasses, finally said the poor *Fraulein* had been in the place for two weeks.

"And where was she before?"

He looked at me pityingly. "Why, England, of course. I have been to super-Mare. I found it most bracing."

"Just what he needs, bracing," said Emily. "This woman had only just come out from Britain then, and not from some other foreign hotel?"

The way she pronounced the word 'foreign' was most offensive. I would never have been surprised if the manager asked us to leave. He was probably only restrained from doing so by the thought of what the German authorities might say. Yet she had been adamant after leaving Kate Witney about not mixing with the British.

233

We went up to Agnes Greenfield's suite and found everything in apple-pie order. Which was a pity. With all surfaces scrubbed clean, the woman's belongings removed and the windows flung open, all clues to her murder had been obliterated. I asked the manager why this was done. He shrugged his shoulders and said in an off-hand way, "We have other guests to consider."

"Yes, but you could simply have shut this suite off until we came." What was the point of asking us to travel all the way to Baden-Baden, and then tidying things up before we arrived?

"Our own police were sent for immediately the body was discovered. I think you will find their reports extremely thorough. In spite of being foreigners," he added, glaring at Emily.

"We still ought to search the rooms," said that damsel after the man had gone back downstairs. "Look for fingerprints, bits of thread. The weapon."

"If you take a good look at these surfaces you'll see no fingerprint has a hope of survival. The knife is, I hope, down at headquarters. It wasn't still in the body."

The police were very helpful as soon as we got down to the station and showed us all the files appertaining to the murder, including statements from visitors who had last seen Miss Greenfield alive. "At least they appear to have all their digits," said Mrs. St. Clair, referring to the coppers. They were willing for us to take away everything temporarily, providing we were also willing to sign a vast number of official forms. I asked if any of the people interviewed were staying in the same hotel as the murdered woman and received the information that they were not. Except perhaps Mrs. Farintosh.

So it was back to the clerk who, earlier in the day, had irritated us so much and watching him thumb laboriously through the Hotel Register again. "If this is the best *Gasthof* in Baden-Baden I would hate to see the worst," said Emily. "One has the right to be served by young, well-trained men with more idea of what they're doing, not by superannuated old codgers left over from the Franco-Prussian War."

"Perhaps they think it adds to the 'old worlde' charm. Too much efficiency, being too slick, would spoil the atmosphere of a watering-place like this. Which has been, after all, popular with tourists for at least two thousand years."

"When our friend here no doubt was as slow then as he is now."

"I know this *Frau* Farintosh," said the clerk suddenly. "A very charming lady who was mentioned by your Great Detective Sherlock Holmes when he investigated something concerning a Speckled Band. She wanted to put an opal tiara into a safe-deposit box. It caused me a great deal of bother I remember. That is, until I managed to find the key. Opals are very unlucky.

I have wondered since if that is why we are having so much trouble."

"But is she in the hotel now?" asked Miss Fanshaw impatiently.

"Indeed yes. She has the suite next to the unfortunate *Fraulein* Greenfly."

"Greenfield," said Emily automatically.

A woman of iron nerve apparently, if she still occupied the same suite as she had done before the murder. I asked the clerk to send a page to ascertain if Mrs. Farintosh would receive us. The answer came back almost at once. The lady would be only too happy. She turned out to be the thinnest woman I ever saw in my life, and sat twisting her handkerchief in her fingers all the time we were with her. Miss Greenfield was – had been – a most charming girl. They often went for walks in the Black Forest or visited the thermal baths together.

"Of course, she was a *little* younger than I am," said Mrs. Farintosh mendaciously. "But it didn't seem to make any difference to our friendship."

I asked if she had met with the girl on the day of her death. Yes, she said, twisting her handkerchief more than ever. They had had a light supper in Agnes's rooms at about eight o'clock. "The staff are very good you know, especially if one stays here regularly. They appreciate guests don't always want to face the hurly-burly of the dining-room after a tiring, and maybe stressful, day."

Miss Fanshaw's expression showed, as clearly as if she had spoken, that hurly-burly was the last thing she'd associate with this particular *Gasthof*. Aloud she said, "I thought these deep springs relieved stress?"

"So they do, my dear," said Mrs. Farintosh. "But I had lost heavily at cards and..." She pulled herself up short and asked hastily if we would like some tea? She would ring down at once.

"What time did you leave this Agnes Greenfield?" asked Mrs. St. Clair.

"It wouldn't have been much after half-past nine."

We already knew the time of death for the murdered English woman had been estimated at around ten. Had Mrs. Farintosh heard anything?

"As I told those German policemen, I am a very bad sleeper and have to take chloral to get off to dreamland."

"The woman has a queer way of expressing herself," I said to Miss Fanshaw after we left the suite and the hotel.

"And if what she said is true then there was no chance of her hearing as much as a pin drop," said Emily.

We were sitting in the gardens of the Kurhaus watching people going in to sample the spa waters. I was enjoying the sunshine and she was trying to make up her mind whether or not to try

237

them herself. "I know those habitual users of chloral. They have to increase the dose over time until they are finally as dead to the world as Miss..."

"So do we write off Mrs. Farintosh as a suspect?" I asked, hastily interrupting her before she could complete such an odious comparison.

"Certainly not. She may be the biggest liar on earth."

"She didn't strike me that way," I said worriedly.

"Would you like me to tell you a story? It's about a holiday we once had in Arles. The children spotted a vehicle with the words 'Dog Taxi' on the back of it and were most amused."

I idly wondered how it would work. After a long, interesting ramble round the market stalls of the *Boulevard des Lices* did the animal stand by the curb and hold up a languid paw to signal it was ready to be taken home? Emily said the owner of the taxi weaved through the traffic and spoke to the dog before it jumped on board the cart. Was it a regular fare then, and would this be charged to someone waiting anxiously at home for this particular *chien;* and almost on the point of phoning the police? Did the owner of the dog order the taxi himself after someone told him Fido was caught up in a card game with a set of disreputable mongrels and was losing every time. Or, because a haughty bitch refused his advances, had he been seen drowning his sorrows in glass after glass of *Châteauneuf-du-Pape*?

"You'll find him lying in a drunken stupor on the pavement outside *Le Café Chat.*"

I hurriedly shook myself awake and said brusquely, "I'd like to know what relevance any of this has. We're investigating a murder."

"So we are," said Miss Fanshaw equably. "I just thought I'd lighten things up a bit."

"It was probably the man's own dog, and a lazy one at that."

"And the owner had a sense of humour? Definitely British!"

We sat in silence for a while and then Miss Fanshaw said pettishly, "Everyone and everything in this town is charming. Charming guests, charming friends, charming hotels, charming scenery..."

"It people convince themselves, and others, that they frequent only charming places and associate only with charming people it adds to their status – or so they think," I said. "When the Queen came to Baden-Baden she said it was 'full of gambling dens housing the worst characters of both sexes in Europe'."

"Well, you can't say she needed to borrow status."

"No, and I dare say when Baden-Baden became part of the German Empire in 1871 (the year before the Queen 's visit) the authorities were already beginning to clean it up."

"You know," said Emily, as if she had been part of my day-dream, "Mrs. F. said something about losing at cards."

"And pulled herself up pretty sharply. I wonder if that has any significance?"

"Muriel, my dear, we have been sitting here among the flowers, in what the guide book calls 'expensively groomed gardens', for far too long. It's time to interview some more friends of the charming Miss Greenfield."

One of the friends, a short fluffy girl with red-rimmed eyes and a tight bodice, said she had known Agnes Greenfield in Weston-super-Mare and was absolutely devastated to hear of her dreadful death. Why, they'd been walking in the Black Forest only the day before and...

"Did everyone go walking with Miss Greenfield in these blasted woods?" asked Emily at dinner that evening. We were busy trying to digest the *Gasthof's* gastronomic speciality, at the same time affecting not to notice all the curious glances from *bona fide* guests. "If you ask me, little Goldilocks is the one 'wot done her in'."

"Why wait until she met her in Germany when she probably had an equal opportunity to 'do her in' as you call it at Weston-super-Mare?"

"There you have me. Those English seaside resorts are ideal places for genteel crime."

"Hardly genteel. Surely you saw the knife down at Police Headquarters?"

"Yes, and the officious policeman who showed us the rest of the exhibits. Including the torn nightgown."

"I thought him rather handsome myself, and quite helpful."

"The weapon was a bit of a facer though, wasn't it?" Miss Fanshaw looked disgustedly at her half-finished meal and pushed the plate aside. With an imperious wave of the hand she signalled the waiter to take it away and asked loudly for two large portions of *kirschentorte*, telling the man to be generous with the cherries and on no account to forget the double cream. Then "It's the casino for us this evening," she said.

As I half expected, she appeared in the foyer dressed as a man, and I saw she was wearing a remarkably elegant set of evening clothes. Clothes which wouldn't have disgraced A. J. Raffles. Even the shoes looked good. Offering me her arm, she said with a sly grin, "Remember Whitechapel? You'll be safe as houses with me in this rig as your escort."

We arrived early at the venue in order to have a good look round, but the huge room soon filled up. It no longer appeared to contain 'the worst characters in Europe'. Indeed, it was far too grand to be called anything remotely approaching a 'den'. There were so many eminently respectable people there. Including a number of diplomats and a few crowned heads, "of the minor sort," as Mrs. St. Clair remarked. But, beautifully dressed as they all were, with jewels, ostrich feathers, sashes and decorations, an air of desperation emanated from them all like a miasma. A feeling of despondency behind their bright smiles and clever quips impossible to ignore. And not dispelled by the many glittering chandeliers hanging from the richly decorated ceiling.

Were the clothes in hock? Would the jewels go back in pawn after the evening? Could the medals on the men's chests be genuine? Did that 'garter ribbon' come from some Far Eastern back street? In addition to the general unease, of the kind generated by grave uncertainties about position and money, everyone seemed over anxious to get to the tables. Both men and women seized their chips almost frantically, placed their bets in a fever and watched the little ball bounce round the roulette wheel with something approaching frenzy.

Emily and I marched into a little back room away from all the row to keep our appointment with a croupier who had said he would make himself available for ten minutes only. She showed him a photograph of the dead girl and asked if the man recognised her.

"The noise, the crowds." He shrugged his shoulders, raising his hands almost to shoulder height. "The heat, the need to concentrate on how the betting was going."

"Take another look," said Miss Fanshaw abruptly, peering at him as if she would like to give him a whack with her parasol if only she hadn't had to leave it behind in the hotel. "The eyes, the hair, the expression." The way she aped him suddenly galvanised the German into more voluble speech.

"I have seen her here," he said. "Every night and all night since she has been in Baden-Baden. Last year too, and the year before that. Hooked on gambling, and leading others down the same path."

"Not all night surely?" whispered my companion. "Or how could she be having supper with Mrs. Farintosh?"

"Did you find her a charming young lady?" I asked quietly, expecting the usual response.

"I found her a ravening she-devil," said the croupier and walked out of the room.

"Well," said Emily very tartly as we strolled arm-in-arm ('for appearance's sake,' said my 'escort' with a grin) through the warm night on our way back to the *Gasthof*, "if that doesn't beat all."

"It certainly suggests a motive. In fact several motives. It sounds as if we might end up with too many suspects."

"Including that insomniac, tiara-toting Mrs. Farintosh," said Emily.

"If Greenfield has caused her to lose all her money the opal headdress won't be any use to the woman. It's probably a family heirloom which she can't sell."

"Is that why she 'lost' it on one occasion do you think, for the insurance money? Wouldn't that be enough to get her out of a fix?"

"And into another one with trustees breathing down her neck?" In any case that arch-busybody Holmes found it for her. As he would, of course. Helen Stoner, when she came to tell him about the frightening behaviour of her guardian, the Squire of Stoke Moran (he of 'The Speckled Band', that is), said Sherlock had helped her acquaintance Mrs. Farintosh 'in the hour of her sore need'. Her sore need for money maybe, since she could offer it as collateral for a loan if she ever became sufficiently desperate."

"If you are right about the dratted thing being a family heirloom," said Miss Fanshaw, "she would have to be pretty certain of being able to pay back this imaginary loan of yours. And now she keeps the trinket in a safe-deposit box in a foreign hotel. Which is hardly wise. Why not leave it at home in a British bank?" continued Emily in xenophobic mood. "But, since she does stay here, it looks as if she still has a considerable amount of funds."

"Perhaps. However, funds or not, no-one's allowed to leave at present."

"We can't keep everybody in Baden-Baden prisoner while we find the murderer."

244

"The weather is getting you down, Emily. It's only those who are known to have had a direct contact with Agnes, for example the guests in this hotel, who have been told not to leave."

"If she was as mad about gambling as that croupier said then she could have been murdered by almost anybody. By now he, the killer, is probably half-way to the Isles of the Blessed." It was hardly an appropriate choice of expression and I couldn't help thinking she ought to have chosen another that would have been.

"Or she," I said, walking slowly upstairs to our suite.

It was quite a surprise to see Kate Witney in our sitting-room, and I was struck once again by the physical similarity between her and Emily. "I persuaded the powers that be to let me come up and wait for you both," she said. "The manager used a skeleton key."

"Then he took more upon himself than he should have done," I said tartly. "What if you were a thief –or even a murderer?"

"Do I look like a thief or a murderer?" said Mrs. Witney, her face flushing up angrily.

"Does anybody? But they could still be quite capable of being either."

"Have you a particular reason for coming to see us?" asked Emily, trying, but not altogether succeeding, in hiding her usual impatience.

"Indeed I have. Isa has disappeared. I went with him to the thermal baths at the Kurhaus for his usual session with the doctors. But after they finished with him he seems to have forgotten our arrangement to meet for a stroll in the Black Forest; and he hasn't come back to the hotel."

"When did you last see your husband?" enquired Mrs. St. Clair.

"At half-past ten yesterday morning."

"You seem to have been mighty slow in doing anything about his disappearance," I said.

Looking daggers at me, my former school-fellow and tormentor said crossly, "Isa does have a habit of wondering off on his own sometimes. But he isn't usually gone for this length of time."

"What was he wearing?"

"A policeman's uniform." She said this without so much as a blink. Then seeing our astonished faces continued, "Mr. Witney likes to dress up. The doctor's tell me it will do no harm. Could even help to take his mind off drugs."

"You told us he hadn't been into that opium den in Upper Swandam Lane for some time," I said accusingly.

"He does, however, take a crafty puff now and again. Especially when my back's turned and he thinks I'm too busy to notice."

"Do you want us to find him?" asked Mrs. St. Clair. "We have a murder investigation on at the moment but will do our best."

"That's all anyone can do," said Kate Witney wearily, getting up and retrieving her parasol prior to sailing out of the room.

"She sure has her hands full with that guy," said Emily.

"What a way to talk in civilised society! As Sherlock Holmes once said, when he came back from America after his trip to Chicago and inadvertently used the word 'stunt', 'I beg your pardon, Watson, my well of English seems to be permanently defiled'."

"Well I'm not going to beg *your* pardon," she said. "And to think of that man Witney's brother being the Principal of a Theological College!"

The following morning, as Emily was sitting at the dressing-table trying to decide exactly what to do with her hair and I was wondering which dress to put on, I said, "We've interviewed the Farintosh woman, and the girl from Weston-super-Mare. I have a hunch we ought to speak to the manager of this hotel again while things are fresh in his mind."

"That will please him," said Emily with a grin.

When we finally waylaid the man and secured seats in his office I asked him if many visitors were taken up to Miss Greenfield's suite, and did she sometimes come down to the vestibule to welcome them herself.

"Many visitors," he said. "Sometimes shown up to her suite, or finding their own way there. Often graciously met here in the foyer. As one would expect from such a charm..."

"Both sexes?" Miss Fanshaw interrupted abruptly.

"Only with their wives," exclaimed the manager in a scandalised voice. "But mainly young ladies very like *Fraulein* Greenfield herself."

"Charming. All of them," said Emily sarcastically.

"But of course!"

"Would you recognise any?" I said, briskly opening my notebook.

"I would recognise all of them."

"And can give us their names, and the names of the hotels where they are staying?"

"It was difficult yes, but I believe the police already have those details."

"Damn and blast," said Miss Fanshaw as we went back to our suite. "Take another look at those police reports, Muriel, before you land us in any more embarrassing situations."

"It says here that four people visited Agnes in the hotel on the day she was murdered, including someone who came in at about nine-fifty that evening."

"Man or woman?" asked Emily in a startled voice.

"You heard what the manager said."

"Man and woman then?"

"According to what I'm reading at the moment the person who came to see Greenfield at that time was a woman, and alone."

"But it was so close to the time she was killed."

"And the crime isn't likely to have been committed by a female. The knife blade seemed sharp, but it would take considerable force to drive it into the body in that fatal way. Even if the girl was asleep and offered no resistance."

"How could she be asleep and expecting a visitor? Come to that, she wouldn't even be in her night clothes."

"Perhaps she wasn't expecting a visitor and had gone to bed. If not, the murderer did her work, undressed her and..."

"The police would know if that happened by comparing the gash in the nightdress with the position in the chest of the knife-thrust. It would be impossible to get them to correspond exactly with one another in the kind of circumstances you envisage . Even if the killer was the most cold-blooded brute possible, and could work calmly enough. Also, what happened to the bloody clothes, if you'll pardon the expression? They could hardly be left behind by the assassin. And in this puritanical place," went on my dear friend and colleague, "The only way a lone man could enter the suite would be in disguise. Not only that, but disguised as a woman. You have already said it seems unlikely that a real woman could have wielded the knife, even though you keep saying 'her' in that idiotic way."

"I trust you have quite finished?" I said coldly.

"No. This so-called *Gasthof* seems to be incredibly slack. It's a wonder all the guests haven't been slaughtered in, and out, of their beds. Not checking that Agnes expected, or did not expect, a caller. Letting whoever turned up make his or her own way upstairs..."

"I'm going to have a word with that clerk in Reception," I said, jumping up and running to the door.

"Getting us into more bother," said Emily, picking up her parasol. "I suppose I'd better come with you."

After scratching his head for a few moments, and then fiddling with some keys as if he wasn't quite sure what to do with them, the clerk said he knew all *Fraulein* Greenfly's visitors by sight and had seen many of her friends – her *charming* friends (Emily could be heard standing behind me grinding her teeth and tapping her parasol on the floor) – go up to her suite at different times. Was he on duty the night of the murder? Unfortunately, yes. His old mother had been eager to hear all about it. He had had to repeat the details over and over again. Which had been very tiring.

"Probably deaf as a post, and as old as the hills," hissed Mrs. St. Clair. "A female Methuselah."

I asked if the man recognised the last visitor Agnes had before she died. Yes, he said. From the back as she went up the stairs. "And you have seen her often?" asked Emily.

"Certainly. She came every day. But more usually in the afternoon."

"You've spoken to her?"

"Well, no." She was an extremely quick and agile lady who usually ran up the stairs..."

"Two at a time, no doubt," sneered Miss Fanshaw.

"...before I could say anything. Besides, German ladies do not go up a staircase in that way."

"She wasn't English then?" I said. That could be a breakthrough. I asked if the manager of the hotel had been on duty that evening. He'd said he would be able to recognise all Agnes's visitors. That would corroborate what was being said now. By a doddery old clerk who had been too lazy, or too infirm, to check first if a late-night visitor was expected or welcome.

No, said the clerk, the manager hadn't been in the hotel that night. Then where was he? At his grandmother's funeral. Which I took to mean the man hadn't a clue.

Back in our rooms Emily leafed through the police reports more and more impatiently. "Whoever she was, the police don't seem to have interviewed her. According to this rubbish the last

251

person to see Agnes alive *was* Farintosh. The other woman has vanished without trace."

"That doesn't surprise me," I said.

"You mean she escaped the town before the police arrived? It wouldn't be difficult if it's true the body wasn't discovered until the maid brought in the early morning tea. I wonder if there's a report from her?"

"Talking of that, for heaven's sake ring for some, and a *torte*. Then I'll tell you what I think."

After a waiter had wheeled in the tea, poured it out, cut the cake into slices and taken himself off, I looked at Miss Fanshaw and said, "Do you recall how struck I was by the resemblance between you and Kate Witney when you were standing together?"

"A superficial one," she said sourly.

"But enough to deceive anyone who didn't know either of you very well."

"You're not suggesting she did the murder, I hope. Or me!"

"Don't be ridiculous. When every night I've been disturbed either by your none-too-gentle snores. Or having to have the light on while you finish some salacious French novel or other."

"How can you utter such a frightful slander? I'm reading *A Chaplet of Pearls* by Charlotte M. Yonge."

"You would be."

"Can we get on with it?" said Emily. "I'm in danger of falling asleep."

"My guess is that, from the back, this late-night visitor strongly resembled somebody else. Perhaps Mrs. Farintosh. However, it couldn't have been her. If she had, for example, left something in Miss Greenfield's sitting-room she wouldn't have had to go up and down the stairs to fetch it."

"She took supper with the girl, left the suite after slamming the door so hard it could be heard all over the hotel and then crept back to kill her."

"Why not do the deed during supper?"

"The two had a furious row, maybe because Greenfield wouldn't part up with any money. Mrs. F. went and fetched a knife and stuck it frenziedly into her former friend. How's that for deduction? "

"The kind of knife an English gentlewoman always carries in her luggage," I said scornfully. "That cock won't fight. The timing's all wrong to start with."

"We only have Mrs. Farintosh's word that she left Agnes well before ten."

"Then how do you account for the clerk in Reception seeing someone later going upstairs? Someone he had noticed on other occasions and knew to be an acquaintance of the unfortunate woman?"

"If you're going to spill the beans, as the vulgar saying is, I wish you'd get a move on."

"If you must know, I think the late-night caller was a man. A man dressed as a woman."

"The lengths some people will go to in order to keep an assignation," said Emily. "I really don't know what the world is coming to. Besides, we have already discussed that possibility."

"Directly after lunch we are going back to the casino to have a word with that croupier," I said. "Put on your trousers and your man's jacket and we'll exit the hotel by the fire escape."

We saw the man coming out of the building just as we arrived. He was going for a rest, he said, having been up nearly all night at the tables and then spending the morning helping to prepare for that afternoon's session. "I think you will have to have a little talk with my brother first," I said in a menacing tone. The croupier hesitated as if he would have liked to refuse. But meanwhile Emily had adroitly placed herself beside him and was looking at me with a rakishly raised eyebrow. I could not, however, see any likeness either in figure or in feature between them. They were the same height, more or less, but that was all. But then, of course, I never expected to see any likeness between this person and Emily. Or between this person and Kate Witney. Certainly not between this person and myself. However, whereas she was slim, he was bone thin.

And so, I recalled with a start, was Mrs. Farintosh.

I walked towards some seats in a shaded part of the garden and willed the others to follow me. Once we were settled I grabbed the bull by the horns and said abruptly, "Young man, you said Miss Greenfield was a ravening she-devil. That suggests to me she had you in her clutches. An inveterate gambler, did she notice you had fixed one of the roulette tables and threatened to give you away unless she got her cut? During her second and third visits to Baden-Baden did she demand a larger and larger part of the proceeds?"

I could see by his face that I had hit the mark. Miss Fanshaw, who could also see it, said wonderingly, "Why didn't you make a run for it?"

"On a false passport?" he asked bitterly. "The woman wasn't here all the year round. And I could make plenty of money during her absence. Money I kept for myself."

"It's a wonder she didn't ask for some of it when she did appear," said Mrs. St. Clair. "But perhaps she did, and you felt unbearably threatened."

I was busy thinking to myself, "So the man isn't a German National after all. Which might make a difference to the situation. Aloud I said, "Is that why you killed her?"

"I never said a word about killing her. But she told me she'd been to a revival meeting in Weston-super-Mare and 'seen the light', whatever that means. She would turn me over to the police to ease her conscience."

"If you ask me," said Emily, using an expression usually applied to the kind of household waste normally sold to pig-farmers, "that was nothing but absolute hog-wash. She'd found something more lucrative and..."

"She informed me that her engagement to a member of the English Aristocracy was about to be announced, and she must do something fast to stop the ugly rumours about her. Her fiancé wanted to spend the honeymoon in Baden-Baden, and people were beginning to talk about her here as well as in Somerset."

At that moment two very large policemen marched towards us along the garden's gravel paths and stood one on either side of the croupier's seat. The largest of the two put his hand heavily on the young man's shoulder and said, "Our orders are to take you in for questioning."

Before he could say anything more, the croupier sprang up with a scream. "These women, they have nothing to go on. No proof. It is all in their imagination."

"Shut up," hissed Miss Fanshaw in his ear. She too had sprung to her feet and was busy adjusting her cap.

"Count von Kramm has lodged a complaint about the casino, saying a roulette table is rigged. That rigging has been traced to you."

As the three men went off, one of the policemen turned to us and said gravely, "You are English?" Emily and I could only nod dumbly, and watched goggle-eyed as he pointed sternly towards a nearby notice. "Remember in Germany people obey the rules. Mind you do not walk on the grass."

"I feel rather odd," muttered Mrs. St. Clair somewhat shamefacedly. "When we present our report there's every chance that young man will be arrested for murder."

"We have to do it, however. Don't forget, we are only private investigators. It's up to the official police what happens next."

"What did you mean by all that talk about Kate Witney and me? It doesn't seem relevant."

"No. But it gave me a clue. If you have two people whose figures and general demeanour are alike one can easily be mistaken for the other, especially by someone not too observant or particularly interested in those persons. I think you'll find that, when the authorities come to search that young man's lodging, they will discover a wig and a set of women's clothes which he used when visiting Miss Greenfield. He had to do this regularly to give her money."

"Not too regularly," said Miss Fanshaw, "or he must have been found out. And where does the emaciated Mrs. Farintosh figure in all this?"

"The clerk would think it was her going up the stairs."

"He must have already seen her come in earlier when she asked for her key."

"Let us put it this way," I said patiently. "Consciously, he knew it couldn't be her. But unconsciously he assumed it was. Have you ever seen in all your years anyone as skinny as she is, apart from the courier himself?"

"She's thinner than that American billed in Sanger's Circus as 'A Living Skeleton'," said Emily with a loud cackle.

We packed our clothes ready for departure the following day and Mrs. St. Clair went to say goodbye to Kate Witney while I pleaded a headache. When she came back, Emily said that Isa Witney was once more in harness. He had been found, in his German policeman's uniform, busily marching round Baden-Baden exhorting people not to walk on the wrong side of the road. Telling them not to hang their bedding out of the window, nor yet anything else; and certainly not to throw anything out of it, not even at cats yowling in the middle of the night. He forbade everybody, in his official capacity, to wear fancy dress and/or to shoot a crossbow in the street, exhorting the dogs to take cognizance of the notice *'Hunden verboten'* whenever they were tempted to walk on the grass. [1]

1. *Three Men on the Bummel* by Jerome K. Jerome

Chapter Eleven

When I arrived home John asked me if we had found time to go to Iffezheim, a suburb of Baden-Baden, for the races. He seemed disappointed to receive an answer in the negative. "But," I said, "we did see the ruins of the baths visited by the Roman Emperor Caraculla in the year two hundred and thirteen. And went for walks along the *Lichtentaler Allee*. Neither of us wanted to bother with the castle ruins or the medieval Cistercian Abbey, although Miss Fanshaw made noises about the wonderful circular pool in the Friedrichbad, and the possibility of sampling the waters in the Trinkhalle. Which is near the casino, one of the places we did visit; and with very positive results as far as detecting is concerned. "

"Nothing beats racing," he said glumly. "Life is very quiet here at the moment."

Emily agreed wholeheartedly with this sentiment when she came into the office. She said that the Watson-Fanshaw Detective Agency had so little work on we might as well start giving advice to young ladies from boarding schools and offer to sharpen their lead pencils for them.

Watson came in at that moment looking for the newspaper and said, "By Jove! I remember Sherlock Holmes saying much the same thing just before we were plunged into the affair of the Copper Beeches. Impersonation, drugs, threatening behaviour, slavering dogs. We had almost too much excitement right after that."

As soon as he had left the room Emily asked if there was any possibility of our being paid for the adventure in Baden-Baden. Miss Greenfield hadn't had any relatives to care what happened to her, the funeral expenses would probably be borne by friends in Weston-super-Mare such as Goldilocks, and the British police weren't involved. "To Lestrade's chagrin," I said. "But I've recently found out that the croupier is wanted for several crimes in his native Austria. There is no reason I can think of why we shouldn't receive a reward from that Government for exposing him."

"Unless it's given to Count Von Kramm," she said, picking up her parasol and preparing to leave. "Let me know if anything turns up."

I promised I would do so immediately and went into the sitting-room to tackle some much needed cleaning. There were dottles all over the hearth from innumerable pipes smoked by John. Dust had been swept under the carpet. The windows were anything but bright. The store cupboard was nearly empty. It was a wonder to me why we kept servants at all and what they imagined they were for. Millie and the Little Nipper were the only two things that sparkled. She had kept him and herself very clean; and the same could be said of the nursery.

When I spoke to Watson about the state of the place he hummed and hawed, coughed, blew his nose and finally asked in a loud voice if I had read all this in the newspaper about the Stalker?

"Stalker? Where does he stalk? How does he stalk? Come to that, why does he stalk?"

"He stalks in the Haymarket and The Strand and jumps out on little children and unaccompanied young females. As to why he stalks, that's a matter for those new-fangled psychiatry people."

"Is he a dipper?"

"I doubt it. Pickpockets work in gangs to shield the one who actually does the fanning. And there's always a stickman to carry away, as fast as he can, what used to be called the 'pogue'. So even if the dipper is caught he'll have nothing incriminating on him."

"Why places like The Haymarket and The Strand? That's usually crawling with coppers. Stalking round Shadwell would be safer. The police have usually got so many other much more important things to keep an eye on there."

"Maybe he gets a bigger thrill stalking in such refined areas, and in Regent Street, than he thinks he would down at the docks."

"And is that all he does, jumping out at people? I wouldn't have thought there was much fun in that."

261

John shrugged his shoulders saying, "It takes all sorts to make a world and it's extremely difficult, my dear Mary, to guess what those kind of people will do. But I haven't read of the man indulging in anything more than that – yet. Of course," he continued, "it's very early days."

"Even so, Lestrade will be on to him before very long. One complaint from a toff is worth more than a thousand from people poor as church mice and living in the East End."

It was some days after this conversation before anything did turn up for the attention of the Watson-Fanshaw Detective Agency, and then only to irritate Emily. "Cats caught in trees and unable to climb down are matters for the fire brigade to deal with," she said, "and little boys losing their spinning tops are certainly no concern of ours."

"Have you heard mention of the Stalker? He tried to set fire to the Northumberland Hotel. The police arrived within the twinkling of an eye, but all newspaper accounts say the man got clean away."

"Then why aren't we there investigating the matter?" she demanded pettishly. "Mr. Mac has gone to Scotland for a holiday with his mother. Hopkins has been sent abroad for a bit to learn a foreign language. Gregson..."

"So, if we can't do better than Chief Inspector Lestrade, we might as well shut up shop," I said merrily.

Watson asked if he might come with us. It would do him good, he said, to see again the place where he had first met Sir Henry Baskerville.

"He's wrong, of course," I hissed in Emily's ear. "Dr. Mortimer brought Sir Henry to Baker Street."

"But he and Mr. Sherlock Holmes later went together to the Northumberland Hotel?"

"So I understand."

"Then don't be so pernickety," said Miss Fanshaw.

My husband spoke at some length as we three strolled down Northumberland Avenue, as Watson insisted we do. Here, he told us, in the drying room on the upper floor of the Turkish Bath establishment, Holmes produced the envelope containing a letter from Sir James Damery. A letter which caused him, John H. Watson, to imitate an expert in ceramics. In spite of all his efforts, however, he hadn't carried things off very well. In fact, he'd had to be rescued by Holmes. But it did lead to the final unmasking of the terrible Baron Gruner. The murderer who had been so violent against John in that court room.

"Holmes asked me to bone up on Chinese porcelain, if you'll pardon the pun. So I went along to The London Library in St. James's Square to consult a friend of mine called Lomax. He was the sub-librarian there at the time, you know. When I went back to Baker Street Sherlock asked me if I had managed to

263

learn anything, and told me to hand him a little box down from the mantelpiece."

"Was it anywhere near the jack-knife?" asked Emily.

"He lifted the lid of the box and took out a small object wrapped carefully in fine Eastern silk. Unwrapping the silk, he exposed an exquisite blue saucer and said it was an example of egg-shell pottery from the Ming Dynasty: 'A priceless object'. I was to take the saucer to Gruner under a false name. Holmes suggested 'Dr. Hill Barton of Half Moon Street'. He said this was an easier alias to assume as I was already a doctor anyway."

"Or so he was supposed to have thought," I said, nearly tripping over Miss Fanshaw's inevitable parasol.

"As I was already known as a doctor," continued John imperturbably. "We discussed the value of the thing: and I said if the Baron was thinking of making an offer I would suggest we consult an expert. At that, Holmes went so far as to say I was absolutely scintillating that morning."

"Very kind of him, I'm sure," I said, angrily quickening my step.

As we drew nearer to the Northumberland Hotel someone suddenly jumped out on us. Emily gave a shriek. I called out in alarm. And John said, "Good Lord, Wiggins! Surely you aren't the Stalker?"

"No, I h'aint," said the young man. "It's Alfred."

"Alfred?"

"The youngest and smallest of the Baker Street Irregulars. Only he aint small any longer. 'Es 'an 'ulking great brute what's suddenly gorn batty."

A stalker and a pyromaniac, I thought idly to myself, and asked Wiggins what he was doing there.

"Trying to save 'im from 'isself. And trying to save this 'ere 'otel."

"Has he still got the – er – incendiary material with him?" asked Watson.

"No," said Wiggins. 'E's got petrol – and lucifers."

"Then we will obviously have to move fast," said Emily. "The combination of an inflammable liquid and lucifers – matches – is hardly salubrious."

Running up the steps of the Northumberland Hotel, she was the first to see the blackened walls of the foyer, and the damp sooty footprints on the carpets where the staff had run around with over-full buckets of water. Had the fire brigade been sent for? No. The men felt they had managed to contain the outbreak quite well themselves, said the manager. There was no need to alarm the guests. Especially some Canadians residing there at present who were anxious to see where the famous Sir Henry Baskerville had stayed before going down to his ancestral home in Devon.

"I wasn't aware that Canadians are of a particularly timorous disposition," remarked Watson. "Quite the opposite in fact."

At that moment Lestrade appeared from the direction of the stairs. "No harm done up above," he said. "But did you ever hear of anything so ridiculous as not sending for a fire engine?" He glared at the manager hovering in the reception area, who glared at him even more fiercely and said, "I hope I can be entrusted with the safety of my own premises?"

"That's it," said Lestrade. "Safety. I wouldn't trust you to cook a rice pudding in a sealed oven, with or without the ground nutmeg."

He shouted an order, and a number of uniformed police appeared from nowhere.

"There's nothing more to be done here," said the Chief Inspector, "since this gentleman thinks he knows better than a senior member of the Force."

"I'm delighted a man of your exalted position should so concern himself with a trumpery fire in my humble hotel that he comes rushing from Scotland Yard with a gang of flat-foots before he's even been sent for," exclaimed the manager sarcastically. "Are there no stolen State Papers? No wanton assassinations of young noblemen with a penchant for gambling? Although I believe Mr. Sherlock Holmes solved those two cases for you, as well as the one concerning a notorious blackmailer. The man he said was as wicked as the Evil One."

"That he didn't," said Lestrade uneasily. "Solve my cases for me, that is. It was my reports that went into the Chief when I was still a simple Inspector, on a par with other Scotland Yard Inspectors."

"Not that humble," I said, referring to the Northumberland Hotel. "Considering the prices you charge for rooms."

"And the way you are always losing the guests' boots," said John.

"Or, more often, boot." said Mrs. St. Clair.

"Missus Watson," chimed in Wiggins, jumping up and down in exasperation and almost tripping over himself. "I would like to respec'fully remind you that Alf is still in 'ere."

"And has probably got plenty of petrol left, as well as matches," gasped John. "The question is, whereabouts in 'ere – *here* – is he?"

"The cellars," said Wiggins decisively. "He was always partial to cellars. Even when we worked for Mr. 'Olmes."

But everybody had rushed down the cellar steps, leaving poor Wiggins to follow as best he could. As I learned later, this was something that didn't quite come off. Just as he had his foot on the top step, and was about to plunge into the semi-darkness, the manager came panting up from the bowels of the earth like the demon king in the pantomime and shouted to him to 'get out of this respectable hotel'. Wasn't it enough to have one vagrant in the place without another hanging about in the foyer? Wiggins, however, stood his ground. He was determined not to leave without Alf.

"Alf," said the manager between clenched teeth as he fought to keep his voice down, "I know nothing about any Alf. What I do know is that three crazed adults, one of whom has almost taken my eye out with a parasol, and a parcel of Peelers led by a lunatic Chief Inspector of Police are at the moment busy running about in the cellars looking for someone who most decidedly isn't there."

"Then where is 'e?" asked Wiggins in alarm.

"How should I know?" asked the man, looking round desperately. "And where are all my staff when they're needed?"

"Half-way 'ome if they've got any sense," said Wiggins. "What with petrol and matches in the vicinity, and certain people refusing to call the fire brigade."

At that moment we all emerged from the cellars. John looked vaguely round the vestibule as if he expected the hulking figure of Alf to be standing in Reception. Emily brushed dust from her clothes. Lestrade marshalled his men and they marched off muttering something about 'a wild-goose chase'. While Wiggins and I went down the steps of the Northumberland Hotel and walked slowly along Northumberland Avenue. I asked him if he would like to come home for tea, waited until the other two had come alongside and commanded Watson to use his whistle to summon a growler.

Miss Fanshaw said she had had enough for one day and would prefer to travel home in a hansom by herself. If anything more exciting than chasing after a street arab turned up she would make herself available for detection. Otherwise she intended to lie down on her day bed with a book.

"If you were so sure Alfred would be in the cellar and he wasn't," said Watson to a disconsolate Wiggins, "where on earth is he?"

"Don't know, Gov'nor. But I intend to find out." With that he went off, with a very determined look on his young face.

That night John asked me if there was anything in the whole episode of use to the Watson-Fanshaw Detective Agency. I had to admit it didn't seem promising. A stalker was jumping out at passers-by. He was later suspected of trying to set fire to a famous hotel. Mistakenly thought to be in the cellars of that hotel, he had now vanished without trace.

"Jumping out at people, although not desirable, is relatively harmless compared to setting fire to somewhere," I said. "Somehow the two characteristics hardly seem to belong to the same person."

"The manager's aversion to fire brigades is also somewhat odd," said John thoughtfully. "Especially as the police were called."

"But were they? Actually summoned, I mean. Ever since that daft gawk became a Chief Inspector he has had spies all over London primed to tell him immediately where the action is."

"You may have something there. But the police don't – they can't – turn up so quickly to every fire, or even take their time over it. Their job is to investigate later, in cases where criminal damage is suspected. Even in that situation Scotland Yard isn't called in automatically, and someone of Lestrade's new rank probably not at all. Unless, of course, a fire is started to hide the fact that there's been a murder."

"Don't you think that, in those circumstances, Tobias Gregson or one of the other Scotland Yard men would investigate first and then report back?"

"It's very strange," muttered Watson. "I'd expect Lestrade to become so full of himself after being promoted that he'd think running about the streets with the constables quite beneath him. Holmes and I found him insufferable enough before that happened."

The next morning at breakfast John, who had been reading the paper while reaching blindly for the toast and smeared butter all over the cuff of his jacket, said that the Stalker was no longer making a nuisance of himself. 'The women of our Great Metropolis are free to walk unmolested down its most fashionable streets without let or hindrance. Small children can bowl their hoops along the pavement safely without being frightened into fits by such un-British behaviour. A circumstance for which all right-minded citizens should be thankful'.

"There can't be much news today if all that ink is being wasted," I said, busy clearing the table. "And surely the Stalker had only one day – yesterday – off?"

"We only have Wiggins' word for it that he was in the Northumberland Hotel. Although when I consider the sterling work that boy did for Sherlock Holmes when a member of the Baker Street Irregulars I'm inclined to trust his word implicitly. But whatever's going on the Stalker appears to have curtailed his non-incendiary activities some days ago."

At that moment there was a knock on the door. When I went to answer it a somewhat subdued Wiggins greeted me on the doorstep with a lop-sided grin.

"I suppose you've come to tell us about your mistake," I said.

"Not exactly," said the boy, taking off his boots and coming into the hall. "I know Alf wasn't in *the* cellar, but I found him in *a* cellar. All trussed up, an' sobbing like a baby."

"I thought you said he was a great hulking brute?"

Wiggins gave me a sheepish look. "I hexaggerated a bit," he said. "But he's still a lot bigger than when we roamed the streets working for Mr. 'Olmes. Even if 'e isn't any match for the likes of them cowards."

"What cowards?"

"Bert Stevens and his gang."

"That rings a few bells," I said. "Come into the kitchen and I'll make you some tea."

"Any chance of some toast wiv it?" asked Wiggins wistfully.

"Certainly. Jam too, if you like."

"Bert Stevens was the cove wot took all yore furniture, if you remember. On that toff's orders, of course."

"Well Mr. Raffles apologised and told his friend Mr. Manners to go round to Bert Stevens' hovel and tell him he was no longer in his (Mr. Raffles') employ. So it all came right in the end."

Wiggins, with his second slice of toast half-way to his mouth, gazed at me goggle-eyed. "An' did 'e go?"

"As far as I know."

"Who would've thought such a milk-sop 'ad it in 'im?" said Wiggins admiringly. "You certainly can't tell the book by the cover. Bert and one of his gang beat up Mr. 'Olmes so badly once that 'e 'ad to be taken to Charing Cross 'Ospital. And then the villain had the cheek..."

272

Pouring myself out a cup of tea I said, "But what's the connection between Bert Stevens and your friend Alfred?"

"None normally, I'm thankful to say. But Bert and his gang were preparing to crack a crib, much bigger than your job, if you don't mind me sayin' so."

"Don't worry about that. It was to be a really 'swell' thing, I take it?"

"So swell, it was a bit out of Bert's line. But what did Alf do but jump out at one of the gang's canaries as she strolled down Regent Street. She was very well-dressed, and so respectable-looking he thought she must be one of the gentry. What was worse, she had a little boy with her and..."

"They do sometimes. It makes the women seem even more law-abiding. Especially if the child is well-behaved and clean."

"This one was certainly behaving 'isself," said Wiggins, giving me a queer look. "Dressed like a Lord, and looking as if 'e 'ad jest come out of the barf."

I could see he was puzzled by my seeming to know all about canaries, but I decided to leave the explanation for some other time. However, I confessed to being curious about one thing.

"And Bert Stevens wasn't having any of it?"

"Well, she was his special..." Wiggins went very red and bit hastily into his cooling piece of toast.

"Judy? Dolly-mop?"

"Missus Watson! What would the Doctor say if 'e 'eard you? That's what comes of all this detectin' business. You end up mixin' with so much low-life."

"And high," I said, thinking of the Duchess of Loamshire and how she had murdered her husband in his own Conservatory with the ornamental scissors she used to snip off dead flowers. "Would you like to come upstairs and help Millie and me give the Little Nipper his bath?"

But Wiggins declined what he called 'the honour'. He really ought to be getting along. After finding Alf and cutting his bonds with his (Wiggins') trusty knife, he had taken his friend home and put him to bed. "I've a nice little place of me own now. A lodging down Camberwell way. We'll both be safe there; and I wouldn't be surprised if he's ready for his breakfast by this time."

Besides, said Wiggins, he wasn't all that keen on baths.

When I went into the sitting-room to tell John what had happened to the Stalker and why, he said that still didn't account for what had gone on at the Northumberland Hotel. "I've already said the behaviour of the manager was odd. Now I think it may even have been criminal."

"You mean he set fire to the place himself? With important people staying there from all over the world?"

"Perhaps not deliberately."

"Then that could only be classed as careless."

"There is such a thing as criminal carelessness," said Watson. "However, if you think carefully, it wasn't much of a blaze. It never really took off, and the staff soon dealt with it."

"Before they disappeared."

"My guess is their boss sent them to their rooms 'to rest and recuperate' in spite of what he said to Wiggins."

"While he did what?"

"Tried to disguise that there had been a fire. But Lestrade and his crew put paid to any hope of doing that by arriving on the doorstep faster than anyone would ever have thought possible."

"What with the manager of the *Gasthof* in Baden-Baden and now this one, I'm beginning to believe eccentricity is an occupational hazard in the hotel trade."

"Well, I never met him, or that desk clerk you spoke of. But I'm inclined to think 'eccentricity' is too mild a term to explain what might be happening in the oh-so-famous Northumberland Hotel. Which will soon be infamous if I'm any judge," said John, lighting another pipe.

At that moment Emily arrived clutching her parasol, and saying her book was so boring instead of finishing it she had come round to see if anything was going on in the detecting line without waiting to be sent for. "Something I might call proper sleuthing, which brings in money and won't involve cellars."

We asked her if she had any explanation for the manager's behaviour. "Dropped on his head when a baby," she said tersely.

"It would make more sense if he'd been frightened by sparklers," said John, "or proper fireworks."

"Sense is not a word I would use lightly in this instance," said Miss Fanshaw. "Since it seems to be a commodity conspicuous by its absence." She pulled a small notebook out of her trouser pocket. "Let me see: the 'woman' in Margate who forgot to powder her nose, the MacQuiver shivering in that fake castle of his. We seem to have had little to exercise my – our – undoubted faculties since the Long Island cave business."

"You've forgotten Geneva," I said, "and the croupier in Baden-Baden."

"As well as nearly killing yourself on Wandsworth Common," said Watson.

"That's as maybe," growled Emily. "But I warn you our next investigation has got to be *big*."

"While we're waiting for the breakthrough you're so keen on I still want to find out why, when, and how the Northumberland Hotel nearly went up in flames," I said loudly.

Telling John I needed to go out on an urgent errand, I drove down to Fulham Palace – practising my demure look as I went along. In the same way I had done before going to see Sherlock Holmes for the first time. Back home, and asked what made my

276

precipitate exit from the house so important, I told Watson I'd been to see the Bishop of London.

"Good Heavens!" he said, using what I thought of as an entirely appropriate expression, "whatever for?"

I told him I'd found a clergyman's collar stud of a peculiar pattern in the foyer of the Northumberland Hotel. "It turns out there has been an unlicensed conference of dubious and unfrocked priests in that establishment. Men like 'Holy Peters' and Williamson, etc. Someone told the owner of the Northumberland Hotel and he threatened to sack the manager."

"Who then had the crazy idea of starting a fire to divert everyone's attention," said John. "Mind you, I didn't smell any gas, or see any paint pots, while we were searching the cellars for signs of what we thought of as the pyrotechnic Alfred."

"Why should you?" I asked, puzzled. "Smell gas and see pots of paint?"

"Well the whole thing reminded me of when Holmes lit a small fire to smoke someone out. The Norwood Builder I think it was. The villain had used fresh paint to hide the smell of gas."

"Holmes may have smoked out the Norwood Builder. But it was the Retired Colourman who tried to hide the smell of gas. Surely you remember Mrs. Marple's lover, Angelo, trying to kill us in a similar way?"

"I didn't see any paint then."

"We didn't stop to see anything then. But you may be right. The manager probably planned to stay up all night disguising the damage before the guests came down to breakfast."

"Then he's dafter than I thought. If the place was repaired so quickly how could that distract the owner from the illegal conference?"

"He would see that something had happened and praise the manager to the skies for averting a tragedy. What a pity Lestrade turned up so promptly."

"Not at all," said John. "The publicity must have helped no end. They'll be giving the manager of the Northumberland Hotel a medal next. By the way, who's Williamson?"

"You've a head like a sieve. Or was that one of the investigations that never really happened? Williamson was the so-called clergyman in the adventure Holmes called 'The Solitary Cyclist.'" I took off my cloak and the conservative bonnet I'd worn to go to Fulham Palace and asked, "Has Emily been in?" .

"You bet she has," said my husband feelingly, "and says she has something big at last."

Full of curiosity, I snatched a hasty sandwich, drank a glass of water and went round to 'The Laurels'.

"Attaboy, Muriel," said Mrs. St. Clair enthusiastically. "The game is afoot!"

278

She had been contacted by an old Russian woman and –

"Just a minute," I said. "Does that mean we have to go to Moscow?" It would be almost as difficult as getting to Afghanistan.

"This person lives in Norfolk. And, by the way, says she did once come into contact with Sherlock Holmes. But it didn't do her a lot of good."

"What does she want?"

"Search me," said Emily somewhat vulgarly. "Don't forget, "You're the senior member of our Agency. I'm only the 'charming assistant'!"

"When it suits you," I said. "And you've a memory like a superannuated elephant."

"Superannuated usually means cast aside because it's no good. You'll have to think of a better adjective than that."

"I'm not here to be taught grammar," I said. I'm here to solve any dastardly crimes."

"Then let's get on with it, seeing as how your humble slave awaits your orders. When do you think we should start?"

"Just as soon as you've bought yourself a new parasol," I said sweetly.

Chapter Twelve

Our journey to a village near the Norfolk Broads passed without incident and we found the old Russian woman in one of a small row of thatched cottages opposite an older farm, and round the corner from The Big House. Outside, the dwelling looked like any other rural retreat. A neat garden full of country-style flowers, white picket fence on three sides, a small windmill by the front door and a sundial on the wall. But when we were invited inside the change was remarkable. Icons everywhere, rich silk hangings from Kiev, large Russian dolls painted to look like peasants and arranged in a rigid row on the sideboard. An arrangement which looked as if it was never disturbed, except perhaps on the day when everything was dusted. One slightly incongruous note was struck by a prayer shawl hanging on the wall, and some phylacteries in pride of place on a table by the window.

"They belonged to my husband, who was murdered in South Russia during the pogroms which followed the Tsar's assassination," said the old woman."Even my name wasn't my own after that dreadful time. The State decreed all Jews must give up their Hebrew names in favour of Russian ones. I chose to call myself Vera Federonova after a woman revolutionary who said publicly how glad she was to hear of the death of Alexander II. It was a dangerous name to adopt. But it sounded passable. Because, you know, if you didn't get a move on the authorities gave you a name which was comic or insulting – and sometimes both. It was better for me to call myself Vera Federonova than to be labelled 'money-bags' or 'fish-face'. Some people chose names which were inoffensive but nonsense. Or ornamental ones like 'Bloom' or 'Mountain Flowers'."

Although Emily looked uncharacteristically serious during this harrowing tale I now saw her yawning behind her hand and fidgeting with her parasol. If we didn't get down to business soon there might be an explosion.

"And, of course, we were already living within the Pale," said the old woman.

"But that's in Dublin," I said, remembering one of my chats with Mrs. Marple on the way to Dundalk. King John's dominions in Ireland, she had said, were marked off: and everywhere else was 'Beyond the Pale'. The 'superior' English fenced themselves in and made sure the 'inferior' Irish were rigidly kept out. It sounded the opposite to what I had just heard. The arrogant Russians put a ring round those they considered beneath them and made sure they themselves kept well outside it.

"In Russia," said Vera Federonova, "it was called 'The Pale of Settlement'. Tracts of poorly cultivated land on which it was difficult to grow much. Like one vast ghetto, only with grass."

"And shops too, surely?" said Emily, "as well as other amenities of civilisation?"

"Indeed my dear. But there were so many restrictions about the jobs one was allowed to have, and where one could or could not live."

"The Tsar wasn't killed all that long ago," said Miss Fanshaw, getting up and moving restlessly round the room. "So what did you call yourself before?"

I could see that the whole situation was becoming too serious for her. Wasn't detecting only an exciting game?

"You won't believe me," said the old Russian woman, "but I've quite forgotten."

"These icons," I began tactfully.

"Are extremely valuable and given to me by my grandmother, who was not a Jewess before she married. They are the reason I have asked you to come down here. But first I should get the samovar going and find some little cakes. You have both had such a long journey and must be very hungry as well as tired."

"The scrapes we get ourselves into," sighed Mrs. St. Clair as our hostess bustled out of the room.

"You wanted something big."

"But is this it? The icons may be very valuable, but nothing seems to have happened to them."

That night we slept in the cottage in a room just large enough for two single beds, but beautifully clean and full of flowers. I annoyed Emily, however, by sitting on my bed by the window with the light on writing a letter to Watson. How could I expect her to do any detecting, she said, if she didn't get enough sleep?

John's answer came during the evening of the following day. He said he hoped Miss Fanshaw wasn't showing any xenophobic tendencies. It reminded him of when Sherlock Holmes wrote about the negro Steve Dixie's 'woolly head' and said 'more lip' was the last thing he needed. "Then there was all that business with the masked child," wrote John. "Lucy Hebron, I think her name was. Anyway, my friend's account did contain racist undertones, whether or not he was fully aware of it. And, of course," added Watson, "Holmes did boast about paying a Jewish pawnbroker fifty-five shillings for a violin which turned out to be a Stradivarius."

"That's just what he would do according to what you've told me about him," said Mrs. St. Clair scornfully. And she wasn't xenophobic in the least. So those remarks in Baden-Baden about foreigners had been merely pleasantries had they?

We spent the day trying to get some information from the old Russian woman which would help us to solve the problem, if there really was one, with Emily growing more and more impatient at her vagueness. The one thing she did say with any

283

certainty (putting her gnarled hand on mine and speaking very slowly) was, "If you and your fellow detective ever come into the cottage and find that I'm not here, Mrs. Watson, be sure to..."

But Miss Fanshaw had jumped up, made a hurried excuse to Vera Federonova and finally hustled me out of the house. She insisted in going for a walk, and would have gone into a public house if I hadn't stopped her.

"The most we will do," I said, "is go for a boat-ride on the Broads."

But the wind annoyed her. The 'hundreds' of ducks squabbling on the grass at the edge of the Broad got on her nerves. Everything became extremely unsatisfactory: and lunch too was a failure.

"Cold food, cold plates, cold coffee. A rural backwater," said Mrs. St. Clair. Even the old Russian woman's cottage was preferable to this.

But when we got back our client was nowhere to be seen. There was no sign of a break-in but Emily, marching in a determined manner through the side gate into the back garden, came back to say the kitchen door was not locked – so we wouldn't have to stand in the cold like a pair of fools for the neighbours to goggle at. Outside, the washing was blowing in the breeze and, inside, the house seemed in perfect order. But of the 'very valuable' icons there was no trace whatsoever. "Well," said Miss Fanshaw, "I've heard of things being pinched, and I've heard of people disappearing. But how often do the two things occur together?"

"Frequently," I said. "And perhaps in this case, too, the twin events aren't entirely separate."

"You mean she's taken her Russian thingies and done a bunk, after bringing us down here for nothing?"

"I think she was warning us this might happen, and was about to tell me what to do if it did. But you were so impatient that..."

"That's right. I have a broad back. Blame me. But it won't bring us any nearer to solving the puzzle. We'd be better off searching the place for clues."

"And not finding any. Everything is exactly as it was when we arrived. Nothing's been moved and..."

"Are you certain?"

"Certain of what?"

"That nothing has been moved. I could have sworn those dolls were in a perfectly straight line when we followed the woman into this room the first time we met."

"And now they're not?"

"Look for yourself."

I went over to the sideboard, stared at the dolls for a moment and then said, "Perhaps this is her day for dusting." Weak, but all I could think of on the spur of the moment.

"When she was expecting visitors from London? You saw for yourself how spick and span everything was. She must have been hard at work the day before we came. In any case, why bother with housework if you are planning to leave?"

"That, if I may say so without sounding patronising (as a certain person often did sound) is a very good point. If you were leaving voluntarily you might tidy up. But I don't think she did disappear of her own accord. Of course, if you were going to leave the house ready for someone else..."

"It would be a great help," snapped Emily, "if you'd only stop all this blathering and take a better look at those dolls."

"Maybe our client accidently brushed one with her elbow if she was in a hurry to get out."

"What, with the others looking as if they've been glued to the sideboard for centuries?" Emily picked up the offending doll and stared at it for a few moments. Then she began to unscrew the body. This revealed another doll and then another, until she had five altogether. Putting the four smaller dolls to one side, she looked carefully at the largest one of the group and ran her finger along the inside of the bottom half. "There's a paper here," she said. "Not stuck, but pressed tightly against the

286

wood by these other dolls. Have you a pair of tweezers? Or a hair-pin might do it."

Taking care not to tear anything, she extracted the flimsy piece of paper, straightened it out and held it up to the window. "It's letters of the alphabet, all jumbled up."

"And in groups," I said, looking over her shoulder.

"Cipher, do you think? Written for us before she was forced out of the house?"

"Look at the yellowing edges of the paper. In my opinion it's been in the doll for some time for anybody to find. Besides, it would take a bit of scribbling down unobserved with kidnappers about. Especially by a woman as ancient as she is, and whose native language isn't English."

"So we don't bother with it?" asked Emily Fanshaw in a disappointed voice.

"I didn't say that. It would be better if we did try to find out what it means." I took a pencil and a piece of paper and wrote out the letters of the alphabet in their proper order.

A B C D E F G H I J K L M N O P Q R S T U V W X Y Z

"Now what?" said Mrs. St. Clair.

"Repeat the letters on the paper you took out of the doll."

"XJHZ   OJ   OCZ   ZHWVNNT   LPDXFGT. It's gobbledegook, But then I suppose it would be, wouldn't it, if it's a code."

"Are you sure?" I said, coming to look over her shoulder once more. "It reminds me of when Holmes was trying to decipher a warning which came to him from Porlock, an agent of Professor Moriarty. Poor Watson had said earlier that he was 'inclined to think' about something or other. Before he could finish, that man – who he thought of as his best friend, mark you – said rudely, 'I should do so'. Sherlock later had the cheek to ask for his help to understand the message."

"I'd like to hear him ask me for anything after that," said Emily. "He must have run out of his seven percent solution."

"Then, having come to the conclusion that the answer lay with a particular book, the great man continued to be abominably impertinent. Watson asked innocently why the title of the book wasn't included with the message. Instead of a straight answer, all he got from Sherlock was 'Your native shrewdness, that innate cunning which is the delight of your friends, would surely prevent you from enclosing cipher and message in the same envelope'."

"Well, you must admit that would be a bit daft," said Mrs. St. Clair.

"That wasn't the end of it. He poured scorn on every book my husband suggested. At the same time as he was extremely patronising. John was 'scintillating' as well as 'brilliant'. One more 'brain wave', one more 'coruscation' from him and the puzzle would be solved. Then, having pooh-poohed two of the books John suggested, the bible and Bradshaw, he accepted without any question that perhaps an almanac might do the trick."

"He'd found a half-empty syringe of cocaine under the sofa," said Emily."And, talking of ciphers, there was all that business with the dancing men."

"Stupid little stick figures," I said.

"Not all of them correct," replied Miss Fanshaw. "Now can we get on with this cipher. If it is one, and not just a load of rubbish."

"What happens if we move the letters two places?"

"What?"

"Make A 'C' and B 'D', etc. Like this, C D E F G II I J K L M N O P Q R S T U V W X Y Z A B

"As far as I can make out we get VHJZ MH MAX XFUTLLW OSGAIJW. A bit more promising since there seem to be two names. 'Max', and what could be 'Oscar' if the message *has* been written in a great hurry."

"We already decided it wasn't a new message," I said, gazing abstractedly at the sideboard. A number of dolls gazed back at me impassively. Four, and then a gap. Three more, and I had reached the end of the row. "I wonder," I mused. "Do you think, Emily, that the number five could be a clue to all this?

The line of letters then becomes V W X Y Z A B C D E F G H I J K L M N O etc."

"And the message 'Come to the Embassy quickly'."

"A simple letter substitution, made even easier by being given a little help," I said. "Thank goodness it wasn't a Playfair."

"A what?"

"A fiendish cipher invented by Admiral Playfair and named after him."

"Oh," said Emily. "I always thought that was a card game. Like cribbage, for instance."

"But which Embassy?" I asked, with the flimsy piece of paper in my hand.

"The one in Belgravia, I imagine, since the old woman is supposed to be Russian."

"Then it's back to Liverpool Street Station for us," I said. "And a brisk ride through the Capital."

"Not before I've had dinner and a good night's sleep," growled Emily, moving to lock the door into the back garden.

After we arrived at Liverpool Street we took a cab to the Russian Embassy, passing through Knightsbridge and skirting Hyde Park Corner. Dropped at our destination, a porter in livery came hurriedly out of his lodge wearing a red waistcoat and knee-breeches. Since neither of us had an appointment, or a letter of introduction, it seemed that our errand could end there and then. It would be back to the Station for our luggage, and an ignominious journey home.

"Since I categorically refuse to go down to Norfolk again," said Mrs. St. Clair, "under any circumstances whatever. Even of the wild horses variety. You had better tell that swine of a porter who you are. Talk about Sherlock Holmes. That always gets everybody going. Even foreigners. Anything to get us in here."

After five long minutes of earnest chat, I finally managed to persuade the man we had a genuine reason for visiting the Embassy. Just as a footman, attracted by the noise, opened the door. Emily and I ran up the steps of the building before anyone could change his mind and stepped into the hall.

"We have come about an old Russian woman," I gasped. The footman looked blank and, I'm sure, would have scratched his head if it hadn't been for his powdered wig. But instead he suddenly decided to have nothing to do with the matter: at the precise moment when a stout and stately-looking gent came walking rather unsteadily down the hall. Dressed in evening clothes and looking as if he had just come from the Café Royal, he said, "We have no women – old or young – in the building at the moment. Except, of course, the cook and a few kitchen maids."

"Then how do you account for this?" I demanded, bending down and picking up a tiny piece of silk which was the exact match of the gown our hostess had been wearing. "You should pay your domestics better. Then perhaps they would clean the place more thoroughly."

Instead of answering, the man opened one of the doors in the passage with an arrogant flourish. Giving an imperious wave, he motioned to us to enter a most elegantly furnished room. One which was obviously his cherished domain. I saw a tall fireplace, a bright fire and some easy chairs – with our client sitting in one and serenely reading a book. The remains of a late breakfast were on a table beside her, and I could see she wasn't in any way the worse for wear. I could also hear Emily cursing quietly, obviously wondering why we had been chasing round the countryside after a chimera.

The old Russian woman rose to her feet and came towards us with a shy smile. "They have taken my icons," she said, "as I always knew they would eventually. Icons which had been in my grandmother's family for generations and are of the greatest sentimental as well as monetary value. But the people here have convinced me they must go back to Holy Russia and..."

"What has all this to do with us?" asked Miss Fanshaw with a frown. "Ours is a very busy Agency. We can't waste time on crimes which are no crimes. Or in chasing after foreigners who don't need chasing after. Women who, in spite appearances, haven't been kidnapped."

"I quite understand, my dear, and will see that neither you nor Mrs. Watson lose by it as soon as the house in Norfolk is sold and I am on my way to Brazil."

"Brazil?" We both looked enquiringly at the Embassy Official.

"We have arranged for Mrs. Federonova – he brought out the name with difficulty – to live with her nephew in that country. You realise," he said, dropping his voice, "that she is no longer fit to look after herself, and now that she has given us the icons..."

"Bevis Marks is arranging for my furniture and all my little treasures to be shipped ahead of me so I shall feel quite at home," said our client. Who had been no client at all because, in a manner of speaking, she'd kidnapped herself.

"Though it beats me," said Emily in a stage whisper, "how she made her way out of her own front door, let alone to London. Did you put Mr. Holmes through the hoop in the same way you have us?" she asked loudly.

"Through the hoop?"

"Getting him down to Norfolk, bringing your icons up to London after leaving behind cryptic messages implying something has happened to you, allowing him to go on a wild-goose chase. Finding you in an embassy when he thought you'd been abducted by aliens. Really," she ended breathlessly, "there seems to be no end to what you may have done."

293

"Oh no," said the old Russian woman merrily. "I was a little younger then. I went to 221B Baker Street to consult Mr. Holmes about something entirely different!"

"And hopefully just as maddening," I said, as Emily and I went down the Embassy steps.

"She's a very pleasant old thing," said Miss Fanshaw between clenched teeth, "and has promised to pay handsomely for our trouble. But I wonder Sherlock Holmes didn't strangle her. A very impatient man, just think of the bother she must have caused *him*..."

"I know," I said. "That's why I like her so much."

"Who's Bevis Marks?"

"I'll tell you something that Sherlock Holmes once said to Watson: 'Matilda Briggs was not the name of a young woman. It was a ship which is associated with the giant rat of Sumatra'. Bevis Marks isn't a person. It's a synagogue."

"Mr. Holmes seemed very fond of giving girl's names to ships in the adventures, don't you think? 'The barque Sophy Anderson', 'The Gloria Scott'."

"Well ships are traditionally female," I said. "Think of the launching ceremonies. 'God bless her, and all who sail in her'. The first name you mentioned was pinched from one of the most famous sea mysteries of all time, the disappearance of the *Marie Celeste*. Come to think of it, so was the other. The captain of that ship had a daughter whose name was Sophia Matilda Briggs."

"There were other mysteries in the stories when it came to names. Although the only one I can think of at the moment is 'Francis Hay Moulton.'

"Hatty Doran's husband in 'The Noble Bachelor'? What's so mysterious about the name Francis Hay Moulton?"

"A Francis Moulton was the go-between in the love affair between Henry Ward Beecher and a much younger married woman," said Emily.

"And one of the adventures begins with a long boring preamble about General Gordon and Ward Beecher. But not 'The Noble Bachelor'. Holmes was careful to separate the contents of the two yarns. Otherwise somebody might have been in the soup. But I see you are very well versed in scandal."

"You ought to write a monogram on the subject."

"I assume you mean 'a monograph'," I said coldly.

"A slip of the tongue," said Miss Fanshaw hurriedly. "I saw from my reading that Mr. Holmes wrote a great many."

"Yes," I said scornfully. "On tattoos, tobacco ash, the polyphonic motets of Lassus."

"Whatever they are," chimed in Mrs. St. Clair.

"Can you give me any reason why I should copy him, of all people? And do you mean write about names or scandals?"

Returning to the subject of the old Russian woman as we were bowling towards Bayswater in a barouche, she said, "And someone will go with her to Brazil. See she comes to no harm?"

"By the sound of it, yes."

"And the person will be from that synagogue? He or she see that Mrs. F. doesn't disappear again after sticking pieces of paper into her little Russian dolls. Doesn't go off leaving washing on the line and the house so clean one could eat off the floor?"

"That's how I read it."

"Let's hope the nephew can cope," said Miss Fanshaw.

Chapter Thirteen

The season of freezing yellow fog and blazing fires being over, the Neville St. Clair and the John H. Watson families embarked on a series of picnics in the London parks. There were so many of us, my husband facetiously suggested hiring what the French call a *charabanc*. It wasn't such a bad idea because, according to custom, we took along almost as much paraphernalia as we would need for afternoon tea in our own sitting-rooms. It didn't happen, however. The men had to cope with carrying the heavy baskets specially designed for such occasions, with straps to hold the crockery in place and all kinds of other fancy fittings.

On one of these outings, while Mr. St. Clair was lying in the sun, his boy was asking me about French irregular verbs and Grizelda was playing with her doll, Mrs. St. Clair began searching in her pocket. Looking very hard at John, she said, "None of us has been to University. Me, you, Neville, Watson..."

"Never mind about Watson," I said. Millie was being very much exercised by the Little Nipper who kept toddling away in search of interesting creepy-crawlies, and John sat fiddling with his pipe – obviously wondering when it would not be impolite to smoke. He made me so fidgety that I signalled him to go ahead in spite of Emily's dirty looks.

Finally she said, "I've a letter here from somebody calling himself The Master of Corpus Christi. He wants The Watson – Fanshaw Detective Agency to go down to Cambridge to investigate a theft,"

"When do we start?"

"As soon as I've finished this sandwich," said Emily with a grin.

"Holmes said he was at University," remarked Watson, who had caught the tail-end of our conversation. "But he was a bit cagey as to which, Oxford or Cambridge. Got bitten on the ankle one morning while on his way to chapel."

"What a very percipient animal," I said. Then, turning to Miss Fanshaw, "On the way home stop at a district messenger's office and send a wire to say we'll be down the day after tomorrow."

When we arrived in at the University and climbed a set of ancient stairs to our rooms in the College, Emily remarked on the small number of rooms with the doors closed, as distinct from the much larger number of rooms where the doors stood open. "Sporting their oak," said The Master jovially, with a passing glance at the flat, thick, silent surfaces.

"What did he mean by that?" asked Mrs. St. Clair, taking off her hat and flinging it into a chair as soon as we were alone, unlacing her boots, padding around in her stockinged feet. Acting for all the world like a thorough bohemian.

"The occupants don't want to be disturbed. They're busy swotting for exams, or wish to imply that they are. By the way, your behaviour in the quadrangle was decidedly embarrassing."

"I don't know what you're talking about. There are no women here except a few decrepit old servants who stick to the kitchens. I was just giving those poor lads a taste of feminine company."

"We're nearly old enough to be their mothers."

"If there's anything I hate," said Miss Fanshaw, "it's exaggeration."

"One doesn't necessarily need brains to be in this place," I continued. "But one certainly needs money. These students are *la crème de la crème* financially as far as most people are concerned. They can well afford to find feminine entertainment without any help from us."

"At the risk of being sent down," she said, looking remarkably smug.

The Master of Corpus Christi told us a manuscript had gone missing from the Library. But when we spoke to the College Librarian he said things were a little different and, if anything, even more serious. "Priceless pages are being cut out of some of our books," he said. "If a complete volume is stolen (as sometimes happens in more lax establishments) and then recovered, it might still be in perfect condition (bearing in mind

299

its age). But books which have pages removed are permanently damaged."

"And there's a market for that kind of thing?" asked Emily wonderingly.

"Most certainly. For example, even one page from Matthew Parker would be worth money."

"Matthew Parker?"

"A former Master of this College and Archbishop of Canterbury, remarkable for his huge collection of books. Which he bequeathed to us," added the Librarian, as if he had personally been around to receive them at the time of the Dissolution of the Monasteries.

"But surely such books are kept under lock and key," I said.

"Of course. But students sometimes need to study them."

"Then they must be signed for."

"And looked at carefully when they are returned. But some of the staff have obviously become too trusting."

"How did you discover certain tomes had been so mutilated?" demanded Miss Fanshaw, using words she obviously thought were the most appropriate to her highly academic surroundings.

"When the present Master of the College asked to see a copy of one of them."

"That must have caused a devil of a row," said Emily.

"He nearly blew his top," said the Librarian.

"You would like us to discover the perpetrator of this ghastly deed, or deeds?"

"I have been given to understand that's what both you women are in Cambridge for."

I drew Mrs. St. Clair to one side and hissed, "If you would only stop talking like a dictionary we might get the chance to examine things and see how anyone could be so busy with the scissors in such a closely guarded place as this. We only got in here by the skin of the teeth ourselves."

"And If you would stop talking utter rot it would also help. Didn't I receive a personal letter from the Head of this place, and hasn't he just escorted me to my room with the utmost courtesy? Even if he does have a fancy name."

"When you have finished your acrimonious discussion," said the Librarian, "I am perfectly willing to show you all our books, and anything else you are desirous of looking at."

"See what I mean?" hissed Miss Fanshaw in her turn. "Proper English."

"Too proper," I said, preparing to follow the man into the furthest recesses of his domain. "He sounds like a pedant of the worst kind."

The man allowed us to look in every nook and cranny, explained the system by which books could be borrowed, showed us the area where they could only be studied in situ and allowed us to sit in the stalls occupied by students when they used the Library to work in. The building, he explained, was never left unattended. There was always someone to supervise the students. Who, although not completely visible all the time, were subjected to a number of spot checks.

"This is going to be a tough nut to crack," I said to Emily as we walked towards the dining-hall, a long room dominated by portraits of past Masters and highly polished refectory tables.

"I saw that Mr. Watson was tickled pink when he heard we were to follow in Mr. Holmes' footsteps," she said.

"How so?"

"Don't you remember the story of the missing three-quarter, and the one about the three students? If ever you write up this investigation for 'The Century Magazine'..."

"It would be much better if Holmes followed in our footsteps," I said crossly. "At least we aren't making most of it up."

"We'll go along the Backs in the morning and have a good think about what to do next. It will be quiet there even if the students are practising their rowing. It's not often one sees a man cry. But the Librarian was almost in tears when he showed us one or two of the damaged books."

"They didn't look too damaged to us, of course. Not torn in any way. Just some very clean cuts. Which means it wasn't done out of spite, or for some sort of crazy revenge."

"In that case I don't think it has happened because someone failed his exams, or was threatened with expulsion."

"No," I said. "Removing the pages was an act of vandalism. But it was vandalism in order to make a profit. If the pages were not treated like precious relics after that then the whole operation would be a waste of time."

"So, somewhere inside this University, pages from priceless books are being lovingly looked after by a common thief?"

"Or outside this University. And not such a common thief when you come to think of it. Someone who knows the value of what he has, and how and where to get the most money for it."

"I'm sure you think he's done a bunk already, Muriel."

"I strongly suspect it," I said. "He'd be silly not to."

"What if *he* can't get away without being suspected?"

"In that case he will still be here and all we have to do is find him."

"And the thing, or things, that he's stolen," said Miss Fanshaw.

We were walking by the river when she suddenly waved her arm as a portly man with a large moustache came strolling towards us. "Colonel Clay! How delightful to see you," she called out as soon as she thought he'd spotted her. "I would have recognised that cane and that handsome moustache anywhere. How long have you been in England and how is Africa?"

"What, all of it?" He stopped and looked at her with a little gleam in his eye, gently swishing the cane to and fro so that it just skimmed the top of his boots.

"Dear me," said Mrs. St. Clair roguishly. "As waggish as ever, I see."

"It was still there when I left," said this strange man with a sly smile. "And I dare say will still be there if ever I go back." He turned round to accompany us on our walk and the two chatted away while yours truly trotted along behind them, trying desperately to keep up. Until the Colonel said he had important business to attend to and must, most reluctantly, leave two such charming ladies to their own devices for the time being.

"Do you know who that man is?" I asked as soon as he was out of sight.

"A friend of Neville's."

" He's known as 'The African Millionaire' – another Raffles. Grant Allen writes about him in 'The Strand Magazine.'"

"Well, I never," said Emily. "Do you think he's pinched the palimpsests, or whatever they are? We could do with having S. H. here."

"No we could not," I said loudly.

"Keep calm for goodness sake," said Miss Fanshaw, "or those rowers carrying their boat on their heads will wonder what's going on. I was only trying to get your rag out."

"You would do better to concentrate on the job in hand," I said. "One thing we need to find out is where Clay is staying."

This proved much easier than I expected. When we went into dinner that evening we were surprised to see that he was a guest of the Master and sitting at the High Table. Emily and I, at our own request, were seated somewhat apart so that we could study everyone without their being too aware of it. The atmosphere was rather tense. Fresh mutilations of the manuscripts and other books in the College Library had been discovered that afternoon, one less than an hour ago. "When I had been in the Library myself," said the Master gravely.

I heard Colonel Clay say, in a most sincere voice, "Then the whole thing is inexplicable."

That night, when I was busy creaming my face and Emily was taking a last look at the moon, she suddenly signalled me to come to the window. Creeping across the Quad was the unmistakable figure of the Colonel. "He's bribed the porter to open the gate for him," she hissed. "Quick, into your outdoor clothes and away."

There then followed a frantic rush down to the gate. Where we bribed the porter in our turn and ran as fast as we could out into the street to find a cab. "Double fare," shrieked Miss Fanshaw, running like the wind as soon as she spotted one, "if you can get us to the station it ten minutes."

"Can't be done. Station's out of town. On account of the Proctor and his bull-dogs don't want young gentlemen slipping up to London when they feel like it. Not that it stops some of the varmints..."

"I'll treble the fare," I said desperately, while Emily looked as if for two pins she'd jump up onto the box herself.

"Then what the devil are you waiting for?" said the cab driver, whipping up his horses. "I can't hang about here all night."

Somehow, parasol and all, Mrs. St. Clair scrambled into the cab, pulled me in with her and banged on the roof. But the horses hadn't waited until we were settled and were racing towards Cambridge Station while we were still struggling into our seats.

"The swine didn't even have the courtesy to get down from the box and lower the step," said Emily. "I'm sure I've sprained my ankle."

"Why are you so certain the Colonel is going to the station?" I asked.

"Because if he is up to no good that is the best place for him to go. I hope he hasn't already caught a train."

"Are we going to Liverpool Street or St. Pancras?"

"That depends," said Emily, jumping out of the cab and flinging some money at the driver. "I can see a train already getting up steam and moving off. Take a look at that indicator to

306

see where it's going. I must say the ticket examiner working it looks remarkably handsome and efficient."

"We've no time for that," I said. "But it would be useless to wait for another. Our quarry, if he is on this train, would be half-way to his destination by then."

We raced down the long platform, with Emily frantically signalling to the guard not to lower his flag. But it was much too late. As we passed a door he wrenched it open, yelled to a passing porter to help him and we were both picked up and thrown bodily into the guard's van. Once we had recovered our breath we went along the corridor looking for seats and finally found two in an empty carriage.

"Did you ever see anything like it?"said Miss Fanshaw, laughing hysterically .

"We must have looked pretty desperate," I said. "Otherwise they would have made us wait for the next train."

"I think this is the last one to London tonight. Did you bring the tickets?"

"What tickets?"

"We came down by train so I assumed you have the other half of two returns."

"You've no business to assume any such thing," I said, rooting in my bag. "It's a wonder I've got my wits, what with you rushing me out of the College in that way."

"An occupational hazard. Detectives must be prepared for anything. Though Sherlock Holmes never seemed to be so harassed."

"That's because he hardly ever went anywhere. But he was very fond of telling John to get a move on when it suited him. Anyway, the tickets *are* here, by a piece of luck."

"We turned right when we got into the station. The London train would then be on our left. So I hope this is the one. It was such a rush, I hardly knew where I was."

"And absolutely miraculous that we managed to board without showing our tickets."

"I'm going along the train to see if I can spot Colonel Clay. Sit tight until I come back."

"I can hardly do anything else," I said as the train sped through the countryside. We would be in London almost before we realised it.

When Mrs. St. Clair returned she said she had seen the African Millionaire, swathed in wraps and with his hat pulled well down over his eyes, sitting in the corner of a crowded compartment. I asked if he had spotted her? She said she didn't think so. But if he was going all the way to London then we would have to keep a weather eye open for what he did next. "St. Pancras is pretty near the British Museum. I wonder if the man could be going there?"

"Well that won't be open at this time of night. My feeling is he has an appointment with a well-known antiquarian who lives in Camberwell. Either that, or he's going up to Town to sample the fleshpots. This, by the way, is a non-stop train. So he won't be able to give us the slip by leaving it before we get to the Metropolis. As he might have done by catching the train to Liverpool Street and changing at Bishop's Stortford."

"This is the first time I've heard about any antiquarian," said Emily testily.

"A well-known book collector. He specialises in Shelley and Keats. But there have been some ugly rumours about him lately."

"What rumours?"

"He may be forging first editions. Nothing's been proved but..."

"I can't see him being interested in anything that belonged to that Matthew Parker person."

"If he has been offering good money for single pages from medieval manuscripts it must be that he has changed tack and intends to fashion them into a whole folio. He may even be almost there except for one or two pages, and employing agents to scour the country for the ones which are missing."

"You mean men are creeping about Britain armed with scalpels and going into university libraries, museums and country houses craftily cutting out pages from priceless manuscripts – all on behalf of this bloke? But, according to the Librarian we spoke to in that College, there has been a great deal of mutilation of books going on there."

"True enough. Perhaps I'm wrong about there being a great many opportunist thieves. It can't be being done on a large a scale. It's sometimes difficult to get into a university library if you aren't a student there."

"Apart from London University, which used to be called 'That Godless Institution in Gower Street' and 'Stinkomalee Triumphans', there *are* only two universities in England."

Now who had told her that? Considering she had never heard of Doctor Johnson, and her knowledge of geography was almost non-existent. To say nothing of the other gaps in her education. Didn't she know about the universities in Scotland or the new University of Wales, with its five constituent Colleges?

By this time the train had pulled into St. Pancras. Getting up to retrieve her parasol from the luggage rack, Emily looked out of the window and said, "There he is. Colonel Clay, disappearing round a corner."

Not waiting for the guard to reach our compartment, she struggled with the strap, pulled down the window, stuck her hand out to grasp the door handle and leapt out on to the platform. Racing towards the Concourse, as she had done when chasing after the thief with the aluminium crutch, she flung our tickets at an examiner and shouted loudly for a growler.

We had lost sight of the Colonel while we were trying to get out of the train. But he had only gone down some steps and now stood in the street signalling for a hansom. While we waited for our own conveyance he drove slowly out of the station.

As soon as our growler arrived and we had piled into it, Miss Fanshaw stuck her head out of the window and yelled to the driver to keep close to the vehicle in front, promising any amount of money if he kept it in sight without letting the driver know he was being followed. "Muriel," she said excitedly, "this is what I call real detective work."

I reflected sourly that there was nothing very subtle about Emily Fanshaw.

The Colonel's vehicle drove to Holborn Viaduct, with us in hot pursuit. As soon as his cab stopped, its occupant jumped out and ran to catch a train to Camberwell. We did the same, keeping well away from his compartment.

"You know the area well, Miss Morstan," said Mrs. St. Clair. "As you were a governess here with Mrs. Forrester."

"At least I worked for my living," I retorted, stung to the quick and wondering how I ever had the stupidity to put up with the woman. "I didn't grab the first man I saw who I thought would keep me in idleness for the rest of my life."

"There's nothing idle about running a house and bringing up two children."

"Rubbish. Anyone could do it with an army of servants."

"After Sherlock Holmes stopped..."

"Yes, yes," I said impatiently, "you had to cut down on the number of servants. But it still seems to me you have more than enough."

"And you can't say we've been idle tonight. Although your contention that the Colonel has stolen a valuable manuscript may still have led us on a wild-goose chase."

"It was you who spotted him in the Quad and started it all."

By this time the train had stopped at our destination and, still trailing Colonel Clay, we followed him as unobtrusively as possible down several streets before he stopped at a certain gate. "I was right," I said. "He has got something for that antiquarian."

Giving a yell enough to wake the dead, Emily sprang forward and grabbed our quarry by the back of his coat. "I'm here to make a citizen's arrest," she said. And, just at that moment, who should come round the corner but Wiggins!

"You, young man," screamed Emily, "give me a hand with this villain."

"Are you in trouble, Mrs. Watson?" asked Wiggins, ignoring her completely. I could only nod dumbly.

"'Ere, Alf", he shouted. "Lend us a hand wiv this cove wot's annoying the Doctor' wife."

Alf emerged from the shadows and, in less than a minute, the two lads had pinned the man to the ground. Alf grabbed his legs in a vice-like grip, and Wiggins sat on his chest. Emily meanwhile had found a constable on the beat and convinced him she had captured a thief. He called up reinforcements and Colonel Clay was hauled away for questioning.

Only it wasn't Colonel Clay. The man's hat had come off in the struggle and his many scarves had fallen away to reveal – the Master of Corpus.

Two days later, when we were safely back in Bayswater and I was yet again taking tea with Mrs. St. Clair, I asked her how she could possibly have mistaken the Master of Corpus Christi College, Cambridge for Colonel Clay when she went down the corridor of the train.

"I didn't," she said. "That was definitely Colonel Clay. So he *must* have been going up to London to visit the fleshpots."

"Of Camberwell?" I said, remembering how boring the place had been. "Don't make me laugh."

"We obviously missed the Master at St. Pancras Station because we were concentrating so much on the African Millionaire. And our fool of a cab driver followed the wrong man to Holborn Viaduct."

"Not such a fool," I said. "If we'd been behind the Colonel's cab we would have more than likely landed up in The Radcliffe Highway."

"I wonder why he did it? The Master, I mean."

"The maximum of temptation combined with the maximum of opportunity, as somebody once said. Nobody would possibly suspect him. He could come and go as he liked. But now the poor man has been put into some sort of private asylum by his loving family."

"And the things he stole?"

"I heard that the latest page, from a priceless medieval manuscript belonging to Richard II, was found inside his shirt taped to his chest."

"And Wiggins sat on it!" shrieked Emily, nearly dropping her cup.

"Damaged beyond all repair," I said. "We must hope he never realises what he's done."

"He won't," she said. "And neither will the College. I didn't tell you, but there was such a struggle the page came adrift and landed on the pavement. I picked it up as soon as I could after the Master was carried away by those coppers, stuffed it in my bag and the maid used it yesterday morning to light the fire."

When I managed to stop laughing I said, "I would hate dear Wiggins to spend time in jug for something he would think of as a quite useless piece of paper not even big enough to wrap a pie in. Or Alf, who seems to have got over the urge to jump out at people."

"Out of evil cometh good," said Miss Fanshaw piously.

A week after my return from Cambridge I met Chief Inspector Lestrade slouching along the street which passed in front of our house. I was on my way home from the dressmaker's with my head full of silks, satins and the latest fashions. "Just like Mrs. St. Clair in one of her more frivolous moods," I thought to myself. The Scotland Yard man was in mufti, as if he was having a day off. But he looked so crestfallen I invited him in for a stiff drink. John sat the policeman in an armchair by the fire, pressed a glass of whisky into his hand and asked how things were going.

"None too well," said Lestrade morosely. "I've been demoted."

"Back to Inspector?"

He shrugged his shoulders.

"Become a desk-wallah?"

Our guest took a swig at the whisky, studied his shoes – and looked sadder than ever. "I'm back on the beat," he said. "A common constable. Goodness knows what Mrs. Lestrade will say when I tell her."

Mrs Lestrade? John and I exchanged glances.

"We married on the strength of my becoming a Chief Inspector. A superior lady's-maid, formerly in a very good establishment."

"To quote Mr. Sherlock Holmes, more like a typical specimen of a boot-slitting slavey, judging by the state of your foot-ware," said Watson. "How did it happen?"

"The marriage or the demotion?"

My husband coughed loudly, and said he wouldn't dream of enquiring into such a delicate matter as how another man conducted his love affairs. Of course he meant the change of employment.

"I wrongly arrested that kitchen maid in the Loamshire business and nearly had John Hector MacFarlane hanged. Then there was James McCarthy, and this latest affair at the Northumberland Hotel. The Assistant Commissioner said my running about all over London to get myself a mention in the newspapers was undignified and brought the force into disrepute. He'd been studying my record more carefully than his predecessor and that was the last straw."

After Lestrade had finished his third whisky and left the house, looking as if he had all the troubles in the world to contend with, Watson amazed me by saying he had received a letter, with a Sussex postmark, from Holmes asking if he would care to travel with him to America.

"That was a short retirement," I said bitterly, thinking what a pity it was the Reichenbach Falls had failed so dismally to do its work.

"It was an early retirement when all is said and done," replied John soothingly. "Do you mind if I go?"

"Not now Black Gorgiano's gang has been taken care of. Have you any idea what Holmes wants to do in The United States?"

"Become a double-agent I think. In case there's a war."

"What foresight," I said sarcastically, "since there hasn't been even a whisper of one since 1878."

"He says he needs to visit Chicago to learn the ropes, and then become a member of an Anglo-Irish secret society in Buffalo. After that he means to cause some serious trouble to the constabulary at Skibbareen, develop an Irish-American accent and call himself by the Irish-sounding Altamont, a name I believe is in some way connected with Arthur. He also says that's his way of preparing for a war, and that he has to do his bit since so many others are too complacent to consider the possibility of such a thing ever happening."

"And where do you come in all this?"

"Once I book his passage, pay for it and see him safely on the steamer to Cork I'm to go to Australia. At least, they were Holmes' instructions."

"It's me you went to Australia with," I said, "when we rescued the Gold King. Are you sure you won't be taking up with some red-headed American tart, [1] marrying the woman illegally and carrying *her* off to Ballarat ?"

"I do wish you wouldn't use such expressions," said Watson in a pained voice. "I have an idea Holmes means me to meet someone special in Melbourne. A meeting he implied would be a tremendous surprise to all of us. But I don't think it's a woman."

Some months later, during which I was beginning to think Watson *had* been snared by a red-haired hussy, Emily sent a note to say she'd received a letter from Arthur asking if he could call at 'The Laurels' and bring a friend. "The last time that happened," I thought to myself, "the 'friend' turned out to be Holmes. I wonder who that so-called literary agent has in tow this time?"

Miss Fanshaw had fixed the meeting for the following day. Was there any chance I could be there too? Certainly I could and, with a hansom cab ready at the door, I skipped out of the house like a two year old filly and made my way to Bayswater. By the time I arrived the best china had been laid out, the tea urn bubbled and Neville St. Clair was already pouring out strong

1. *Angels of Darkness*. A play by Sherlock's literary agent, Arthur.

drinks for himself and the men. What threw me was that these included not only Arthur, John and Sherlock but, of all people, James Moriarty. He and Holmes sat together on a sofa chatting away like old friends, while Watson stood beaming down on them like a Dutch Uncle.

Seeing my raised eyebrow, Mrs. St. Clair shrugged her elegantly clad shoulders and began delicately fiddling with the tea cups. Taking a small silver bell from a side table a little to her right, she gave it a modest tinkle and, as soon as a servant appeared, ordered more cake and some toasted muffins. It seemed she was as much at sea as I was. And her husband also seemed more than a little puzzled, although he went on playing the assiduous host.

It turned out that my husband had been sent to Australia by Sherlock to find Moriarty. Holmes had sworn him to secrecy in case the plan failed and damaged his reputation. John wasn't even allowed to write to his family. "That worried me, Mary, especially as the whole thing took longer than I thought it would."

"Of all the people in that circus tent," said Mr. St. Clair to Moriarty, "most got out safely. The two Poirots were taken to hospital and then deported as soon as they had recovered from their injuries. Black Gorgiano's grandson was killed. And you were nowhere to be seen. What happened?"

The Professor smiled gently. "I saw what was coming, rolled under the bench and, when the coast was clear, crept out from under the canvas sideways and skidaddled damn quick. Sebastian helped me get to Australia. But to tell the truth I was beginning to be a little homesick and felt quite glad when dear Dr. Watson here turned up. All the same," he continued, looking at Emily with a glint of malice in his grey eyes, "I received an extremely nasty jolt from that episode. Which was not good for a man of my years."

I sat there thinking someone must surely wake me up soon from some kind of fantastic dream. Sherlock chatting in that friendly way with his arch-enemy. Moriarty suddenly gentle and almost complaisant. All seven of us in the same room and taking refreshment together as if there had never been such an occurrence as that which had taken place in Switzerland, or any such person as a 'Napoleon of Crime'.

I stared at the old man and saw that he had indeed mellowed. His grip on things was considerably lessened. The great intellect didn't seem to be diminished in any way, but he no longer stood at the centre of things. Had he abdicated his Throne in favour of somebody else? Turned over his great Empire to Colonel Sebastian Moran or one of his less well-known but equally evil lieutenants? If so, that jolt certainly was considerable. In spite of what he said, it must have almost cost him his life.

Neville St. Clair suddenly asked Holmes how he was enjoying his retirement. I guess they had all been talking about it before I arrived. I was glad to hear Sherlock say he had no intention of returning to London, "Unless there is a war at some time." His bees kept him fully occupied, including the ones in his bonnet. "I think you would find their behaviour quite mathematical Professor," he said genially. "The little dances they do on returning to the hive, to indicate the position and distance of various kinds of nectar, are remarkably precise and follow a most intricate pattern. I see no reason why you shouldn't come back with me to study it. In fact, I would be quite happy to share my sweet little cottage with you and my housekeeper Mrs. Hudson *ad infinitum*. She cooks the most delicious dinners, and knows her place."

"In that case," said James Moriarty eagerly, "I would be very happy to start straightaway. Do you think these two charming ladies and these three delightful gentlemen would think it impolite if we went at once?"

They could be heard carolling away together as they walked arm in arm into the outer hall to collect their belongings prior to whistling for a growler to take them to Victoria to catch a train to the South Downs. Sherlock remarked with glee that their plan was sure to work. Moriarty, moving a little unsteadily, said more softly, "My dear Holmes, there isn't a lot of money in bee-

321

keeping. I have several little scams – that is, ideas which will help us if we run short at any time."

Emily rang for the maid to take away the tea things. Neville St. Clair poured himself another strong drink. Arthur said he must be off to check the time of the next train to London Bridge – while John and I stood looking out of the window as the cab which was carrying Mr. Sherlock Holmes and Professor James Moriarty away from the door moved at a rattling pace towards the railway station. With the two new friends smiling away at each other as if they hadn't a care in the world.

"I give it six months," said Watson.

Also from MX Publishing:

Molly Carr

The Sign of Fear

**The adventures of Mrs.Watson with a supporting cast
including Sherlock Holmes, Dr.Watson and Moriarty**

Also from MX Publishing:

John H Watson

Edited by Tony Reynolds

The recent decease of one of the descendents of Dr. Watson has brought to light his personal papers. These include a number of stories that Dr. Watson suppressed at the time for various reasons. As all involved are long dead, the inheritor has agreed to the publication of a set of eight of the most interesting adventures.

Also from MX Publishing:

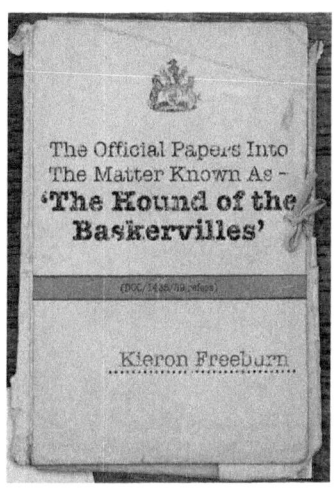

Kieron Freeburn

The Official Papers Into The Matter Known As The Hound of the Baskervilles (DCC/1435/89 refers)

The original police papers from the Hound of The Baskervilles case discovered by real-life 'Sherlock Holmes', former Metropolitan Police detective Kieron Freeburn.

Also from MX Publishing:

Alistair Duncan

Close To Holmes

A Look at the Connections Between Historical London, Sherlock Holmes and Sir Arthur Conan Doyle

Also from MX Publishing:

Alistair Duncan

Eliminate the Impossible

An Examination of the World of Sherlock Holmes on Page and Screen

Also from MX Publishing:

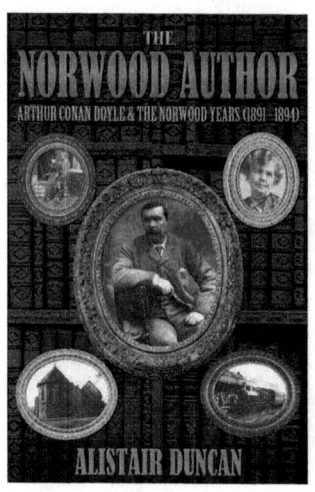

Alistair Duncan

The Norwood Author

Arthur Conan Doyle
and the Norwood Years (1891 - 1894)

Also from MX Publishing:

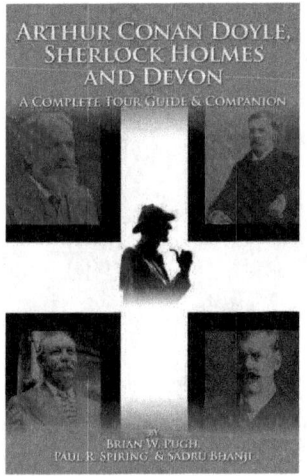

Brian W. Pugh and Paul R. Spiring

Arthur Conan Doyle, Sherlock Holmes and Devon

A Complete Tour Guide and Companion

Also from MX Publishing:

Brian W. Pugh

A Chronology of The Life Of
Sir Arthur Conan Doyle

A Detailed Account Of The Life And Times Of The Creator
Of Sherlock Holmes

Also from MX Publishing:

Paul R. Spiring

Aside Arthur Conan Doyle

Twenty Original Tales By Bertram Fletcher Robinson

Printed by BoD™in Norderstedt, Germany

9 781907 685408